Samuel Hubbard Scudder

Catalogue Of The Orthoptera Of North America

Samuel Hubbard Scudder

Catalogue Of The Orthoptera Of North America

ISBN/EAN: 9783741147371

Manufactured in Europe, USA, Canada, Australia, Japa

Cover: Foto ©Andreas Hilbeck / pixelio.de

Manufactured and distributed by brebook publishing software
(www.brebook.com)

Samuel Hubbard Scudder

Catalogue Of The Orthoptera Of North America

SMITHSONIAN MISCELLANEOUS COLLECTIONS.

—————— 189 ——————

CATALOGUE

OF THE

ORTHOPTERA

OF

NORTH AMERICA

DESCRIBED PREVIOUS TO 1867.

PREPARED FOR THE SMITHSONIAN INSTITUTION

BY

SAMUEL H. SCUDDER.

WASHINGTON:
SMITHSONIAN INSTITUTION.
OCTOBER, 1868.

This Report upon the present state of knowledge of the Orthoptera of North America and the West Indies, has been prepared by Mr. S. H. Scudder, at the request of this Institution. The work is designed to call attention to a much neglected order of our insects, and to facilitate their study by the student of Entomology.

The Institution proposes at some future time, to publish Monographs of the Orthoptera of this Country, and, in view of this, would be pleased to receive specimens from any quarter which may serve as material for investigation.

JOSEPH HENRY,

Secretary S. I.

ACCEPTED FOR PUBLICATION, JULY, 1867.

PREFACE.

In preparing this Catalogue, at the request of the Smithsonian Institution, for the benefit of those who wish to examine our native Orthoptera, I have adopted a purely alphabetical arrangement. The list is not in any sense a synonymical one, involving the expression of personal views, but a hand-book for the student, in which is collected every reference to any species of Orthoptera stated to have been found on the continent of North America or in the West Indies — a groundwork upon which he may erect a superstructure of his own.

It would be difficult to extend its scope and retain uniformity of design without making it a complete synonymical list, scarcely differing from an index to an elaborate monograph, and necessitating nearly all the labor which that would require. Such a monograph I am preparing for the Smithsonian Institution, but the earlier publication and distribution of this list will assist me to obtain material for my purpose, and further the interests of science, by calling attention to this neglected group of insects.

The list furnishes an index to the exact names given to the insects in the original descriptions; if an author has described the same species, at different times, under different generic or specific names, although confessedly synonymous, they will not be found together, but distributed through the book in alphabetical order; so, too, the species of Linné and Fabricius are given under the ancient genera in which these authors placed them and not under the modern ones to which they have since been referred. When an author has used sub-genera, retaining the generic name in connection with the specific, as Burmeister, De Haan and de Saussure have frequently done, the specific will be placed under the generic name, the name of the sub-genus enclosed in brackets, and under the sub-genus will be found a reference to the genus; for example: under the genus *Phalangopsis* we find the species *gracilipes*, which was referred by Halderman to the sub-genus *Daihinia*; this is made clear in the following way:—

Phalangopsis.

gracilipes [Daihinia] HALD. Proc. Amer. Ass. Adv. Sc. II, 346, Penn.

while under the genus *Daihinia*, after the mention of the different species, will be found the words, *See also Phalangopsis.*

Great pains have been taken to give the localities in full and to include in the list all references to such general localities as "America" or "the Indies," even when it was uncertain whether *North* America or the *West* Indies — the field embraced in my scheme — was intended. References to "meridional" America are also included, because authors have frequently embraced in this term Honduras and other parts of Central America. I have excluded every case where no reference to my field was made, even if subsequent investigations proved that the insect occurred within those limits or the name itself suggested the locality. *Œdipoda carolina* presents an exaggerated instance of this kind. Stoll figured the insect under the name of *Locusta carolina*, but did not state where it was found; this is indicated by the name, but I have omitted reference to it and similar cases, for the sake of making the work strictly one of compilation.

In the sequence of authorities under each specific name, a chronological arrangement has been attempted, but works quoted from a single author will succeed one another.

Finally, to assist the young naturalist in the more ready use of the list, I have added a tabular view of an Orthopteran System, derived mainly from Burmeister's Handbuch der Entomologie, but including only the genera mentioned in this list. I have, however, altered the sequence of the families to what I conceive to be a more natural method.

SAMUEL H. SCUDDER.

Boston Society of Natural History,
Boston, Mass., July, 1867.

AUTHORITIES.

AFZELIUS, A.—Achetæ Guineenses quas consensu exp. Fac. med. Ups. proponunt Adamus Afzelius et Fredericus Wilhelmus Brannius. 4to. Upsaliæ, 1804.

AUDOUIN, J. V., et BRULLÉ, A.—Histoire naturelle des Insectes, traitant de leur organisation et de leurs mœurs en général; et comprenant leur classification et la description des espèces. Tome IV-VI, IX. 4 vols. 8vo. Paris, 1834-8. (Orthoptera, Vol. IX, 1835.)

BILLBERG, G. J.—Enumeratio Insectorum in Museo Gust. Joh. Billberg. 4to. Holmiæ, 1820.

BLANCHARD, E.—In Guérin-Méneville, Magasin de Zoologie, Journal destiné à faciliter aux Zoologistes de tous les pays les moyens de publier leurs travaux et les espèces nouvelles ou peu connues qu'ils possèdent. Tome V. 8vo. Paris, 1835.

    "   Monographie du genre Phoraspis de la famille des Blattiens, précédée de quelques observations sur les Blattes des anciens; in the Annales de la Société entomologique de France. Tome VI, 8vo. Paris, 1837.

    "   Histoire naturelle des Insectes Orthoptères, Nevroptères, Hémiptères, Hyménoptères, Lépidoptères et Diptères; avec une introduction par M. Brullé. 3 vols. 8vo. Paris, 1840-1 (Orthoptera, Vol. III, 1840).

BROWNE P.—The civil and natural history of Jamaica, containing I, an accurate description of that island; its situation and soil; with a brief account of its former and present state, Government, Revenue, Produce and Trade. II, An history of the natural productions, including the various sorts of native fossils, perfect and imperfect vegetables; Quadrupeds, Birds, Fishes, Reptiles and Insects; with their properties and uses in Mechanics, Diet and Physic. Illustrated with forty-nine copperplates in which the most

curious productions are represented of their natural sizes and
delineated immediately from the objects by George Dionysius
Ehret. There are now added complete Linnean Indexes and a
large and accurate map of the Island. Fol. London, 1789.

BRUNNER VON WATTENWYL, C.— Orthopterologische Studien. 8vu.
Wien, 1861.

"　Ditto, in the Verhandlungen der k. k. zoologisch-botanischen
Gesellschaft in Wien. 8vo. Wien, Jahrgang 1861.

"　Nouveau Système des Blattaires. 8vo. Vienne, 1865.

BURMEISTER, H.—Handbuch der Entomologie. Band II, Abtheil. II,
Gymnognatha; erste Hälfte, Orthoptera. 8vo. Berlin, 1838.
See also Germar, E. F.

"　Audinet-Serville, Histoire naturelle des Orthoptères. Paris,
1839, 8. verglichen mit H. Burmeister, Handbuch d. Entomologie. II Bd. II Abth. 1 Hälfte (vulgo Orthoptera). Berlin, 1838.
8. von Verfasser des Letzteren; in Germar, Zeitschrift für die
Entomologie. II. Bd. 8vo. Leipzig, 1840.

CATESBY, M. — The natural history of Carolina, Florida and the
Bahama Islands, containing the figures of Birds, Beasts, Fishes,
Serpents, Insects and Plants, etc. Together with observations on
the air, soil and waters, with remarks upon agriculture, grain,
pulse, root, etc. 2 vols. Fol. London, 1743. 2d Edition, London, 1754. See also Mortimer, C.

CHARPENTIER, T. DE—Orthoptera descripta et depicta. 4to. Lipsiæ, 1841-5.

"　Bemerkungen zu A. A. H. Lichtenstein's Abhandlungen über
die Mantis-Arten in den Transactions of the Linnean Society.
Vol. VI. Lond., 1802; in Germar, Zeitschrift für die Entomologie. Bd. V. 8vo. Leipzig, 1844.

DALLAS, W. S.—Insecta; in Gunther, The Record of Zoological Lit-
erature. Vol. I (1864). 8vo. London, 1865.

DALMAN, J. W.—Analecta Entomologica. 4to. Holmiæ, 1823.

DE GEER, C.—Mémoires pour servir a l'histoire des Insectes. 7
Tom. 4to. Stockholm, 1752-78 (Orthoptera, Tome III, 1773).

DE HAAN, W.—Bijdragen tot de Kennis der Orthoptera; in the Verhande-
lingen over de Natuurlijke Geschiedenis der Nederlandsche over-
reesche Bezittingen door de Leden der natuurkundige Commissie
in Indie en andere Schrijvers. Uitgegeven door C. J. Temminck.
Fol. Leiden, 1835-44. (Orthoptera, 1842.)

DOHRN, W. L. H.—Die Dermapteren von Mexico; in the Entomologische Zeitung, herausgegeben von dem entomologischen Vereine
zu Stettin. Jahrgang 23. 8vo. Stettin, 1862.

"　Versuch einer Monographie der Dermapteren; in the Entomologische Zeitung, herausgegeben von dem entomologischen Vereine
zu Stettin. Jahrgang 24-26. 8vo. Stettin, 1863-5.

DOUBLEDAY, E.—Communications on the Natural History of North

America; in the Entomological Magazine. Vol. V. 8vo. London, 1838.

DRURY, D.—Illustrations of Natural History, wherein are exhibited upwards of two hundred and forty figures of exotic insects, according to their different genera; very few of which have hitherto been figured by any author, being engraved and colored from nature, with the greatest accuracy, and under the author's own inspection; with a particular description of each insect. 3 vols. 4to. London, 1770–82. See also Panzer, G. W. F., and Westwood, J. O.

DUNCAN, J.—Introduction to Entomology; comprehending a general view of the metamorphoses, internal structure, anatomy, physiology, and systematic arrangement of the various orders, and a tabular view of the whole class of Insects. 8vo. London, 1840. (Jardine's Naturalists' Library, Entomology, Vol. I.)

EMMONS, E.—Agriculture of New York; comprising an account of the classification, composition and distribution of the soils and rocks, and of the climate and agricultural productions of the State; together with descriptions of the more common and injurious species of insects. Vol. V. 4to. Albany, 1854.

ERICHSON, W. F.—Bericht über die Leistungen in der Entomologie; in Wiegmann, Archiv für Naturgeschichte. Jahrgang III. 8vo. Berlin, 1838.

"   Bericht über die wissenschaftlichen Leistungen in der Entomologie. 10 vols. 8vo. Berlin, 1838–47. See also Gerstaecker, C. E. A., and Schaum, H. B.

"   Ditto, in Wiegmann, Archiv für Naturgeschichte. 8vo. Berlin.

FABRICIUS, J. C.—Systema Entomologiae sistens Insectorum classes, ordines genera species, adjectis synonymis, locis, descriptionibus, observationibus. 8vo. Flensburgi et Lipsiae, 1775.

"   Species Insectorum exhibentes eorum differentias specificas, synonyma auctorum, loca natalia, metamorphosin adjectis observationibus, adumbrationibus. 2 vols. 8vo. Hamburgi et Kilonii, 1781.

"   Mantissa Insectorum sistens eorum species nuper detectas adjectis characteribus genericis, differentiis specificis, emendationibus, observationibus. 2 vols. 8vo. Hafniae, 1787.

"   Entomologia Systematica emendata et aucta, secundum classes, ordines, genera, species, adjectis synonymis, locis, observationibus, descriptionibus. 4 vols. in 7. 8vo. Hafniae, 1792–4 (Orthoptera, Tom. II, 1793).

"   Epitome Entomologiae Fabricianae sive Nomenclator Entomologicus emendatus sistens Fabricini systematis cum Linnaeano comparationem adjectis characteribus ordinum et generum, speciebus novis aliorum entomologorum insectorum habitationibus nominibus germanorum francogallorum anglorum cum indicibus et bibliotheca fabriciana. 8vo. Lipsiæ, 1797. Editio nova. 8vo. Lipsiæ, 1810.

FABRICIUS, J. C.—Supplementum Entomologiæ systematicæ. 8vo. Hafniæ, 1798.

F(ABREAU), A. S.—*in* Ferrussac, Bulletin des Sciences naturelles et de Géologie. 1º Section du Bulletin universel publié par la Société pour la propagation des connaissances scientifiques et industrielles. Tum. XVII. 8vo. Paris, 1829.

FELTON, S.—An account of a singular species of Wasp and Locust; in *the* Philosophical Transactions, giving some account of the present undertakings, studies and labours of the ingenious in many considerable parts of the world. Vol. LIV. 4to. London, 1764.

FISCHER VON WALDHEIM, G.—Sur les Spectres ou Phasmides; in *the* Bulletin de la Société Impériale des Naturalistes de Moscou. Tome X. 8vo. Moscou, 1837.

" Locustarum quædam genera aptera novo examini submissa; *in the* Bulletin de la Société Impériale des Naturalistes de Moscou. Tome XII. 8vo. Moscou, 1839.

" Index Orthopterorum societati traditorum. 8vo. Moscou, 1846.

" Ditto, *in the* Bulletin de la Société Impériale des Naturalistes de Moscou. Tome XIX. 8vo. Moscou, 1846.

FISCHER, L. H.—Orthoptera Europæa. 4to. Lipsiæ, 1853.

FITCH, A.—List of Noxious Insects; *in the* American Journal of Agriculture and Science, conducted by Dr. E. Emmons and A. Osburn. Vol. VI. 8vo. New York, 1847.

" Third Report on the noxious and other insects of the State of New York; *in the* Transactions of the New York State Agricultural Society. Vol. XVI, for 1856. 8vo. Albany, 1856.

" Third, fourth and fifth Reports on the noxious, beneficial and other insects of the State of New York, made to the State Agricultural Society, pursuant to an annual appropriation for that purpose from the Legislature of the State. 8vo. Albany, 1859.

" Eighth Report on the noxious and other insects of the State of New York; *in the* Transactions of the New York State Agricultural Society. Vol. XXII, for 1862. 8vo. Albany, 1863.

" Sixth, seventh, eighth and ninth Reports on the noxious, beneficial and other insects of the State of New York, made to the State Agricultural Society, pursuant to an annual appropriation for this purpose from the Legislature of the State. 8vo. Albany, 1865.

FLOR, G.—*In* von Sivers, Ueber Madeira und die Antillen nach Mittelamerika. 8vo. Leipzig, 1861.

GERMAR, E. F.—*In* Germar, Magazin der Entomologie. T. III. 8vo. Halle, 1818.

" *In* Burmeister, Handbuch der Entomologie.

GERMAR, E. F.—*In* Germar, Zeitschrift für die Entomologie. Tom. I. 8vo. Leipzig, 1839.

GERSTAECKER, C. E. A.—Bericht über die wissenschaftlichen Leistungen im Gebiete der Entomologie. 11 vols. 8vo. Berlin, 1853–65. See also Erichson, W. F. and Schaum, H. R.

" Ditto, *in* Wiegmann und Tröschel, Archiv für Naturgeschichte. 8vo. Berlin, 1853–65.

" Ueber die Locustinen-Gattung Grillacris; *in* Wiegmann, Archiv für Naturgeschichte. Bd. XXVI. 8vo. Berlin, 1860.

" Sepaeus und Phyllocyrtus, zwei Käferähnliche Gryllodeengattungen; *in the* Entomologische Zeitung, herausgegeben von dem entomologischen Vereine zu Stettin. 21 Jahrgang. 8vo. Stettin, 1862.

" *In* Peters, W. C. H., and Carus, J. V., Handbuch der Zoologie. Zweiter Band, Arthropoden, bearbeitet von A. Gerstaecker. 8vo. Leipzig, 1863.

GIRARD, C.—Appendix F. Zoology. Orthopterous Insects; *in* Marcy, R. B., assisted by McClellan, G. B., Exploration of the Red River of Louisiana in the year 1852. 8vo. Washington, 1853. Executive [Document] No. 54, 32d Congress, 2d Session. Robert Armstrong, public printer, 1853.

" The same, Executive Document, 32d Congress, 1st Session, Senate. Beverly Tucker, Senate Printer, 1854.

GMELIN, J. F.—Caroli a Linné Systema Naturae per regna tria naturae secundum classes, ordines, genera, species cum characteribus, differentiis, synonymis, locis. Editio decima tertia, aucta, reformata. III Tomi in 10 vols. 8vo. Lipsiæ, 1788–93. (Orthoptera, Tom. I, Pars IV, 1788.)

" Ditto, X Tomi. 8vo. Lugduni Batavorum, 1789–96. (Orthoptera, Tom. IV, 1789.)

GOSSE, P. H.—The Canadian Naturalist; a series of conversations on the natural history of Lower Canada. 12mo. London, 1840.

" Letters from Alabama (U. S.) chiefly relating to natural history. 16mo. London, 1859.

GOEZE, J. A. E.—Entomologische Beiträge zu des Ritter Linné zwölften Ausgabe des Natursystems. 3 vols. in 5. 8vo. Leipzig, 1777–81. (Orthoptera, T. II, 1778.)

" Des Herrn Baron Karl de Geer Abhandlungen zur Geschichte der Insecten aus dem Französischen übersetzt und mit Anmerkungen herausgegeben von J. A. E. Goeze. 7 vols. in 8. 4to. Nürnberg, 1776–83. (Orthoptera, T. III, 1780.)

GRAY, G. R.—Synopsis of the species of insects belonging to the family of Phasmidæ. 8vo. London, 1835.

GUÉRIN-MÉNEVILLE, F. E.—Iconographie du Règne Animal de G. Cuvier, ou représentations d'après nature de l'une des espèces les plus remarquables et souvent non encore figurées de chaque genre d'; animaux; pouvant servir d'Atlas à tous les traités de Zoologie. Insectes. 8vo. Paris, 1829-38.

GUÉRIN-MÉNEVILLE, F. E.—In Sagra, Ramon de la. Histoire physique, politique et naturelle de l'île de Cuba. Animaux articulés à pieds articulés. Text 8vo, planches folio. Paris. 1857.

GUILDING, L.—The natural history of Phasma cornutum, and the description of a new species of Acrolophus; in the Transactions of the Linnean Society of London. Vol. XIII. 4to. London, 1822.

HAHN, C. W.—Icones Orthopterorum. 4to. Nürnberg. 1836.

HALDEMAN, S. S.—Remarks on the Insects of Mexico; in the American Journal of Science and Arts. 2d Series. Vol. V. 8vo. New Haven, 1848.

    " History of Phalangopsis, a genus of Orthoptera, with three new species, two of which form a subgenus; in the Proceedings of the American Association for the Advancement of Science. Vol. II. 8vo. Boston, 1850.

    " Appendix C. Insects; in Stansbury, H., Exploration and Survey of the Valley of the Great Salt Lake of Utah, including a reconnoisance of a new route through the Rocky Mountains. Printed by order of the Senate of the United States. 8vo. Washington, 1852. (Another edition with same title printed by order of House of Representatives of the United States. 8vo. Washington, 1853.)

    " Description of some new species of insects, with observations on described species; in the Proceedings of the Academy of Natural Sciences of Philadelphia. Vol. VI. 8vo. Philadelphia, 1853.

HARRIS, T. W.—A Catalogue of the Animals and Plants in Massachusetts. VIII. Insects; in Hitchcock, E., Report on the Geology, Mineralogy, Botany and Zoölogy of Massachusetts. Made and published by order of the government of that State. 8vo. Amherst, 1833.

    " Ditto, in Hitchcock, Report, &c. 2d edition, corrected and enlarged. 8vo. Amherst. 1835.

    " Ditto, in Hitchcock, Catalogue of the Animals and Plants of Massachusetts, with a copious index. 8vo. Amherst. 1835.

    " Article Locust; in the Encyclopædia Americana. Vol. VIII. 8vo. Philadelphia, 1835. Boston, 1856.

    " A Report on the Insects of Massachusetts Injurious to vegetation, published agreeably to an order of the Legislature, by the Commissioners on the Zoological Survey of the State. 8vo. Cambridge, 1841. (Another impression of the same, printed at the charge of the Author, entitled: A Treatise on some of the Insects of New England which are injurious to vegetation. 8vo. Cambridge, 1842.)

HARRIS, T. W.—A Treatise on some of the Insects of New England which are injurious to vegetation. Second edition. 8vo. Boston, 1852.

" A Treatise on some of the Insects Injurious to vegetation. Third edition. 8vo. Boston, 1862 (posthumous).

" In Scudder, S. H., Materials for a Monograph of the North American Orthoptera (posthumous).

HERBST, J. F. W.—Fortsetzung des Verzeichnisses meiner Insectensammlung. Zweyte Classe; in Fuessly, Archiv der Insectengeschichte. Heft 7 und 8. 4to. Zürich, 1784.

JAEGER, B.—The life of North American Insects; illustrated by numerous colored engravings and narratives. 8vo. Providence, 1854.

" The life of North American Insects. Assisted by H. C. Preston, M. D., with numerous illustrations from specimens in the cabinet of the author. 12mo. New York, 1859.

JOHNSTONE, J. C.—In the Transactions of the Entomological Society of London. Vol. II. 8vo. London, 1837.

JONES, J. M.—The Naturalist in Bermuda. A sketch of the geology, zoology and botany of that remarkable group of Islands. 8vo. London, 1859.

KALM, P.—Travels into North America, containing its natural history, and a circumstantial account of its plantations and agriculture in general, with the civil, ecclesiastical and commercial state of the country, the manner of its inhabitants, and several curious and important remarks on various subjects; translated into English by J. R. Forster, enriched with a map, several cuts for the illustration of natural history, and some additional notes. 3 vols. 8vo. 1770-1. (Orthoptera, Vol. II, 1771.)

" Ditto, in Pinkerton, J., a general collection of the best and most interesting voyages and travels in all parts of the world, many of which are now first translated into English. Digested on a new plan. Vol. XIII. 4to. London, 1812.

KIRBY, W.—Fauna Boreali-Americana, or the Zoology of the northern parts of British America, containing descriptions of the objects of natural history, collected by John Richardson on the late northern land expeditions under command of Captain Sir John Franklin. 4 vols. Part fourth and last. The Insects. 4to. London, 1837.

KIRBY, W., AND SPENCE, W.—An Introduction to Entomology, or Elements of the Natural History of Insects. 4 vols. 8vo. London, 3d Edition, 1818-26.

" Ditto, 7th Edition. 1 vol. 8vo. London, 1858.

LAMARCK, J. B. P. V. DE—Histoire naturelle des animaux sans vertèbres présentant les caractères généraux et particuliers de ces animaux, leur distribution, leurs classes, leurs familles, leurs genres, et la citation des principales espèces qui s'y rapportent;

précédés d'une Introduction offrant la détermination des caractères essentiels de l'animal, sa distinction du végétal et des autres corps naturels; enfin l'exposition des principes fondamentaux de la Zoologie. 7 vols. 8vo. Paris, 1815–22. (Orthoptera, Vol. IV, 1817.)

LAMARCK, J.B.P.V. DE.—Ditto, 2° édition, revue et augmentée de notes présentant les faits nouveaux dont la science s'est enrichie jusqu'à ce jour par MM. G. P. Deshayes et H. Milne-Edwards. 11 Tom. 8vo. Paris, 1835–15. (Orthoptera, Tom. IV, 1835.)

" Ditto, 3° Edition. 3 vols. Roy. 8vo. Bruxelles, 1837–9. (Orthoptera. Vol. II, 1839.)

LATREILLE, P. A.— Histoire naturelle, générale et particulière des Crustacés et des Insectes. Ouvrage faisant suite aux œuvres de Leclerc de Buffon et partie du cours complet d'Histoire naturelle rédigé par C. S. Sonnini. 14 vols. 8vo. 1802–5. (Orthoptera, Vol. XII, 1804.)

" Genera Crustaceorum et Insectorum secundum ordinem naturalem in familias disposita, iconibus exemplisque plurimis explicata. 4 vols. 8vo. Parisiis et Argentorati, 1806–9. (Orthoptera, Tom. III, 1807.)

" In Humboldt, A. de, et Bonpland, A., Recueil d'observations de zoologie et d'anatomie comparée, faites dans un voyage aux tropiques dans les années 1799–1804. 2 vols. Fol. Paris, 1811–32.

" In Cuvier, G., Le Règne animal distribué d'après son organisation, pour servir de base à l'histoire naturelle des animaux et d'introduction à l'anatomie comparée. Tome III. 8vo. Paris, 1817.

" Ditto, 2° Édition. Tome V. 8vo. Paris, 1829.

" Ditto, Édition accompagnée de planches gravées représentant les types de tous les genres, les caractères distinctifs des divers groupes et les modifications de structure sur lesquelles repose cette classification, par une réunion de disciples de Cuvier. MM. Audouin, Blanchard, Deshayes, Alcide D'Orbigny, Doyère, Dugès, Duvernoy, Laurillard, Milne-Edwards, Roulin et Valenciennes. Insectes. Tome III. Roy. 8vo. Paris. No date. See also Guérin-Méneville, F. E., and Westwood, J. O.

" Ditto, American Edition, translated from the French, with notes and additions by H. M'Murtrie. 4 vols. 8vo. New York, 1831.

LEACH, W. E.—Article Entomology; in the New Edinburgh Encyclopædia. Vol. IX. 4to. Edinburgh, 1830.

" Ditto, American Edition. Vol. VIII. 4to. Philadelphia, 1816.

LEFEBVRE, A.—In Serville, Histoire naturelle des Insectes Orthoptères.

LEIDY, J.—On the anatomy of Spectrum femoratum Say; *in the Proceedings of the Academy of Natural Sciences of Philadelphia.* Vol. III. 8vo. Philadelphia, 1846.

"   *In the Proceedings of the Academy of Natural Sciences of Philadelphia.* Vol. V. 8vo. Philadelphia, 1851.

LHERMINIER, F. J.—Observations sur les habitudes des Insectes de la Guadeloupe; *in the* Annales de la Société entomologique de France. Tome VI. 8vo. Paris, 1837.

LICHTENSTEIN, A. A. H.—A dissertation on two natural genera, hitherto confounded under the name of Mantis; *in the* Transactions of the Linnean Society. Vol. VI. 4to. London, 1802.

LINNÉ, C. von.—Museum Adolphi Frederici Regis Suecorum etc. in quo animalia rariora imprimis et exotica: Quadrupedia, Aves, Amphibia, Pisces, Insecta, Vermes, describuntur et determinantur latine et suecice cum iconibus. Fol. Holmiae, 1754.

"   Systema Naturæ per regna tria naturae, secundum classes, ordines, genera, species, cum characteribus, differentiis, synonymis, locis. Editio decim reformata. 3 Tom. Holmiae, 1758-9. (Orthoptera, Tom. I, 1758.)

Ditto, Editio duodecim reformata. 3 Tom. 8vo. Holmiae, 1766-7. (Orthoptera, Tom. II, 1767.)

Ditto, Editio decima tertia ad editionem duodecimam reformatam Holmianam. 3 Tom. in 4 vols. 8vo. Vindobonae. 1767-70. (Orthoptera, Tom. I, 1767.)

See also Gmelin, J. F., Goeze, F. A. E., Turton, W., Villers, C. de, and Müller, P. L. S.

"   Centuria Insectorum rariorum. 4to. Upsaliae, 1763.

"   Ditto, *in the* Amœnitates Academicae seu dissertationes physicae, medicae, botanicae antehac seorsim editæ nunc collectae et auctae cum tabulis aeneis. Tom. VI. 8vo. Holmae, 1763.

"   Museum S. R. M. Ludovicae Ulricae Reginae etc. in quo animalia rariora, exotica, imprimis insecta et conchylia describuntur et determinantur, prodromi instar editum. 8vo. Holmiae, 1764.

LUCAS, H.—*In the* Annales de la Société entomologique de France. 3ᵉ Sér. Tom. IV. 8vo. Paris, 1856.

MACQUART, J.—Catalogue du Musée d'histoire naturelle de la ville de Lille. Animaux invertébrés. 8vo. Lille, 1850.

MARSCHALL, A. F. von.—Decas Orthopterorum novorum; *in the* Annalen des Wiener Museums der Naturgeschichte, herausgegeben von der Direction derselben. Tom. I. 4to. Wien, 1836.

MORTIMER, C.—A continuation of an account of an essay towards a natural history of Carolina and the Bahama Islands, by Mark Catesby, with some extracts out of the tenth set; *in the* Philosophical Transactions. Vol. XLIV. 4to. London, 1748.

"   Ditto, with some extracts out of the appendix; *in the* Philosophical Transactions. Vol. XLV. 4to. London, 1748.

MÜLLER, P. L. S.—Des Ritters Carl von Linné vollständiges Natursystem nach der zwölften lateinischen Ausgabe und nach Anleitung des holländischen Houttuynischen Werks mit einer ausführlichen Erklärung. 8vo. 6 Theilen in 9 Bänden. Nurnberg, 1773-4. (Orthoptera, V Theil, 1774.)

NIÉTO, J.—Note sur une nouvelle espèce d'Orthoptère du Mexique. 8vo. Paris, 1857.

"   Ditto, in Guérin-Méneville, Revue et Magasin de Zoologie pure et appliquée. Recueil mensuel destiné à faciliter aux savants de tous les pays les moyens de publier leurs observations de zoologie pure et appliquée à l'industrie et à l'agriculture, leurs travaux de paléontologie, d'anatomie et de physiologie comparées, et à les tenir au courant des nouvelles découvertes et des progrès de la science. XX° année. 8vo. Paris, 1857.

OKEN, L.—Lehrbuch der Naturgeschichte. 3 vols. in 6. 8vo. Leipzig, 1813-26. (Orthoptera, Bd. III, i, 1815.)

"   Allgemeine Naturgeschichte für alle Stände. 7 vols. in 14. 8vo. Stuttgart, 1833-43. (Orthoptera, Bd. V, C, 1836.)

"   Isis. 4to. Leipzig.

OLIVIER, V. G.—In the Encyclopédie méthodique, dictionnaire des insectes. 10 vols. 4to. 1789-1825. (Orthoptera, Vol. IV, 1789; VI, 1791; VII, 1792.)

PACKARD, A. S., Jr.—Report on the insects collected on the Penobscot and Alleguash Rivers during August and September, 1861; in the Preliminary Report upon the natural history and geology of the State of Maine for 1861, embodied in the Sixth Annual Report of the Secretary of the Maine Board of Agriculture for 1861. 8vo. Augusta, 1861; also entitled: Sixth Annual Report of the Secretary of the Maine Board of Agriculture; embracing also the Reports on the Scientific Survey, 1861. 8vo. Augusta, 1861.

"   How to collect and observe insects. From the Report of the Maine Scientific Survey for 1862. 8vo. Augusta, 1862.

"   Ditto, in the Second Annual Report upon the natural history and geology of the State of Maine, 1862. 8vo. Augusta, 1863.

PALISOT DE BEAUVOIS, A. M. F. J.—Insectes recueillis en Afrique et en Amérique dans les royaumes d'Oware à Saint Domingue et dans les États-unis pendant les années 1786-97. Fol. Paris, 1805-21.

PALLAS, P. S.—Spicilegia Zoologica quibus novæ imprimis et obscuræ animalium species iconibus, descriptionibus atque commentariis illustrantur. Tom. I. 4to. Berolini, 1767-74. Tom. II, fasc. XI-XIII. 4to. Berolini, 1774-79. Tom. I, also entitled: Spicilegia Zoologica, Tomus I. Continens quadrupedium, avium, amphibiorum, piscium, insectorum, multorumque aliorumque marinorum fasciculos decem. (Orthoptera, Fasc. IX, 1772.)

PANZER, G. W. F.—Rob. Drurys Abbildungen und Beschreibungen exotischer Insecten mit fein illuminirten Kupfertafeln. Aus dem Englisch übersetzt mit vollständiger Synonymie und erläuternden Bemerkungen versehen. 4to. Nürnberg, 1785–88. See also Westwood, J. O.

PERCHERON, A. R.—*In* Guérin-Méneville, F. E., et Percheron, A. R., Genera des Insectes ou exposition détaillée de tous les caractères propres à chacun des genres de cette classe d'animaux. 8vo. Paris, 1835–8.

PERTY, M.—De Insectorum in America meridionali habitantium vitae genere, moribus ac distributione geographica observationes nonnullas; in Delectus animalium articulatorum quae in itinero per Brasiliam annis 1817–20 jussu et auspiciis Maximiliani Josephi I. Bavariae regis augustissimo peracto collegerunt Dr. J. B. de Spix et Dr. C. F. Ph. de Martius. Digessit, descripsit, pingenda curavit Dr. Maximilianus Perty, praefatus est et edidit C. F. Ph. de Martius. Fol. Monachii, 1830–34.

ROEMER, J. J.—Genera Insectorum Linnaei et Fabricii iconibus illustrata. 4to. Vitoduri, 1789.

SAUSSURE, H. DE—Orthoptera nova americana (Diagnoses praeliminaires). Series I–III. 8vo. Paris, 1859–61.

  "   Ditto, *in* Guérin-Méneville, Revue et Magasin de Zoologie. 8vo. Paris, 1859–61.

  "   Études sur quelques Orthoptères du Musée de Genéve nouveaux ou imparfaitement connus; *in the* Annales de la Société entomologique de France. 4ᵉ Série. Tome I. 8vo. Paris, 1861.

  "   Blattarum novarum species aliquot. 8vo. Paris, 1864.

  "   Ditto, *in* Guérin-Méneville, Revue et Magasin de Zoologie. 8vo. Paris, 1864.

  "   Orthoptères de l'Amérique moyenne. 4to. Genéve, 1864. Also entitled: Mémoires pour servir à l'histoire naturelle du Mexique des Antilles et des États-unis. 3ᵉ et 4ᵉ Livraisons. Orthoptères. Blattides. 4to. Genéve et Paris, 1864–65.

SAY, T.—*In* Keating, W. H., Narrative of an expedition to the source of St. Peter's River, Lake Winnepeek, Lake of the Woods, etc., etc., performed in the year 1823, by order of the Hon. J. C. Calhoun, Secretary of War, under the command of Stephen H. Long. Messrs. Say, Keating and Calhoun. 2 vols. 8vo. Philadelphia, 1824. (Orthoptera, Vol. II. Appendix. Part 1, Natural History. § 1, Zoölogy.)

  "   Description of new Hemipterous Insects, collected in the expedition to the Rocky Mountains, performed by order of Mr. Calhoun, Secretary of War, under command of Major Long; *in the* Journal of the Academy of Natural Sciences of Philadelphia, Vol. IV. 8vo. Philadelphia, 1825.

  "   American Entomology, or Descriptions of the Insects of North

America; Illustrated by colored figures from original drawings executed from nature. 3 vols. 8vo. Philadelphia, 1824–8.

SAY, T.—The complete writings of Thomas Say on the Entomology of North America, edited by John L. LeConte, M. D. 2 vols. 8vo. New York, 1859 (posthumous). See also Uhler, P. R.

SCHAUM, H. R.—Bericht über die wissenschaftlichen Leistungen im Gebiete der Entomologie. 5 vols. 8vo. Berlin, 1850–4. See also Erichson, W. F., and Gerstaecker, C. E. A.

"   Ditto, in Troschel, Archiv für Naturgeschichte. 8vo. Berlin, 1850–54.

SCUDDER, S. H.—On the Genus Rhaphidophora, Serville; with descriptions of four species from the caves of Kentucky, and from the Pacific coast. 8vo. Boston, 1861.

"   Ditto, in the Proceedings of the Boston Society of Natural History. Vol. VIII. 8vo. Boston, 1861.

"   List of Orthoptera collected on a trip from Anticosti to Cumberland; in the Canadian Naturalist and Geologist and Proceedings of the Natural History Society of Montreal. Vol. VII, No. 4. 8vo. Montreal, 1862.

"   Materials for a monograph of the North American Orthoptera, including a catalogue of the known New England species; in the Boston Journal of Natural History, containing Papers and Communications read to the Boston Society of Natural History. Vol. VII, No. III. 8vo. Boston, 1862. See also Harris, T. W., and Uhler, P. R.

"   Remarks on some characteristics of the Insect Fauna of the White Mountains, New Hampshire; in the Boston Journal of Natural History. Vol. VII, No. IV. 8vo. Boston, 1861.

SELLS, W.—Entomological Notes; in the Transactions of the Entomological Society of London. Vol. III. 8vo. London, 1842.

SERVILLE, J. G. AUDINET.—In the Dictionnaire classique d'histoire naturelle par M. M. Audouin, Isid. Bourdon, Ad. Brongiart, DeCandolle, Daudebard de Férussac, A. Desmoulins, Drapiez, Edwards, Flourens, Geoffroy St. Hilaire, A. de Jussieu, Kunth, C. DeLafosse, Lamouroux, Latreille, Lucas fils, Prevôt-Duplessis, C. Prévost, A. Richard, Thirbaut de Berneaud et Bory. de Saint Vincent. Ouvrage dirigé par ce dernier collaborateur, et dans lequel on a ajouté pour le porter au niveau de la science, un grand nombre de mots qui n'avaient pu faire de la plupart des dictionnaires antérieurs. Tom. I–XVII. 8vo. Paris, 1822–31. (Orthoptera, T. II, 1827.)

"   In Férussac, Bulletin des Sciences naturelles et de Géologie. Vol. I. 8vo. Paris, 1824.

"   Revue méthodique des Orthoptères; in the Annales des Sciences naturelles. T. XXII. 8vo. Paris, 1831.

SERVILLE, J. G. AUDINET.—Histoire naturelle des Insectes, Orthoptères. 8vo. Paris, 1839.[1] See also Lefebvre, A.

SHAW, G. and NODDER, P.—Vivarium Naturæ, or the Naturalist's Mis-
cellany. 24 vols. 8vo. London, 1790–1813.

STÅL, C.—Entomologiska Notiser; in the Öfversigt af Kongliga Vetens-
kaps-Academien Förhandlingar. XII Årg., 1855. 8vo. Stockholm, 1856.

"   Orthoptera species novas descripsit C. Stål; in the Kongliga
Svenska Fregatten Eugenies Resa omkring Jorden under Befäl
af C. A. Virgin Åren 1851–3. Vetenskapliga iakttagelser På H.
Maj. Konung Oscar den Förstes Befallning utgifna af K. Svenska
Vetenskaps-Akademien, Haft 10, Zoologi, V. (Insekter, 4.) 4to.
Stockholm, 1861.

STOLL', C.—Natuurlijke en naar 't Leven naauwkeurig gekleurde Af-
beeldingen en Beschryvingen der Spooken, wandelende Bladen,
Zabelspringhaanen, Krekels, Treksprinkhaanen en Kakkerlakken
in alle vier Deelen der Waereld Europa, Asia, Afrika en Amerika huishoudende, by een verzameld en beschreeven; also entitled:
Representation exactement colorée d'après nature des Spectres,
des Mantes, des Sauterelles, des Grillons, des Criquets, et des
Blattes qui se trouvent dans les quatre parties du monde, l'Europe,
l'Asie, l'Afrique et l'Amérique rassemblées et décrites. 4to. Am-
sterdam, 1787–1813.

SULZER, J. H.— Die Kennzeichen der Insekten nach Anleitung des
Rittern Karl Linnaeus durch 24 Kupfertafeln erläutert und mit
derselben natürlichen Geschichte begleitet. Mit einer Vorrede
des Herrn Johannes Gessners. 4to. Zürich, 1761.

TAYLOR, A. S.—An account of the Grasshoppers and Locusts of America; in the Annual Report of the Board of Regents of the Smithsonian Institution, showing the operations, expenditures and condi-
tion of the Institution for the year 1858. 8vo. Washington, 1859.

THOMAS, C.—In the Proceedings of the Entomological Society of Philadelphia. Vol. I. 8vo. Philadelphia, 1862.

"   Insects injurious to vegetation in Illinois; in the Transactions of
the Illinois State Agricultural Society, with Reports from County

[1] The Author's proof copy of this work was shown to me in Paris by M. Lucas, of
the Jardin des Plantes. The signatures bore the impress of the printer's stamp as fol-
lows:—"Imprimerie de Fain. Rue Racine No. 4, 1er Auteur." In the middle of each
stamp was written the date at which the impression was sent, showing that the whole
work was printed in 1838, between the 20th of July and the 30th of December. The
title-page also bore the printed date, 1839.

Burmeister's Handbuch II, ii (containing the Orthoptera), has always been granted
priority of publication over Serville's Orthoptères; but while the title-page of that por-
tion of Burmeister's second volume bears the date of 1838, the first half (on the Neurop-
tera) is dated 1839. These dates compared with the completion of Serville's work late
in 1839, seem to throw some doubt upon the priority of authority in the two cases. The
time of the actual publication of Burmeister's Orthoptera may perhaps be decided by
reference to the periodicals of the day.

b

Agricultural Societies and kindred Associations. Vol. V. 1861-64. 8vo. Springfield, 1865.

THOMPSON, W.—Notice of the Blind-fish, Cray-fish and Insects from the Mammoth Cave of Kentucky; in the Annals and Magazine of Natural History. Vol. XIII. 8vo. London, 1844.

THON, T.—Entomologisches Archiv. 2 Bänden. 4to. Jena, 1827-9.

THUNBERG, C. P.—Nägra nya Species af Blattas-slägtet beskrifna; in the Kongliga Vetenskaps-Academiens nya Handlingar. Tom. XXXI. 8vo. Stockholm, 1810.

    "   Descriptio Acridii; in the Nova Acta Regiae Societatis Upsaliensis. T. VII. 8vo. Upsaliæ, 1815.

    "   Hemipterorum maxillosorum genera Illustrata; in the Mémoires de l'Académie Impériale des Sciences de St.-Pétersbourg. Tomo V. 4to. St.-Pétersbourg, 1815.

    "   Dissertatio entomologica de Hemipteris maxillosis Capensibus. 4to. Upsaliæ, 1822.

    "   Grylli monographia Illustrata; in the Mémoires de l'Académie Impériale des Sciences de St.-Pétersbourg. T. IX. 4to. St.-Pétersbourg, 1824.

    "   Blattarum novae species descriptae; in the Mémoires de l'Académie Impériale des Sciences de St.-Pétersbourg. T. X. 4to. St.-Pétersbourg, 1826.

    "   Truxalis insecti genus Illustratum; in the Nova Acta Regiae Societatis Upsaliensis. Tom. IX. Upsaliæ, 1827.

TURTON, W.—A general system of nature, through the three grand kingdoms of animals, vegetables and minerals, systematically divided into their several classes, orders, genera, species and varieties, with their habitations, manners, economy, structure and peculiarities. Translated from Gmelin's last edition of the celebrated Systema Naturae, by Sir Charles Linné, amended and enlarged by the improvements and discoveries of later naturalists and societies, with appropriate copperplates, in seven volumes. 8vo. London, 1800-6. (Orthoptera, Vol. I, 1802.)

    "   A general system of nature through the three grand kingdoms of animals, vegetables and minerals, systematically divided into their several classes, orders, genera, species and varieties, with their habitations, manners, economy, structure and peculiarities. By Sir Charles Linné. Translated from Gmelin, Fabricius, Willdenow, etc., together with various modern arrangements and corrections derived from the transactions of the Linnean and other societies, as well as from the classical works of Shaw, Thornton, Abbot, Donovan, Sowerby, Latham, Dillwyn, Lewin, Martyn, Andrews, Lambert, etc., etc., with a life of Linné, appropriate copperplates, and a 'dictionary, explanatory of the terms which occur in several departments of natural history, in seven volumes. 8vo. London, 1806. (Orthoptera, Vol. II, which has the additional title, Animal Kingdom, Vol. II. Insects, Part I).

UHLER, P. R.—*In* Say, T., The complete writings of Thomas Say on the Entomology of North America, edited by John L. LeConte. M. D.

"   *In* Harris, T. W., A Treatise on some of the insects injurious to vegetation. 3d edition.

"   *In* Scudder, S. II., Materials for a Monograph of the North American Orthoptera.

"   Orthopterological contributions; *in the* Proceedings of the Entomological Society of Philadelphia. Vol. II. 8vo. Philadelphia, 1864.

"   *In* Thomas, C., Insects injurious to vegetation in Illinois.

VILLERS, C. DE—Caroli Linnaei Entomologia, faunae suecicae descriptionibus aucta; D. D. Scopoli, Geoffroy, De Geer, Fabricii, Schrank, etc., speciebus vel in systemate non enumeratis, vel nuperrime detectis, vel speciebus Galliae australis locupletata, generum specierumque rariorum iconibus ornata. 4 Tomi. 8vo. Lugduni, 1789.

VOIGT, F. S.—Das Thierreich geordnet nach seiner Organisation als Grundlage der Naturgeschichte der Thiere und Einleitung in die vergleichende Anatomie vom Baron von Cuvier. Nach der zweiten vermehrten Ausgabe übersetzt und durch Zusätze erweitert. Bände I–VI. 8vo. Leipzig, 1831–43. (Orthoptera, Band V, 1839.)

WALSH, B. D.—On certain entomological speculations of the New England school of naturalists; *in the* Proceedings of the Entomological Society of Philadelphia. Vol. III. 8vo. Philadelphia, 1864.

"   On phytophagic varieties and phytophagic species; *in the* Proceedings of the Entomological Society of Philadelphia. Vol. III. 8vo. Philadelphia, 1864.

"   Grasshoppers and Locusts; *in the* Transactions of the Illinois State Agricultural Society. Vol. V, 1861–64. 8vo. Springfield, 1865.

WEBER, F.—Observationes Entomologicae, continentes novorum quae condidit generum characteres et nuper detectarum specierum descriptiones. 8vo. Kiliae, 1801.

WESTWOOD, J. O.—*In* Guérin-Méneville, Magasin de Zoologie. Vol. VII. 8vo. Paris, 1837.

"   *In the* Proceedings of the Zoological Society of London. Part V. 8vo. London, 1837.

"   Drury, Dru. Illustrations of Exotic Entomology, containing upwards of six hundred and fifty figures and descriptions of foreign insects, interspersed with remarks and reflections on their nature and properties. A new edition, brought down to the present state of the science, with the systematic characters of

each species, synonyms, indexes, and other additional matter, in
3 vols. 4to. London, 1837–42.

WESTWOOD, J. O.—On Hymenoptera, a group of exotic orthopterous
insects; in the Magazine of Natural History. 2d series. Vol.
III. 8vo. London, 1839.

"   An introduction to the modern classification of insects, founded
on the natural habits and corresponding organizations of the different families. 2 vols. 8vo. London, 1839–40. (Orthoptera,
Vol. I, 1837.)

"   Arcana Entomologica, or Illustrations of new, rare and interesting exotic insects. 2 vols. 8vo. London, 1841–5.

"   Catalogue of Orthopterous Insects in the collection of the
British Museum. Part I. Phasmidae. 4to. London, 1859.

"   The Animal Kingdom, arranged after its organisation, forming
a natural history of animals, and an Introduction to comparative
anatomy, by the late Baron Cuvier. Translated and adapted to
the present state of science. New edition with considerable additions, by W. B. Carpenter and J. O. Westwood. Roy. 8vo.
London, 1863.

WHITE, A.—In Richardson, Sir J., Arctic Searching Expedition through
Rupert's Land and the Arctic Sea in search of Sir J. Franklin.
2 vols. 8vo. London, 1851.

WILSON, J.—A Treatise on Insects, general and systematic, being the
article Entomology from the seventh edition of the Encyclopædia
Britannica, with five hundred and forty woodcuts. 4to. Edinburgh, 1835.

"   Ditto, in the Encyclopædia Britannica. 8th Ed. Vol. IX.
4to. Boston, 1855.

ZIMMERMAN, C.—Zur Naturgeschichte der Mantis Carolina; in Erichson,
Archiv für Naturgeschichte. Tomo IX. 8vo. Berlin, 1843.

ZINCKEN, J. L. T. F.—In Germar, Magazin der Entomologie. Bd. I,
Heft II. 8vo. Halle, 1813.

CATALOGUE

OF

NORTH AMERICAN ORTHOPTERA.

Acanthoderus.

adumbratus [Xylicus] SAUSS. Orthopt. nov. amer. I, 4:—In. Rev. et Mag. de Zool. 1859, 62, *Porto Rico.*—[Xylodus] GERST. Archiv f. Nat. XXVI, II, 404;—In. Bericht, 1859–60, 48, *Porto Rico.*

cornatus BURM. Handb. d. Entom. II, 569, *Aus Westindien von St. Thomas.*—GUÉR. Sagra, Hist. nat. de Cuba, 351, *Cuba, St. Thomas et Martinique.*—WESTW. Catal. Orthopt. 56, *In Insula St. Thomas.* See also *Phasma cornutum.*

mexicanus SAUSS. Orthopt. nov. amer. I, 4:—In. Rev. et Mag. de Zool. 1859, 62, *Mexico.*—GERST. Archiv f. Nat. XXVI, II, 404;—In. Bericht, 1859–60, 48, *Mexico.*

rosarius WESTW. Catal. Orthopt. 56, *America meridionalis?*
See also PHASMA.

Acanthodis.

aquilina SERV. Ann. Sc. Nat. XXII, 151, *Indes.*—In. Orthopt. 451, *Amérique méridionale, Cayenne.*—BLANCH. Hist. nat. Ins. III, 21, *Amérique méridionale.*

azteca SAUSS. Orthopt. nov. amer. I, 10:—In. Rev. et Mag. de Zool. 1859, 206, *Mexico.*—GERST. Archiv f. Nat. XXVI, II, 405; —In. Bericht, 1859–60, 49, *Mexico.*

coronata SERV. Ann. Sc. Nat. XXII, 151, *Indes.*

Imhoffiana [Calamoptera] SAUSS. Orthopt. nov. amer. II, 5:—In. Rev. et Mag. de Zool. 1861, 130, *Mexico.*—[Calamoptera] GERST. Archiv f. Nat. XXVIII, II, 316;—In. Bericht, 1861, 44, *Mexico.*

2   CATALOGUE OF DESCRIBED

macrocera FITCH, Trans. N. Y. St. Agric. Soc. XVI, 406;—Ia. 3d
  —5th Rep. 3d Rep. 171, *Acapulco, Mexico.*
mexicana SAUSS. Orthopt. nov. amer. I, 9;—In. Rev. et Mag. de
  Zool. 1859, 206, *Tellus mexicana.*—GERST. Archiv f. Nat.
  XXVI, II, 405;—In. Bericht, 1859–60, 49, *Mexiko.*
specularis SERV. Ann. Sc. Nat. XXII, 151, *Amérique.*
toltoca SAUSS. Orthopt. nov. amer. I, 10;—In. Rev. et Mag. de Zool.
  1859, 206, *Mexico.*—GERST. Archiv f. Nat. XXVI, II, 405;
  —In. Bericht, 1859–60, 49, *Mexiko.*
  See also LOCUSTA.

Acanthops.

antocus SAUSS. Orthopt. nov. amer. I, 2;—In. Rev. et Mag. de Zool.
  1859, 60, *Merkoaran.*—GERST. Archiv f. Nat. XXVI, II, 402;
  —In. Bericht, 1859–60, 46, *Mexiko.*
mexicanus SAUSS. Orthopt. nov. amer. I, 2;—In. Rev. et Mag. de
  Zool. 1859, 60, *Mexico.*—GERST. Archiv f. Nat. XXVI, II,
  402;—In. Bericht, 1859–60, 46, *Mexilo.*
  See also MANTIS.

Acheta.

abbreviata HARR. Treat. Ed. 1841–2, 172; Ed. 1852, 133; Ed. 1862,
  152, fig. 69, *Massachusetts.*—ERICHS. Archiv f. Nat. IX, II,
  276;—In. Bericht, 1842, 82, *Massachusetts.*—FITCH, Amer.
  Journ. Agric. and Sc. VI, 146, *New York.*—Ews. Agric. of
  N. Y. V, 143, *New York.*—THOMAS, Trans. Ill. St. Agric.
  Soc. V, 442, *Illinois.*
arachnoides DEGE. Introd. Entom. 243, pl. vi, fig. 1, *Jamaica.*
  —ERICHS. Archiv f. Nat. VII, II, 196;—ID. Bericht, 1840,
  53, *Jamaica.*
assimilis FABR. Syst. Entom. 280, *Jamaica.*—In. Spec. Ins. I, 354,
  In America meridionalis insulis.—In. Entom. Syst. II, 29;—In.
  Nom. Entom. emend. Ed. 1797, 80; Ed. 1810, 80, *Jamaica.*
  —BILL. Enum. Ins. 63, *Ind. occ.* See also *Gryllus assimilis.*
bipunctata ? HARR. Hitchc. Rep. 2d Ed. 578;—In. Catal. 56, *Mass.*
  See also *Gryllus bipunctatus.*
brevipennis [Gryllotalpa] JÄGG. N. Amer. Ins. Ed. 1854, 164, *N.
  America.*
crucis FABR. Mant. Ins. I, 232;—In. Entom. Syst. II, 82, *Insula St.
  Crucis.*—In. Nom. Entom. emend. Ed. 1797, 80; Ed. 1810,
  80, *Ind.* See also *Gryllus crucis.*
cylindrica HARR. Hitchc. Rep. 2d Ed. 576;—In. Catal. 56, *Mass.*
domestica JÄGG. N. Amer. Ins. Ed. 1854, 161; Ed. 1859, 115, *N.
  America.*—THOMAS, Trans. Ill. St. Agric. Soc. V, 443, *Illinois.*

exigua Say, Journ. Acad. Nat. Sc. Philad. IV, 309;—In. Entom. of
N. Amer. Ed. Leconte, II, 232, *Missouri.*

flavipes Fabr. Entom. Syst. II, 30, *Insula St. Thomas.* — In. Nom.
Entom. emend. Ed. 1797, 80; Ed. 1810, 80, *St. Thomas.* See
Gryllus flavipes.

gigas Boxm. Gen. Ins. 53, tab. viii, fig. 8, *America.* See also *Gryllus
gigas.*

gryllotalpa Fabr. Syst. Entom. 279;—In. Entom. Syst. II, 28; — In.
Spec. Ins. I, 353, *In Europa, America borealis cultis.*—In. Nom.
Entom. emend. Ed. 1797, 80; Ed. 1810, 80, *Eur. Am.*—Jaeg.
N. Amer. Ins. Ed. 1859, 117, *N. America.* See also *Gryllus
gryllotalpa.*

guadaloupensis Fabr. Entom. Syst. II, 32, *Guadeloupe.* See also
Gryllus guadaloupensis.

hospes Fabr. Syst. Entom. 281;—In. Spec. Ins. I, 355;—In. Entom.
Syst. II, 32;—In. Nom. Entom. emend. Ed. 1797, 80; Ed.
1810, 80, *America.* See also *Gryllus hospes.*

marginata Thomas, Trans. Ill. St. Agric. Soc. V, 444, *Illinois.*

membranacea Westw. Drury, Ins. II, 91, pl. xliii, fig. 2, *Bay of Honduras, Musquito Shore.*

minuta Fabr. Syst. Entom. 282, *America.* — In. Spec. Ins. I, 355, *In
America meridionali.*—In. Entom. Syst. II, 33;—In. Nom. En-
tom. emend. Ed. 1797, 80; Ed. 1810, 80, *America.* See also
Gryllus minutus.

monstrosa Fabr. Nom. Entom. emend. Ed. 1797, 80; Ed. 1810, 80,
Ind.—Dill. Entom. Ins. 65, *Ind.*

nigra Harr. Treat. Ed. 1841-2, 123; Ed. 1852, 131; Ed. 1862, 132.
Massachusetts. — Erichs. Archiv f. Nat. IX, ii, 222;—In. Bericht, 1842, 82, *Massachusetts.* — Fitch, Amer. Journ. Agric.
and Sc. VI, 346, *New York.*—Jaeg. N. Amer. Ins 1854, 160;
1859, 113, *N. America.*—Thomas, Trans. Ill. St. Agric. Soc.
V, 443, *Illinois.*

nivea Harr. Hitchc. Rep. 582;—In. (Œcanthus) Hitchc. Rep. 2d Ed.
576;—In. Catal. 56, *Mass.* — Jaeg. N. Amer. Ins. 1854, 159,
pl. v, fig. 26; 1859, 113, fig. 25, *N. America.* See also *Gryllus niveus.*

pennsylvanica Uhler, Harr. Treat. Ed. 1862, 132, *Massachusetts.*

aurvilla Harr. Hitchc. Rep. 2d Ed. 576;—In. Catal. 56, *Mass.*

tripunctata Harr. Hitchc. Rep. 2d Ed. 576;—In. Catal. 56, *Mass.*

vastatrix Auss. Achet. Guin. 15, *Et America sinu Honduras et litore
Muskito, Freetown.*

vittata [Nemobius] Harr. Treat. Ed. 1841-2, 123; Ed. 1852, 134; Ed.
1862, 133, fig. 70, *Massachusetts.*—[Nemobius] Erichs. Archiv
f. Nat. IX, ii, 226; — In. Bericht, 1842, 82, *Mass.* — Fitch,

Amer. Journ. Agric. and Sc. VI, 146, *New York.*—Jaeg. N.
Amer. Ins. 1854, 160; 1859, 113, *N. America.*
See also GRYLLUS.
ACHURUM, see TRUXALIS.
ACONTISTES, see MANTIS.
ACRIDA, see GRYLLUS.

Acridium.

alutaceum HARR. Treat. Ed. 1841-2, 139; Ed. 1852, 150; Ed. 1862,
173, *Martha's Vineyard.*—ERICHS. Archiv f. Nat. IX, π, 329;
—IB. Bericht, 1842, 85, *Mass.*—SCUDD. Bost. Journ. Nat.
Hist. VII. 466, *Martha's Vineyard, Conn.*
americanum SCUDD. Bost. Journ. Nat. Hist. VII, 466, *N. Carolina,
Southern States, Florida, Alabama, Texas, Southern Illinois.*—
THOMAS, Trans. Ill. St. Agric. Soc. V, 448, 452, *Illinois.*
annulatum OLIV. Encycl. méth. VI, 225, *Amérique méridionale.*
aeneosum [Tetrix] DE HAAN, Bijdr. Kenn. Orthopt. 143, *Tennessee.*
bivittatum [Opomala] DE HAAN, Bijdr. Kenn. Orthopt. 144, *Caro-
lina.*—[Calopterus] UHLER, Harr. Treat. Ed. 1862, 174, *New
England and western sections of the Union.*—THOMAS, Trans.
Ill. St. Agric. Soc. V, 449, *Illinois.*
Boreckii [Podisma] STÅL. Orthopt. Eug. Res. 332, *California, San
Francisco.*—[Podisma] GERST. Archiv f. Nat. XXVIII, II.
318;—IB. Bericht. 1863, 46, *California.*
carolinum DE GEER, Mém. III, 491, pl. xlvii, figs. 2, 3, *Amérique
septentrionale et en particulier la Caroline et la Pensylvanie.*—
GÖZE. De Geer, Geschh. Ins. III, 319, tab. xli, figs. 2, 3, *In
nordlichen Amerika.*—OLIV. Encycl. méth. VI, 225, *Amérique
septentrionale.*—(carolinianum) PAL. DE BEAUV. Insectes, 147,
pl. iv, fig. 6, *Caroline du Sud.*—HAHN, Icon. Orthopt. tab.
A. Genus Acridium, fig. 3, *America.*—[Edipoda] DE HAAN,
Bijdr. Kenn. Orthopt. 113, *Tennessee.*
centurio [Rhomalea] DE HAAN, Bijdr. Kenn. Orthopt. 144, *Carolina.*
clavuligerum [Oxya] SERV. Orthopt. 676, pl. xiv, fig. 11, *Amérique septentrionale.*—DE HAAN, Bijdr. Kenn. Orthopt. 144,
Carolina.
coloratum BURM. Germ. Zeitschr. f. Entom. II, 61, *Amerika.*—SERV.
Orthopt. 671, *Une partie de l'Amérique voisine de la Caroline du
Sud.*—DE HAAN, Bijdr. Kenn. Orthopt. 144, *Carolina.*
compressum THUNB. Nov. Act. Upsal. VII, 162, *In insula Jamaica.*
—GERM. Germ. Mag. d. Entom. III, 408, *Jamaica.*
cristatum LAM. Hist. nat. Anim. sans Vert. IV, 211; 2e Ed. IV, 413;
2e Ed. II, 132, *Amérique méridionale.*—SERV. Ann. Sc. Nat.
XXII, 283, *Amérique.*—IB. Orthopt. 650, *Amérique méridi-*

ionale, Cayenne principalement.—Fitch. W. Index Orthopt.
13;—In. Bull. Soc. Imp. Nat. Mosc. XIX, 11, 480, *Am. Mer.*—
Fitch. Trans. N. Y. St. Agric. Soc. XVI, 307; —In. 3d-5th
Rep. 3d Rep. 172, *Tropical America.*

cubense Saues. Orthopt. nov. amer. II, 14;—In. Rev. et Mag. de
Zool. 1861, 163, *Cuba.*

cucullatum [Tetrix] De Haan, Bijdr. Kenn. Orthopt. 143. *Tennessee.*

cyanipes Oliv. Encycl. méth. VI, 228, *Amérique méridionale.*

damniflcum Saues. Orthopt. nov. amer. II, 14;—In. Rev. et Mag. de
Zool. 1861, 164, *America borealis, Tennessee.*—Gerst. Archiv
f. Nat. XXVIII, 11, 317;—In. Bericht, 1861, 45, *Tennessee.*

dentatum De Geer, Mém. III, 496, pl. xlii, fig. 5, *India.*

differentiale Uhler, Thomas, Trans. Ill. St. Agric. Soc. V, 450,
Illinois.

discoideum [Edipoda] De Haan, Bijdr. Kenn. Orthopt. 143, *Tennessee.*

dux Oliv. Encycl. méth. VI, 215, pl. cxxvi. fig. 1, *Amérique méridi-
onale à la baie de Honduras.*—Serv. Ann. Sc. Nat. XXII, 283,
Amérique méridionale, Brésil.—Fitch, Trans. N. Y. St. Agric.
Soc. XVI, 307;—In. 3d-5th Rep. 3d Rep. 172, *Tropical
America.*—? Flor, v. Siv. Antill. xii, *Honduras, Senegita.*

ensicornu De Geer, Mém. III, 499, pl. xlii, fig. 7, *Pensylvanie.*—
Goez, De Geer, Gesch. Ins. III, 375, Tab. xlii, fig. 7, *Pensylvanien.*

femorale Oliv. Encycl. méth. VI, 226, *Pensylvanie.*

femoratum [Caloptenus] De Haan, Bijdr. Kenn. Orthopt. 144, *Carolina.*

femur rubrum De Geer, Mém. III, 498, pl. xlii, fig. 5, *Pensylvanie.*—Goez, DeGeer, Gesch. Ins. III, 324, tab. xlii, fig. 5,
Pensylvanien.—Harr. Hitchc. Rep. 583; 2d Ed. 576;—In.
Catal. 58, *Mass.*—In. Treat. Ed. 1841-2, 141; Ed. 1852, 151;
Ed. 1862, 174, *United States.*—[Caloptenus] De Haan, Bijdr.
Kenn. Orthopt. 143, *Tennessee.*—Fitch, Amer. Journ. Agric.
and Sc. VI, 146, *New York.*—Emm. Agric. of N. Y. V, 146,
pl. In, fig. 4, *New York.*—Uhler, Harr. Treat. Ed. 1862,
174, *United States.*—Thomas, Trans. Ill. St. Agric. Soc. V,
451, 452, *United States.*

flavofasciatum Serv. Orthopt. 663, *Amérique méridionale, Brésil.*—
Harr. Hitchc. Rep. 583, 2d Ed. 576;—In. Catal. 56, *Mass.*—
De Haan, Bijdr. Kenn. Orthopt. 143, *Tennessee.*

flavovittatum Harr. Treat. Ed. 1841-2, 140; Ed. 1852, 151; Ed.
1862, 173, *Massachusetts.*—Erichs. Archiv f. Nat. IX, 11, 229;
—In. Bericht, 1842, 85, *Mass.*—Fitch, Amer. Journ. Agric.
and Sc. VI, 146, *New York.*—Emm. Agric. of N. Y. V, 147,
New York.

giganteum [Rhomalea] De Haan, Bijdr. Kenn. Orthopt. 143, Tennessee.

granulatum Kirby, Fauna Bor. Amer. IV, 251, N. America, Lat. 65°.—[Tetrix] De Haan, Bijdr. Kenn. Orthopt. 143, Noord-America.—White, Rich. Arct. Search. Exp. II, 360, Borders of Mackenzie and Slave Rivers, Fort Simpson.

hemipterum Pal. de Beauv. Insectes, 145, pl. iv, fig. 3, États unis d'Amérique, Caroline du Sud.

laterale Oliv. Encycl. méth. VI, 226, Les isles de l'Amérique méridionale.—Say, Amer. Entom. pl. v;—Ia. Entom. of N. Amer. Ed. Leconte, I, 10, pl. v, Georgia, East Florida.—Thon, Entom. Archiv, I, 41, Georgien und West-florida.

Latreillei Fitch, Trans. N. Y. St. Agric. Soc. XVI, 507;—Ia. 2d —5th Rep. 3d Rep. 172, pl. iii, iv, Tropical America.

leucostomum [Locusta] De Haan, Bijdr. Kenn. Orthopt. 143, Noord-America.

lunum Oliv. Encycl. méth. VI, 216, Amérique méridionale.

marginatum Oliv. Encycl. méth. VI, 229, Pennsylvania.

marginicolle [Opomala] De Haan, Bijdr. Kenn. Orthopt. 143, Tennessee.

micropterum Pal. de Beauv. Insectes, 146, pl. iv, fig. 4, États unis d'Amérique, Caroline du Sud.—[Rhomalea] De Haan, Bijdr. Kenn. Orthopt. 144, Carolina.—Ia. 151, Georgia, Carolina.

Milberti Serv. Orthopt. 649, Amérique septentrionale.—De Haan, Bijdr. Kenn. Orthopt. 144, Carolina.

miliare Oliv. Encycl. méth. VI, 218, Amérique méridionale.

obliteratum [Œdipoda] De Haan, Bijdr. Kenn. Orthopt. 144, Carolina.

obscurum Harr. Hitchc. Rep. 583; 2d Ed. 576;—Ia. Catal. 56, Mass.—Burm. Handb. d. Entom. II, 632, Südcarolina.—De Haan, Bijdr. Kenn. Orthopt. 144, Carolina, Cuba.—Guér. Sagra, Hist. nat. de Cuba, 356, Cuba, Amérique septentrionale.—Scudd. Bost. Journ. Nat. Hist. VII, 467, Texas.

olivaceum Serv. Orthopt. 666, Cuba, Amérique septentrionale.—De Haan, Bijdr. Kenn. Orthopt. 144, Cuba.—Guér. Sagra, Hist. nat. de Cuba, 356, Cuba, Amérique septentrionale.

ornatum Say, Amer. Entom. pl. v;—Ia. Entom. of N. Amer. Ed. Leconte, I, 10, pl. v, Philadelphia.—Thon, Entom. Archiv, I, 41, Philadelphia.—Hald. Amer. Journ. Sc. [2] V, 435, Chihuahua, Santa Fé.

oxycephalum [Tetrix] De Haan, Bijdr. Kenn. Orthopt. 143, Tennessee.

pellidnum [Gomphocerus] De Haan, Bijdr. Kenn. Orthopt. 144, Carolina.

phœnicopterum [Œdipoda] De Haan, Bijdr. Kenn. Orthopt. 144, Carolina.

polymorphum [Tetrix] DE HAAN, Bijdr. Kenn. Orthopt. 144, *Carolina.*

punctipenne [Opsomala] DE HAAN, Bijdr. Kenn. Orthopt. 144, *Carolina.*

purpurascens OLIV. Encycl. méth. VI, 234, *L'Ile de la Trinité.*

quadrimaculatum THUNB. Nov. Act. Upsal. VII, 160, *In insula Bartholomei Americæ.*—GERM. Germ. Mag. d. Entom. III, 407, *St. Bartholemy.*

rhombeum [Choriphyllum] DE HAAN, Bijdr. Kenn. Orthopt. 144; —[Hymenotes] Ib. Bijdr. Kenn. Orthopt. 163, *Jamaica.*

rubiginosum HARRIS, Scudd. Bost. Journ. Nat. Hist. VII, 467, *Cape Cod, Conn. S. Car. Southern States, Alabama.*—GERST. Archiv f. Nat. XXIX, II, 358;—Ib. Bericht, 1862, 44, *Nord America.*

rusticum OLIV. Encycl. méth. VI, 228, *Les Iles de l'Amérique méridionale.*—BURM. Handb. d. Entom. II, 633, *Nord Amerika.*—DE HAAN, Bijdr. Kenn. Orthopt. 144, *Carolina.*

Sagrai [Choriphyllum] DE HAAN, Bijdr. Kenn. Orthopt. 144, *Cuba.*

sanguinipes HARR. Hitchc. Rep. 583; 2d Ed. 576;—Ib. Catal. 56, *Mass.*—SERV. Orthopt. 670, *Amérique méridionale, Brésil.*

semirubrum FITCH, Trans. N. Y. St. Agric. Soc. XVI, 507;—Ib. 3d-5th Rep. 3d Rep. 172, *Tropical America.*—SAUSS. Orthopt. nov. amer. II, 13;—Ib. Rev. et Mag. de Zool. 1861, 162, *In campis americanis.*

serratum LAM. Hist. nat. Anim. sans Vert. IV, 241; 2° Ed. IV, 443; 3° Ed. II, 152, *Cap de Bonne Espérance, l'Amérique méridionale.*

sordidum [Œdipoda] DE HAAN, Bijdr. Kenn. Orthopt. 143, *Tennessee.*

speciosum BURM. Germ. Zeitschr. f. Entom. II, 61, *Amerika.*

spretum UHLER, Thomas, Trans. Ill. St. Agric. Soc. V, 450, (apreès?) *Illinois.*

sulphureum OLIV. Encycl. méth. VI, 227, *Amérique septentrionale.*—PAL. DE BEAUV. Insectes, 145, pl. iv, fig. 2, *Etats unis d'Amérique, Virginie.*—[Œdipoda] DE HAAN, Bijdr. Kenn. Orthopt. 143, *Tennessee.*

toltecum SAUSS. Orthopt. nov. amer. II, 14;—Ib. Rev. et Mag. de Zool. 1861, 163, *Mexico temperata.*—GERST. Archiv f. Nat. XXVIII, ic, 217;—Ib. Bericht, 1861, 45, *Mexiko.*

torvum HARR. Hitchc. Rep. 2d Ed. 576;—Ib. Catal. 56, *Mass.*

tuberculatum PAL. DE BEAUV. Insectes, 145, pl. iv, fig. 1, *Etats unis d'Amérique.*

variegatum OLIV. Encycl. méth. VI, 222, *Amérique méridionale.*

varipes [Opsomala] DE HAAN, Bijdr. Kenn. Orthopt. 144, *Carolina.*

Velasquezii NIETO, Nouv. Orthopt. 2;—Ib. Rev. et Mag. de Zool. 1857, pl. xii, *Dans les bois des Haciendas, du l'oterro et de San*

Francisco, Etat de Vera Cruz.—GERST. Archiv f. Nat. XXIV,
II, 343;—Ib. Bericht, 1857, 153, *Vera Cruz.*—LUCAS, Ann.
Soc. Ent. France, [3] IV, lxvii, *Mexique, particulièrement les
bois des Haciendas, du Potrero et de San Francisco, aux environs de Cordora (Etat de Vera Cruz).*

verrucosum DE GEER, Mém. III, 486, pl. xl, fig. 6, *Amérique.*—GÜER,
De Geer, Gesch. Ins. III, 315, tab. xl, fig. 6, *Amerika.*

verruculatum [Locusta] DE HAAN, Bijdr. Kenn. Orthopt. 143, *Noord-
Amerika.*

virginianum OLIV. Encycl. méth. VI, 224, *L'Amérique septentrionale,
Virginie*—[Œdipoda] DE HAAN, Bijdr. Kenn. Orthopt. 143,
Tennessee.

viridifasciatum GÜER, De Geer, Gesch. Ins. III, 325, tab. xlll. fig. 6,
Pennsylvanien.

vitreipenne [Oxya] DE HAAN, Bijdr. Kenn. Orthopt. 114, *Carolina.*

vittatum PAL. DE BEAUV. Insectes, 146, pl. iv, fig. 5, *A la côte occidentale d'Afrique à St. Domingue et dans les Etats unis d'Amérique.*

xanthopterum [Œdipoda] DE HAAN, Bijdr. Kenn. Orthopt. 143,
Tennessee.

See also GRYLLUS.

Amblerus.

Haldemanii GIRARD, Marcy, Expl. Red River, Zol. 1853, 259, pl. xv,
fig. 5-8; Ed. 1854, 246, pl. xv, fig. 5-8, *Red River.*—GERST.
Archiv f. Nat. XX, II, 214;—Ib. Bericht, 1853, 38, *Louisiana.*

purpurascens UHLER, Proc. Entom. Soc. Philad. II, 550, *Minnesota,
Texas, Washington Territory.*—DALLAS, Zool. Record, I, 373,
Minnesota, Washington Territory.

simplex HALD. Stansb. Expl. Utah, 372, pl. x, fig. 4, *Utah.*—SCHAUM,
Archiv f. Nat. XIX, II, 271;—Ib. Bericht, 1852, 130, *Utah.*

Amplecta.

dorsalis BRUNN. Blatt. 63, *Portorico.*

fallax SAUSS. Orthopt. nov. amer. III, 2;—Ib. Rev. et Mag. de Zool.
1862, 163.—Ib. Orthopt. Amér. moy. 51, *Guatemala.*—BRUNN.
Blatt. 66, *Guatemala.*

fulgida SAUSS. Orthopt. nov. amer. III, 2;—Ib. Rev. et Mag. de Zool.
1862, 163;—Ib. Orthopt. Amér. moy. 50, *Guatemala.*—BRUNN.
Blatt. 66, *Guatemala.*

Ametrogaster.

spinax DOHRN, Entom. Zeitschr. Stett. XXIII, 279, taf. i, fig. 1, *Mexico.*—GERST. Archiv f. Nat. XXIX, II, 339;—Ib. Bericht, 1862,
45, *Mexiko.*

Anisomorpha.

buprestoides Gray, Synops. Phasm. 19, *Georgia.*—Burm. Handb.
d. Entom. II, 570, *Georgia.*—Westw. Introd. Class. Ins. 1, 424,
America.—In. Catal. Orthopt. 17, *Georgia.*—Uhler, Say,
Entom. of N. Amer. Ed. Leconte, I, 196, *Falls of Niagara,
Missouri River.*—In. Harr. Treat. Ed. 1862, 146, *Florida and
Southern States.* See also *Phasma buprestoides.*

ferruginea Gray, Synops. Phasm. 18, *Carolina.*—Burm. Handb. d.
Entom. II, 570, *Carolina.*—Westw. Catal. Orthopt. 16, *Carolina, Virginia.* See also *Phasma ferruginea.*

See also PHASMA.

Anophelepis.

Scythrus Westw. Catal. Orthopt. 68, pl. II, fig. 3, *Mexico.*
vittata Westw. Catal. Orthopt. 68, pl. III, fig. 3, *Mexico.*

Anostostoma.

tolteca Sauss. Orthopt. nov. amer. II, 5;—In. Rev. et Mag. de Zool.
1861, 130, *Mons Orizaba, Mexico.*—Gerst. Archiv f. Nat.
XXVIII, II, 316;—In. Bericht, 1861, 41, *Orizaba.*

See also LOCUSTA.

Apterygida.

ruficeps Dohrn, Entom. Zeitschr. Stett. XXIII, 231, *Cordova.*—
Gerst. Archiv f. Nat. XXIX, II, 359;—In. Bericht, 1862, 43,
Mexiko.

Arcyptera.

gracilis Scudd. Can. Nat. VII, 286, *Red River Settlements, British
America.*—In. Bost. Journ. Nat. Hist. VII, 463, *Maine, Red
River Settlements.*—Gerst. Archiv f. Nat. XXIX, II, 358;—In.
Bericht, 1862, 44, *Nord Amerika.*

lineata Scudd. Bost. Journ. Nat. Hist. VII, 462, *Mass.*—Gerst.
Archiv f. Nat. XXIX, II, 358;—In. Bericht, 1862, 44, *Nord
Amerika.*

platyptera Scudd. Bost. Journ. Nat. Hist. VII, 464, *New England.*—
Gerst. Archiv f. Nat. XXIX, II, 358;—In. Bericht, 1862, 44,
Nord Amerika.

10   CATALOGUE OF DESCRIBED

Bacteria.

Ætolus WESTW. Catal. Orthopt. 27, pl. xxii, fig. 3, *Mexico*.

arumatia GRAY, Synops. Phasm. 16, *In India occidentali*—WESTW.
Catal. Orthopt. 22, pl. xxiii, fig. 4, *In India occidentali, Guadeloupe*.

asteca [Bacunculus] SAUSS. Orthopt. nov. amer. I. 3;—In. Rev. et
Mag. de Zool. 1859, 62, *Litus mexicanum*—GERST. Archiv f.
Nat. XXVI, 11, 404;—In. Bericht, 1859–60, 45, *Mexiko*.

baculus [Bacunculus] SAUSS. Orthopt. nov. amer. I, 3;—In. Rev. et
Mag. de Zool. 1859, 62, *America*—GERST. Archiv f. Nat.
XXVI, 11, 404;—In. Bericht, 1859–60, 48, *America*.

bicornis GRAY, Synops. Phasm. 16, *In India occidentali*—BURM.
Handb. d. Entom. II, 566, *Westindien und Surinam*—WESTW.
Catal. Orthopt. 23, *In America australi et India occidentali*.

caiamus SERV. Ann. Sc. Nat. XXII, 64, *D'Amérique*—GRAY, Synops. Phasm. 17, *In India occidentali*—WESTW. Catal. Orthopt. 20, *In insula St. Crucis, Surinam, Brazil*. See also
Phasma calamus.

calcarata BURM. Handb. d. Entom. II, 566, *Merida*. See also *Phasma
calcaratum*.

Clinteria WESTW. Catal. Orthopt. 27, pl. xxv, fig. 9, *Am. merid*.

cornuta [Bacunculus] SAUSS. Orthopt. nov. amer. II, 3;—In. Rev. et
Mag. de Zool. 1861, 128, *Mexico calida*—GERST. Archiv f.
Nat. XXVIII, 11, 311;—In. Bericht, 1461, 39, *Mexiko*.

crudelis WESTW. Catal. Orthopt. 24, *In India orientali*.

cubaensis WESTW. Catal. Orthopt. 26, *Cuba*. See also *Phasma cubaense*.

Dryas WESTW. Catal. Orthopt. 27, *St. Domingo*.

faunus WESTW. Catal. Orthopt. 28, *Am. merid*.

ferula SERV. Ann. Sc. Nat. XXII, 64, *Guadeloupe*—BURM. Handb. d.
Entom. II, 564, *Westindien*.

filiformis SERV. Ann. Sc. Nat. XXII, 64, *L'Amérique méridionale*—
GRAY, Synops. Phasm. 17, *In India occidentali*—WESTW.
Catal. Orthopt. 22, *In India occidentalis insulis*.

gracilis WESTW. Catal. Orthopt. 28, *La Guayra*.

Haita WESTW. Catal. Orthopt. 25, pl. xxv, figs. 5, 6, *St. Domingo*.

linearis ?GRAY, Synops. Phasm. 17, *In India occidentali*—WESTW.
Drury, Ins. I, 123, pl. ii, fig. 8, *Antigua*.—In. Catal. Orthopt. 21,
In India occidentali, Antigua—BURM. Handb. d. Entom. II,
567, *Westindien, Portorico und St. Thomas*—GUÉR. Sagra, Hist.
nat. de Cuba, 250, *Antilles*—GOSSE, Alab. 275, *Alabama*.
See also *Phasma lineare*.

mexicana WESTW. Catal. Orthopt. 25, *Mexico*. See also *Phasma
mexicanum*.

rosaria Percu. Guér. et Perch. Gen. Ins. 5ª Livr. No. 3, pl. v, *L'Amérique méridionale.*

Sayii [Bacunculus] Burm. Handb. d. Entom. II, 566, *Nordamerika von Pennsylvanien bis Südkarolina.*—Charp. Orthopt. descr. tab. vi, *America septentrionalis.*

spinosa Burm. Handb. d. Entom. II. 567, *St. Domingo von Prinzenhafen.*

striata Burm. Handb. d. Entom. II, 567, *Mexiko.*—Westw. Catal. Orthopt. 28, *Mexico.* See also *Phasma striatum.*

toltecs [Bacunculus] Sauss. Orthopt. nov. amer. I, 3;—In. Rev. et Mag. de Zool. 1859, 62, *Montes mexicani.*—Gerst. Archiv f. Nat. XXVI, ii, 494;—In. Bericht, 1859-60, 48. *Mexiko.*

tridens Burm. Handb. d. Entom. II, 567, *Mexiko von Oaxaca.*—Westw. Catal. Orthopt. 27, *Mexiko, Oaxaca.* See also *Phasma tridens.*

See also PHASMA.

Bacunculus.

femoratus Uhler, Harr. Treat. Ed. 1862, 146, *United States east of the Mississippi.*

Sayi Thomas, Trans. Ill. St. Agric. Soc. 441, *Illinois.*

See also BACTERIA.

Batrachidea.

carinata Scudd. Bost. Journ. Nat. Hist. VII, 479, *Massachusetts.*—Gerst. Archiv f. Nat. XXIX, ii, 858;—In. Bericht, 1862, 44, *Massachusetts.*

cristata Scudd. Bost. Journ. Nat. Hist. VII, 476, *Mass. Me. N. H. Conn.*—Gerst. Archiv f. Nat. XXIX, ii, 858;—In. Bericht, 1862, 44, *Massachusetts.*

Blabera.

atropos Serv. Orthopt. 71, *Saint Domingue.*—Sauss. Orthopt. Amér. moy. 233, *Les Antilles, Cuba et la côte chaude du Mexique.*—Bruxn. Blatt. 375, tab. xii, fig. 8b, *Jamaique, Venezuela, Colombie, Brésil.* See also *Blatta atropa.*

cranifpes Burm. Handb. d. Entom. II, 816, *Kuba.*

cubensis Sauss. Blatt. nov. 29;—In. Rev. et Mag. de Zool. 347, *Cuba*—In. Orthopt. Amér. moy. 236, *Les Antilles, Cuba.*

deplanata Sauss. Blatt. nov. 30;—In. Rev. et Mag. de Zool. 1864, 348, *Antillae.*—In. Orthopt. Amér. moy. 230, *Les Antilles, Cuba.*—Dallas, Zool. Record. I, 572, *W. Indies.*—Gerst. Archiv f. Nat. XXX, ii, 431;—In. Bericht, 1863-4, 125, *Antillen.*

discoidalis Serv. Orthopt. 76, pl. i, fig. 6, *Saint Domingue.*

ferruginea Saus. Orthopt. Amér. moy. 41, *Mexique.*—Brunn. Blatt. 317, *Mexique, Acapulco.*

fraterna Saus. Orthopt. Amér. moy. 241, *L'Amérique du Sud (les Antilles, Cuba?).*

fumigata Saus. Orthopt. Amér. moy. 244, *Cuba.*—Gerst. Archiv f. Nat. XXIV, 11, 348;—In Bericht, 1857, 156, *Cuba.*—Brunn. Blatt. 381, *Havane.*

fusca Brunn. Blatt. 376, *Brésil, Chile, Cuba.*

gigantea Fisch. Orthopt. Europ. 118, *In America meridionali degens rem morbus et India occidentali in Angliam adverta est.*—Saus. Orthopt. Amér. moy. 238, *L'Amérique méridionale, Brésil, Guyanas.* See also *Blatta gigantea.*

limbata Burm. Handb. d. Entom. II, 816, *Mexiko.*

luctuosa Stål. Öfv. Kongl. Vet. Akad. Forhandl. 1855, 351, *Mexico.*—Gerst. Archiv f. Nat. XXII, 11, 211;—In Bericht, 1855, 91, *Mexiko.*

madera Sells, Trans. Entom. Soc. Lond. III, 104, *Jamaica.*

marmorata Brunn. Blatt. 378, *St. Domingue.*

mexicana Saus. Orthopt. nov. amer. 111, 17;—In Rev. et Mag. de Zool. 1862, 233, *Mexico.*—In. Orthopt. Amér. moy. 234, *Les parties chaudes du Mexique, commune dans la Cordillère orientale, Tampico, Turpan, Cordoba, etc. N. Orleans.*

minor Saus. Orthopt. Amér. moy. 238, *L'Amérique territoriale, le Brésil (Cuba?).*

Sulzeri Gerst. Archiv f. Nat. XXIV, 11, 348;—In Bericht, 1857, 156, *Cuba.*—Saus. Orthopt. Amér. moy. 239, pl. li, fig. 29, *Cuba.*—Brunn. Blatt. 380, *Surinam, Cuba.* See also *Blatta Sulzeri.*

Thunbergii Saus. Orthopt. Amér. moy. 246, *Cuba.*

trapezoides Burm. Handb. d. Entom. II, 816, *Mexiko.*—Saus. Orthopt. Amér. moy. 240, *Mexique.*—Brunn. Blatt. 374, *Mexique, Cuba.*

varians Serv. Orthopt. 78, *Cuba.*
    See also BLATTA.

Blatta.

aegyptiaca Deray, Mém. Nat. Hist. II, 67, pl. xxxvi, fig. 8, *Jamaica.*—[Polyphaga] ? Westw. Drury, Ins. II, 71, pl. xxxvi, fig. 8, *Jamaica, Egypt.*

Alcarrazas Serv. Orthopt. 90, *Amérique.*

americana Mort. Phil. Trans. XLV, 163, *Carolina.* — Linn. Syst. Nat. 10th Ed. I, 431, *America.*—In. Syst. Nat. 12th Ed. II, 687; 13th Ed. I, 687, *America, in Gallia australi.* — Müll. Linn. Natursyst. V, 402, *Westindische Kakerlack.*—Fabr.

Syst. Entom. 271, *America*—Ib. Spec. Ins. I, 512, *America;
nuper incipit in Europa saccharo allata.*—Ib. Entom. Syst. II, 7,
America—GOEZE, Entom. Beytr. II, 7, *Der braune amerikani-
sche Kakerlak.*—GMEL. Linn. Syst. Nat. IV, 2042, *America,
cum saccharo in Europam delata.*—BROWNE, Nat. Hist. Jama-
ica, 432 (Blatta 2), Index, iii, Iv, *America.*— VILL. Linn.
Entom. Fam. Succ. I, 479, *America, Gallia australi*—TURT.
Syst. Nat. Linn. II, 528, *America; has lately appeared in Europe.*—LATR. Hist. nat. Crust. et Ins. XII, 98, pl. xciv, fig. 1,
Portée de l'Amérique méridionale en Europe.—Ib. Cuv. Règne
Anim. Ed. 1817, III, 371; Ed. 1829, V, 175; Ed. Disc. Ins.
II, 10, pl. lxxvii, figs 4, 4ʰ-4ᶜ, *Amérique.*—Ib. Cuv. Règne
Anim. Ed. M'Murtrie, IV, 7, *America.*—LAM. Hist. nat. Anim.
sans Vert. IV, 263; 2° Ed. IV, 462; 3° Ed. II, 159, *L'Amé-
rique, et se trouve en Europe.*—DILLE. Enum. Ins. 63, *America.*
—SERV. Dict. class. d'Hist. nat. II, 542, *Originaire de l'Amé-
rique méridionale, et des Antilles, d'où elle a été importée d'abord
dans les contrées chaudes de l'Afrique et de l'Asie et delà dans le
reste du monde.*—? PERTY. De Ins. in Del. Anim. Artic. 10, *In
India occidentali.*— VOIGT. Thierreich, V, 353, *Amerika.*—
HARR. Hitchc. Rep. 2d Ed. 576;—Ib. Catal. 56, *Mass.*—
AUD. et BRULLÉ, Hist. nat. Ins. IX, 58, *Dans différentes
parties des deux continents*—WILL. Encycl. Brit. 8th Ed. IX,
156;—Ib. Treat. Ins. 190, *South America, Antilles, Asia,
Africa, seaport towns of Europe.*—OKEN, Allg. Naturg. V, C,
1506, *America.*—LUCAS. Ann. Soc. Entom. France, [1] VI,
508, *Guadeloupe.* — [Kakkerlac] BLANCH. Hist. nat. Ins. III,
8, *Univers.*—[Periplaneta] GUÉR. Sagra, Hist. nat. de Cuba,
339, *Cuba*—JONES, Nat. Derm. 110, *Bermuda.*

angustata LATR. Humb. et Bonpl. Rec. d'Obs. Zool. I, 146, pl. xv,
fig. 9, *Vera Cruz.*—PERTY, De Ins. in Del. Anim. Artic. 19, *In
dumibus urbis Mexicanae Vera Cruz.*—ZINCK. Germ. Mag. d.
Entom. I, 11, 109, *Vera Cruz.*

aeolius THUNB. Mém. Acad. St. Petersb. X, 277, tab. xiv, *Ex America
meridionali, et imprimis e Brasilia.*

atropos [Blabera] GUÉR. Sagra, Hist. nat. de Cuba, 333, *Havane.*

australasiae [Periplaneta] GUÉR. Sagra, Hist. nat. de Cuba, 340,
Cuba, Guatimala.

bicolor PAL. DE BEAUV. Insectes, pl. i⁰, fig. 6, *Saint Domingue*—
HARR. Hitchc. Rep. 2d Ed. 576;—Ib. Catal. 56, *Mass.*

biguttata THUNB. Mém. Acad. St. Petersb. X, 276, tab. xiv, *Ex
America meridionali et imprimis e Brasilia.*

bipustulata THUNB. Mém. Acad. St. Petersb. X, 273, *Ex America meridionali et imprimis e Brasilia.*

bivittata [Phyllodromia] SERV. Orthopt. 106, *Sénégal, Cap-de-Bonne-
Espérance, Ile-de-France, Cuba, Perou, etc.*—[Phyllodromia]

c

Guér. Sagra, Hist. nat. de Cuba, 846, *Cuba, Pérou, l'île de France, Cap et Sénégal*—Saur. Orthopt. Amér. moy. 102, *Ceylan, Mexique ; dans la Cordillière orientale du Mexique et sur son revers occidental, dans le Mechoacan, Cuba,*

borealis Saur. Orthopt. nov. amer. III, 4;—In. Rev. et Mag. de Zool. 1862, 166, *America borealis.*—In. Orthopt. Amér. moy. 96, pl. l, fig. 13, *L'Amérique du Nord.*—Germ. Archiv f. Nat. XXIX, ii, 351;—In. Bericht, 1862, 40, *Nord Amerika.*

brasiliensis Lneau. Ann. Soc. Entom. de France, [1] VI, 506, *Guadeloupe.*

brunnea Thunb. Mém. Acad. St. Petersb. X, 278, *Ex America meridionali et imprimis e Brasilia.*

buprestoïdes Saur. Orthopt. nov. amer. III, 5;—In. Rev. et Mag. de Zool. 1862, 166;—In. Orthopt. Amér. moy. 116, pl. l, fig. 20, *Cuba.*—Germ. Archiv f. Nat. XXIX, ii, 351;—In. Bericht, 1862, 40, *Cuba.*

Burmeisteri [Phyllodromia] Guér. Sagra, Hist. nat. de Cuba, 345. *Cuba.*

capitata Saur. Orthopt. nov. amer. III, 5;—In. Rev. et Mag. de Zool. 1862, 167;—In. Orthopt. Amér. moy. 114, pl. l, fig. 19, *Cuba*—Germ. Archiv f. Nat. XXIX, ii, 354;—In. Bericht, 1862, 40, *Cuba.*

cicatricosa [Zetobora] Guér. Sagra, Hist. nat. de Cuba, 335, pl. xli, fig. 5, *Havane.*

cincta Fabr. Mant. Ins. I, 226;— In. Entom. Syst. II, 9, *America.*—In. Nom. Entom. emend. Ed. 1797, 76; Ed. 1810, 78, *Am.*—Gmel. Linn. Syst. Nat. IV, 2014, *America.*—Oliv. Encycl. méth. IV, 318, *Amérique.*— Turt. Syst. Nat. Linn. II, 529, *America*—Billb. Enum. Ins. 163, *Amer.*

cinerea Thunb. Mém. Acad. St. Petersb. X, 277, *Ex America meridionali et imprimis e Brasilia.*

collaris [Holocompsa] Guér. Sagra, Hist. nat. de Cuba, 332, pl. xii, fig. 3, *Cuba, l'île Maurice.*—[Holocompsa] Germ. Archiv f. Nat. XXIV, ii, 348;—In. Bericht, 1857, 156, *Cuba.*

conspersa Serv. Orthopt. 89, *Cuba.*—[Zetobora] Guér. Sagra, Hist. nat. de Cuba, 339, *Cuba, Brésil.*

convexa Thunb. Mém. Acad. St. Petersb. X, 279, *Ex America meridionali et imprimis e Brasilia.*

cubensis Saur. Orthopt. nov. amer. III, 4;—In. Rev. et Mag. de Zool. 1862, 165;—In. [Phyllodromia] Orthopt. Amér. moy. 108, pl. l, figs. 14, 15, *Cuba.*—Germ. Archiv f. Nat. XXIX, ii, 354;—In. Bericht, 1862, 40, *Cuba.*

cylindrica Thunb. Mém. Acad. St. Petersb. X, 279, *Ex America meridionali et imprimis e Brasilia.*

delicatula [Phyllodromia] Guér. Sagra, Hist. nat. de Cuba, 346, *Cuba.*—Saur. Orthopt. Amér. moy. 104, pl. l, fig. 17, *Cuba.*

claphana FABR. Entom. Syst. II, 11, *in Am. merid. insulis.*—In. Nom.
Entom. emend. Ed. 1797, 78; Ed. 1810, 78, *Am. m.*—BURM.
Handb. d. Entom. II, 496, *St. Thomas, Westindien.* — [Hololampra] SAUSS. Orthopt. Amér. moy. 95, *Des Antilles, Saint Thomas.*

disoicollis BURM. Handb. d. Entom. II, 498, 1012, *Mexiko.*

domingensis PAL. DE BEAUV. Insectes. 182, pl. 1*, fig. 4, *Saint Domingue.*—HARR. Illustr. Rep. xi Ed. 576;—In. Catal. 56, *Mass.*

elongata PAL. DE BEAUV. Insectes, 183, pl. 1*, fig. 5, *Saint Domingue.*—[Phyllodromia] SERV. Orthopt. 106, *Saint Domingue.*

fumigata GUÉR. Sagra, Hist. nat. de Cuba. 335, pl. xii, fig. 4, *Havane.*

germanica AUD. et BRULLÉ, Hist. nat. Ins. IX, 55, *Dans toutes les parties du monde.*—GERST. Handb. der Zool. II, 44, *Von Europa aus, aber alle Welttheile verbreitet.*

gibba THUNB. Mém. Acad. St. Petersb. X, 279, *Ex America meridionali et imprimis e Brasilia.*

grossa THUNB. Mém. Acad. St. Petersb. X, 280, *Ex America meridionali et imprimis e Brasilia.*

gigantea LINN. Syst. Nat. 10th Ed. I, 424, *America.*—In. Syst. Nat. 12th Ed. II, 687, *America, Asia.*—In. Mus. Lud. Ulr. Reg. 106, *America.*—DRURY, Illustr. Nat. Hist. II, 66, pl. xxxvi, fig. 2, *Jamaica.*—MÜLL. Linn. Natursyst. V, 402, *America, Asia.*—FABR. Syst. Entom. 271;—In. Entom. Syst. II, 6;—In. Nom. Entom. emend. Ed. 1797, 78; Ed. 1810, 78, *America, Asia.*—GMEL. Linn. Syst. Nat. 13th Ed. IV, 2011, *Asia et America.*—OLIV. Encycl. méth. IV, 314, pl. cxxv, fig. 1, *Toute l'Amérique méridionale, rarement de Cayenne.*—TURT. Syst. Nat. Linn. II, 527, *America and Asia.*—LAM. Hist. nat. Anim. sans Vert. IV, 262; 2° Ed. IV, 462; 3° Ed. II, 159, *L'Amérique méridionale, Cayenne.*—KIRBY and SPENCE, Introd. Entom. 3d Ed. I, 245; 7th Ed. 140, *Asia, Africa, America.*—LUCUM. Ann. Soc. Entom. France. [1] VI, 506, *Guadeloupe.* — [Blabera] WESTW. Drury, Ins. II, 71, pl. xxxvi, fig. 8, *Jamaica, America, Asia, Cayenne.*—In. Introd. Class. Ins. I, 418, *West Indies.*—[Blabera] DUNC. Introd. Entom. 225, pl. vii, fig. 1, *N. American, West Indian Islands.*

guttata THUNB. Kongl. Vet. Akad. nya Handl. XXXI, 188, *In insula Bartholomi.*

indica PAL. DE BEAUV. Insectes, 327, pl. II*, fig. 2, *Saint Domingue et les Indes orientales.*—SERV. Ann. Sc. Nat. XXII, 40, *Ind Indes.*

intercepta BURM. Handb. d. Entom. II, 497, *Mexiko.* — [Eublia] SAUSS. Orthopt. Amér. moy. 113, *Mexico.*

kakkerlac DE GEER. Mém. III, 535, pl. xliv, figs. 1–3, *Amérique méridionale.*—OLIV. Encycl. méth. IV, 315, *Europe et dans*

toute l'Amérique méridionale.—PAL. DE BEAUV. Insectes, 181,
pl. I', fig. 1, Afrique; Iles de l'Amérique.

lævigata PAL. DE BEAUV. Insectes, 228, pl. II', fig. 4, Saint Domingue.
—SERV. Orthopt. 98, Cuba, Martinique.—[Panchlora] GUÉR.
Sagra, Hist. nat. de Cuba, 344, Cuba.—SAUSS. Orthopt.
Amér. moy. 99, pl. I, fig. 16, Les Antilles; Cuba, La Martinique, Saint Domingue.

limbata THUNB. Mém. Acad. St. Petersb. X, 278, Ex America meridionali et imprimis e Brasilia.

lineata PAL. DE BEAUV. Insectes, 228, pl. II', fig. 5, Amérique méridionale.

lineolata DALM. Anal. Entom. 87, In America insulis?

livida FABR. Spec. Ins. I, 341, America, Ins.

maderae OLIV. Encycl. méth. IV, 314, A Madère aux Antilles et dans
l'Amérique méridionale.—HAHN, Icon. Orthopt. tab. A, Gen.
Blatta, fig. 1, Madera et Ins. St. Bartholomæi.—SERV. Orthopt. 87, Madère, Ile de France, Saint Domingue.—BLANCH.
Hist. nat. Ins. III, 3, Afrique, Amérique, Indes orientales.—
[Panchlora] GUÉR. Sagra, Hist. nat. de Cuba, 338, Madère,
Maurice, Sénégal, Cuba.—JONES, Nat. Berm. 110 (maderensis?), Bermuda.

major PAL. DE BEAUV. Insectes, 182, pl. I', fig. 2, Afrique, Iles de
l'Amérique.

mexicana SAUSS. Blatt. nov. spec. 7; — In. Rev. et Mag. de Zool.
1864, 311, Mexico.—DALLAS, Zool. Record, I. 571, Mexico.—
GERST. Archiv f. Nat. XXX, 11, 450; — In. Bericht, 1863-4,
121, Mexiko.

mystoca SAUSS. Orthopt. nov. amer. III, 6; — In. Rev. et Mag. de
Zool. 1862, 167, Mexico calida.—In. [Eclobia] Orthopt. Amér.
moy. 110, Mexique, des terres chaudes de la côte de Véra Cruz.
—GERST. Archiv f. Nat. XXIX, 11, 354; — In. Bericht, 1862,
40, Aus den heissen Gegenden Mexiko's.

nivea LINN. Syst. Nat. 10th Ed. I, 431; 12th Ed. II, 688; 13th
Ed. I, 688, America.—DRURY, Illustr. Nat. Hist. II, 66, pl.
xxxvi, fig. 1, New York. — FABR. Syst. Entom. 272, America.—In. Spec. Ins. I, 343, In America meridionali. — In.
Entom. Syst. II, 8, In Am. insulis. — In. Nom. Entom. emend.
Ed. 1797, 78; Ed. 1810, 78, Am.—GOEZE, Entom. Beytr. II, 8,
Der amerikanische Weissling.—HERBST, Fuessly, Archiv d. Ins.
1786, 185, tab. xlix, fig. 8, Amerika.—GMEL. Linn. Syst. Nat.
IV, 2041, In America meridionali. — OLIV. Encycl. méth. IV,
316, pl. cxxv, fig. 4, Cayenne, Surinam, Antilles. —? BROWN,
Nat. Hist. Jamaica, 431 (Camida, 2) Index, iii, iv, tab. xliii, fig.
13, Jamaica.—THUNB. Mém. Acad. St. Petersb. X, 277, Ex
America meridionali et imprimis e Brasilia.—LUCEM. Ann. Soc.
Entom. France, [1] VI, 306, Guadeloupe.—WESTW. Drury, Ins.

II, 10, pl. xxxvi, fig. 1, *New York*, in *Am. insulis.* — EMM.
Agric. of N. Y. V, 141, pl. xlvi, fig. 7, *New York.*

oblongata LINN. Syst. Nat. 10th Ed. I, 435; 12th Ed. I, 689, *America.* — GOEZE, Entom. Beytr. II, 63, *Die amerikanische längliche Schabe.*

occidentalis FABR. Mant. Ins. I, 225, *America.* — ID. Entom. Syst. II, 7, *in Am. insulis.* — ID. Nom. Entom. emend. Ed. 1797, 78; Ed. 1810, 78, *Am.* — GMEL. Linn. Syst. Nat. 13, Ed. IV, 2041, *America.* — OLIV. Encycl. méth. IV, 314, *Amérique.* — TURT. Syst. Nat. Linn. II, 527, *American islands.*

orientalis LINN. Syst. Nat. 10th Ed. I, 434, *America, Oriente.* — ID. Syst. Nat. 12th Ed. II, 688, *America; hospitatur in Oriente; hodie in Russiæ adjacentibus regionibus frequens; incepit nuperis temporibus Holmiæ 1739 uti dudum in Finlandia.* — ID. Syst. Nat. 13th Ed. I, 688, *America, hospitatur in Oriente.* — SULZ. Kennz. der Ins. 78, Erkl. 18, tab. vii, fig. 47, *America, Turkei; in den Gegenden Russlands, unlängst sind diese ungebetenen Gäste auf ihrer Reise nach Westen, nach Finnland, Schweden, Deutschland und Schwaben gekommen.* — MÜLL. Linn. Natursyst. V, 404, *Eigentlich nur aus America herstammen durch die Handlung und Schiffahrt aber nach Asien gekommen.* — FABR. Syst. Entom. 272; — ID. Spec. Ins. I, 513, *America; hospitatur nunc in oriente adjacentisque Europæ.* — ID. Entom. Syst. II, 9, *America; hospitatur nunc in tota fere Europa.* — GMEL. Linn. Syst. Nat. 13th Ed. VI, 2043, *America; hospitatur in Oriente et Europa, a 200 inde annis in Bohemia, a 1739 in Belgio et antea in Finlandia et Russia.* — VILL. Linn. Entom. Fann. Suec. I, 429, *America, hospitatur in Oriente; hodie in Russiæ adjacentibus regionibus frequens; incepit nuperis temporibus Holmiæ 1739 uti dudum in Finlandia.* — RŒMER, Gen. Ins. 12, tab. viii, fig. 2, *America, hospitatur in Oriente.* — TURT. Syst. Nat. Linn. II, 529, *America; long since naturalized in Europe.* — PAL. DE BEAUV. Insectes, 228, pl. ii°, fig. 3, *Le monde entier.* — LATR. Gen. Crust. et Ins. III, 83, *Europæ, Am. bor.* — ID. Cuv. Règne Anim. Ed. 1817, III, 371; Ed. 1829, V, 175; Ed. Disc. Ins. II, 9, pl. lxxvii, figs. 5, 6, *Russie et la Finland; originaire de l'Asie; quelques auteurs la font venir de l'Amérique méridionale.* — LEACH, New Edinb. Encycl. IX, 120; Am. Ed. VIII, 709, *North America, common in Europe.* — LAM. Hist. nat. Anim. sans Vert. IV, 263; 2° Ed. IV, 463; 3° Ed. II, 139, *Le Levant, toute l'Europe et l'Amérique septentrionale.* — ACD. et BRULLÉ, Hist. nat. Ins. IX, 54, *Il n'est pas de partie du monde où il n'ait été transporté.* — HARR. Hitchc. Rep. 582; 2d Ed. 576; — ID. Catal. 56, *Mass.* — ID. Treat. Ed. 1811-2, 118; Ed. 1852, 126; Ed. 1862, 143, fig. 86, *Maritime towns of the United States.* — OKEN, Allg. Naturg. V, C, 1503, *Aus dem Orient; in nördlichen America,*

in gen. Europa.—LIKERS. Ann. Soc. Entom. France, [1] VI,
506, Guadeloupe.—[Kakkerlac] BLANCH. Hist. nat. ins. III,
6, L'univers.—JACQ. N. Amer. Ins. 1854, 165; 1859, 117, N.
America.—WALSH. Prox. Entom. Soc. Philad. III, 212, S.
Illinois.

otomia SAUSS. Orthopt. Amér. moy. 104, Mexique.

papiliosa THUNB. Mém. Acad. St. Petersb. X, 276, tab. xiv, Ex
America meridionali et imprimis e Brasilia.

parallela HARR. Hitche.-Rep. 2d Ed. 570:—Catal. 56, Mass.

pellucens THUNB. Mém. Acad. St. Petersb. X, 276, tab. xiv, Ex
America meridionali, et imprimis e Brasilia.

pellucida SAUSS. Mant. nov. spec. 7;—In. Rev. et Mag. de Zool. 311;
—[Ectobia] In. Orthopt. Amér. moy. 112, Mexique.—DALLAS,
Zool. Record, I, 571, Mexico.—GERST. Archiv f. Nat. XXX,
II, 430;—In. Bericht, 1863-4, 124, Mexico.

pennsylvanica DE GEER, Mém. III, 537, pl. xliv. fig. 4, Pensylvanie.
—GOEZE, Entom. Beytr. II, 15, Die braune pensylvanische
Schabe.—In. De Geer, Gesch. Ins. III, 318, tab. xliv. fig. 4,
Pensylvanien.—GMEL. Linn. Syst. Nat. 13th Ed. IV, 2046,
Pennsylvania.—OLIV. Encycl. méth. IV, 317, Pensylvanie.—
TURT. Syst. Nat. Linn. II, 531, Pennsylvania.—HARR. Hitche.
Rep. 2d Ed. 570;—In. Catal. 56, Mass.—THOMAS, Trans. Ill.
St. Agric. Soc. V, 410, Illinois.

Petiveriana DESC. Introd. Entom. 276, pl. vii, fig. 2, West Indies.

Posyi SAUSS. Orthopt. nov. amer. III, 2;—In. Rev. et Mag. de Zool.
1862, 164;—[Hololampra] Orthopt. Amér. moy. 84, Cuba.—
GERST. Archiv f. Nat. XXIX, II, 354;—In. Bericht, 1862, 40,
Cuba.

porcellana SAUSS. Orthopt. nov. amer. III, 3;—In. Rev. et Mag. de
Zool. 1862, 164, Cuba.—GERST. Archiv f. Nat. XXIX, II,
354;—In. Bericht, 1862, 40, Cuba.

punctulata PAL. DE BEAUV. Insectes, 183, pl. I[b], fig. 8, Saint Domingue.

pygmaea PAL. DE BEAUV. Insectes, 183, pl. I[b], fig. 9, Saint Domingue.
—SAUSS. Orthopt. Amér. moy. 118, St. Domingo.

reflexa THUNB. Mém. Acad. St. Petersb. X, 278, Ex America meridionali et imprimis e Brasilia.

rufescens PAL. DE BEAUV. Insectes, pl. I[b], fig. 7, Saint Domingue.

rufovallis FABR. Nom. Entom. emend. Ed. 1797, 78; Ed. 1810, 78,
Ind.

Servillei LEF. Serv. Orthopt. 91, Rio Grande.

sexnotata THUNB. Mém. Acad. St. Petersb. X, 276, tab. xiv, Ex
America meridionali et imprimis e Brasilia.

Sulzerii [Blabera] GUÉR. Sagra, Hist. nat. de Cuba, 331, Cuba.

surinamensis LIKERS. Ann. Soc. Entom. France, [1] VI, 506, Guadeloupe.—[Panchlora] Guér. Sagra, Hist. nat. de Cuba, 343, *Cuba.*

taranoa Saus. Orthopt. nov. amer. III, 3;—Ib. Rev. et Mag. de Zool. 1863, 164;—Ib. Orthopt. Amér. moy. 95, *Mexique.*—Gerst. Archiv f. Nat. XXIX, ii, 354;—Ib. Bericht, 1862, 40, *Mexiko.*

Thunbergii [Monachoda] Guér. Sagra, Hist. nat. de Cuba, 337, pl. xii, fig. 6, *Cuba.*

totonaca Saus. Orthopt. nov. amer. III, 4;—Ib. Rev. et Mag. de Zool. 1862, 165, *Mexico calida.*—Ib. Orthopt. Amér. moy. 101, *Mexique (côte du golfe, province de Véra Cruz).*—Gerst. Archiv f. Nat. XXIX, ii, 354;—Ib. Bericht, 1862, 40, *Aus den heissen Theilen Mexiko's.*

translucida Saus. Blatt. nov. spec. 7;—Ib. Rev. et Mag. do Zool. 311; —[Ectobia] Ib. Orthopt. Amér. moy. 113, *Mexique.*—Dallas, Zool. Record, I, 371, *Mexico.*—Gerst. Archiv f. Nat. XXX, ii, 430;—Ib. Bericht, 1863–4, 124, *Mexiko.*

tuberculata Aud. et Brullé, Hist. nat. Ins. IX, 52, *De l'Amérique et des Indes.*

venosa Saus. Blatt. nov. spec. 6;—Ib. Rev. et Mag. de Zool. 1864, 310;—Ib. Orthopt. Amér. moy. 106, *Mexique.*—Dallas, Zool. Record, I, 371, *Mexico.*—Gerst. Archiv f. Nat. XXX, ii, 430; —Ib. Bericht, 1863–4, 124, *Mexiko.*

virescens Thunb. Mém. Acad. St. Petersb. X. 278, *Ex America meridionali et imprimis e Brasilia.*—Serv. Orthopt. 101, *Cuba.* —[Panchlora] Guér. Sagra, Hist. nat. de Cuba, 344, *Cuba.*

viridis Fabr. Syst. Entom. 272;—Ib. Spec. Ins. I, 343, *America.*—Ib. Entom. Syst. II, 6, *In Am. insulis.*—Ib. Nom. Entom. emend. Ed. 1797, 76; Ed. 1810, 76, *Am.*—Gorze, Entom. Beytr. II, 13, *Die amerikanische grüne Schabe.*—Gmel. Linn. Syst. Nat. 13th Ed. IV, 2043, *America.*—Oliv. Encycl. méth. IV, 316, *L'Amérique méridionale, Cayenne.*—Turt. Syst. Nat. Linn. II, 528, *American Islands.*

zapoteca Saus. Orthopt. nov. amer. III, 5;—Ib. Rev. et Mag. do Zool. 1862, 166, *Mexico calida.*—Ib. Orthopt. Amér. moy. 106, *Les terres chaudes du Mexique; l'isthme de Téhuantepec.*—Gerst. Archiv f. Nat. XXIX, ii, 354;—Ib. Bericht, 1862, 40, *Aus den heissen Gegenden Mexiko's.*

Brachytmetus.

maritima Dohrn, Entom. Zeit. Stett. XXV, 293, *Japan, China, Ostindien, Madagascar, Westafrika und den Südstaaten der nordamerikanischen Union.*

Brachypepius.

magnus GIRARD. Marcy, Expl. Red River, 1853, 260, pl. xv, figs. 1–4;
1854, 249, pl. xv, figs. 1–4, *Red River of Louisiana.*—GERST.
Archiv f. Nat. XX, II, 246;—In. Bericht, 1853, 50, *Louisiana.*

virescens CHARP. Orthopt. descr. tab. II, *Mexico.*—GIRARD. Marcy,
Expl. Red River. 1853, 261; 1854, 250. *Red River of Louisiana.*—ERICHS. Archiv f. Nat. X, II, 399;—In. Bericht, 1853,
51, *Mexiko.*

Bradyporus.

spinulosus SERV. Ann. Sc. nat. XXII, 165, *Des Indes.*

BULLA, see GRYLLUS,
CACERLACA, see PERIPLANETA.
CALAMOPTERA, see ACANTHODIS.

Caloptenus.

bivittatus UHLER, Say, Entom. of N. Amer. Ed. Leconte, II, 238,
Atlantic States, western part of the country, Baltimore. —
SCUDD. Can. Nat. VII, 287, *Lake Winnipeg.*—In. Bost. Journ.
Nat. Hist. VII, 465, *Mass. Maine, Conn. Maryland, Texas, S.
Illinois, Nebraska, Minnesota, Lake Winnipeg.* See also
Acridium bivittatum.

borealis BRUNN. Orthopt. Stud. 3;—In. Verhandl. zool. bot. Gesellsch.
Wien, 1861, 233, *Labrador.*

femoratus BURM. Handb. d. Entom. II, 638, *Karolina.*—BRUNN.
Orthopt. Stud. 4:—In. Verhandl. zool. bot. Gesellsch. Wien,
1861, 234, *Süd Carolina.*—GERST. Archiv f. Nat. XXVIII, II,
319;—In. Bericht, 1861, 47, *Süd Carolina.* See also *Acridium
femoratum.*

femur rubrum BURM. Handb. d. Entom. II, 638, *Pennsylvanien.*—
SCUDD. Can. Nat. VII, 287, *Red River.*—In. Bost. Journ. Nat.
Hist. VII, 464, *Massachusetts, Maine, Connecticut, S. Illinois,
Minnesota, Nebraska, Red River Settlements.*—PACK. Rep. Nat.
Hist. Maine, 1861, 374, *Mount Katahdin.*—WALSH, Trans. Ill.
St. Agric. Soc. V, 497, *New England, Rock Island.* See also
Acridium femur rubrum.

punctulatus UHLER. Scudd. Bost. Journ. Nat. Hist. VII, 465, *Maine.*—
GERST. Archiv f. Nat. XXIX, II, 358;—In. Bericht, 1862, 44,
Maine.

sanguinipes SERV. Ann. Sc. Nat. XXII, 284, *Amérique méridionale.*
See also ACRIDIUM.

Campsnotus.

Scudderi UHLER. Proc. Entom. Soc. Philad. II, 549, *Maryland, Delaware.*—DALLAS, Zool. Record, I, 573, *Baltimore.*

CARDIOPTERA, *see* MANTIS.

Ceratinoptera.

diaphana BRUNN. Blatt. 76, *Indes occidentales, St. Thomas.*
porcellana BRUNN. Blatt. 79, *Cuba.*

Ceuthophilus.

Agassizii SCUDD. Bost. Journ. Nat. Hist. VII, 439, *Gulf of Georgia, Washington Territory.*
brevipes SCUDD. Bost. Journ. Nat. Hist. VII, 434, *Grand Menan.*—GERST. Archiv f. Nat. XXIX, II, 357;—Jn. Bericht, 1862, 43, *Grand Menan.*
californianus SCUDD. Bost. Journ. Nat. Hist. VII, 438, *San Francisco, California.*—GERST. Archiv f. Nat. XXIX, II, 357;—Jn. Bericht, 1862, 43, *San Francisco.*
divergens SCUDD. Bost. Journ. Nat. Hist. VII, 436, *Nebraska.*—GERST. Archiv f. Nat. XXIX, II, 357;—Jn. Bericht, 1862, 43, *Nebraska.*
gracilipes SCUDD. Bost. Journ. Nat. Hist. VII, 439, *Southern Illinois, New York, New Jersey.*
lapidicolus SCUDD. Bost. Journ. Nat. Hist. VII, 435, *Maryland, Penn. Georgia.*
latens SCUDD. Bost. Journ. Nat. Hist. VII, 437, *Illinois.*—GERST. Archiv f. Nat. XXIX, II, 357;—Jn. Bericht, 1862, 43, *Illinois.*
maculatus SCUDD. Bost. Journ. Nat. Hist. VII, 434, *Mass. Vermont, Maine, Anticosti.*—PACK. How to collect, 56;—Jn. Rep. Nat. Hist. Maine, 1862, 196, *Maine.*
niger SCUDD. Bost. Journ. Nat. Hist. VII, 437, *Illinois.*—GERST. Archiv f. Nat. XXIX, II, 357;—Jn. Bericht, 1862, 43, *Illinois.*
scabripes SCUDD. Bost. Journ. Nat. Hist. VII, 438, *Alabama.*
stygius SCUDD. Bost. Journ. Nat. Hist. VII, 438, *Hickman's Cave, Hickman's Landing, Kentucky.*
Uhleri SCUDD. Bost. Journ. Nat. Hist. VII, 435, *Maryland.*—GERST. Archiv f. Nat. XXIX, II, 357;—Jn. Bericht, 1862, 43, *Maryland.*

Charadodis.

strumaria SERV. Ann. Sc. Nat. XXII, 51, *Amérique méridionale.*

Chloraltis.

conspersa Scudd. Can. Nat. VII, 286, *Dog's Head on Lake Winnipeg.*—In. Bost. Journ. Nat. Hist. VII, 455, *Massachusetts, N. Hampshire, Lake Winnipeg.* — Germ. Archiv f. Nat. XXIX, 11, 358;—In. Bericht, 1862, 41, *Nord America.* See also *Locusta consperra.*

curtipennis Pack. Rep. Nat. Hist. Maine, 1861, 376, *Chamberlain Farm, Me.* See also *Locusta curtipennis.*

punctulata Scudd. Bost. Journ. Nat. Hist. VII, 455, *Connecticut.*—Germ. Archiv f. Nat. XXIX, 11, 358;—In. Bericht, 1862, 41, *Connecticut.*

viridis Scudd. Bost. Journ. Nat. Hist. VII, 455, *Connecticut*—Germ. Archiv f. Nat. XXIX, 11, 358;—In. Bericht, 1862, 41, *Connecticut.*

See also Lacusta.

Chloriphyllum.

Sagrai Burm. Germ. Zeitsch. f. Entom. II, 56, *Cuba.*—Serv. Orthopt. 755, pl. viii, fig. 5, *Cuba.*—Erichs. Archiv f. Nat. VI, 11, 201;—In. Bericht, 1839, 48, *Cuba.* See also *Acridium Sagrai.*

See also Acridium.

Chorisocera.

mysteca Brunn. Blatt. 258, *Mexique.*

Conocephalus.

acuminatus Thunb. Mém. Acad. St. Petersb. V, 273, *In Indiis et Europa australi*—Serv. Ann. &c. Nat. XXII, 149, *Du midi de l'Europe et des Indes suivant Fabricius.*

cinereus Thunb. Mém. Acad. St. Petersb. V, 273, *Jamaica.*

crepitans Scudd. Bost. Journ. Nat. Hist. VII, 450, *Texas, Nebraska.*—Germ. Archiv f. Nat. XXIX, 11, 357;—In. Bericht, 1862, 42, *Texas.*

dissimilis Serv. Orthopt. 518, *Amérique septentrionale.*—Thomas, Trans. Ill. St. Agric. Soc. V, 448, *Illinois.* See also *Locusta dissimilis.*

ensiger Harr. Trent. Ed. 1841-2, 131; Ed. 1852, 149; Ed. 1862, 162, fig. 79, *Mass.*—Erichs. Archiv f. Nat. IX, 11, 227;—In. Bericht, 1843, 85, *Mass.*—Fitch. Am. Journ. Agric. and Sc. VI, 116, *New York.*—Scudd. Bost. Journ. Nat. Hist. VII, 419, *Massachusetts, Cape Cod, Vermont, Connecticut, Illinois, Minne-*

zota, *Nebraska.*—JARO. N. Amer. Ins. 1851, 154; 1859, 109, *N. America*—THOMAS, Trans. Ill. St. Agric. Soc. V, 445. *Illinois.*—See also *Gryllus ensiger.*

guttatus SERV. Orthopt. 518, *Cuba.*—GUÉR. Sagra, Hist. nat. de Cuba, 355, *Cuba.* See also *Locusta guttata.*

mexicanus SAUSS. Orthopt. nov. amer. I, 3;—In. Rev. et Mag. de Zool. 1859, 208, *Mexico.*—GERST. Archiv f. Nat. XXVI, II, 405;—In. Bericht, 1859–60, 49, *Mexico.*

Nietii SAUSS. Orthopt. nov. amer. I, 2;—In. Rev. et Mag. de Zool. 1859, 208, *Mexico.*—GERST. Archiv f. Nat. XXVI, II, 405;—In. Bericht, 1859–60, 49, *Mexico.*

obtusus SCUDD. Bost. Journ. Nat. Hist. VII, 450, *Georgia.* See also *Locusta obtusa.*

occidentalis SAUSS. Orthopt. nov. amer. I, 2;—In. Rev. et Mag. de Zool. 1859, 208, *Haiti.*—GERST. Archiv f. Nat., XXVI, II, 405;—In. Bericht, 1859–60, 49, *Haiti.*

robustus SCUDD. Bost. Journ. Nat. Hist. VII, 449, *Cape Cod.*—GERST. Archiv f. Nat. XXIX, II, 357;—In. Bericht, 1863, 43, *Cape Cod.*

Salléi SAUSS. Orthopt. nov. amer. I, 10;—In. Rev. et Mag. de Zool. 1859, 207, *Mexico.*—GERST. Archiv f. Nat. XXVI, II, 405;—In. Bericht, 1859–60, 49, *Mexico.*

tricornis THUNB. Mém. Acad. St. Petersb. V, 278, *In Insula Bartholemi.*

triops THUNB. Mém. Acad. St. Petersb. V, 278, *In Indiis, ins. Bartholemi, Morocco.*

uncinatus HARR. Treat. Ed. 1841–2, 132; Ed. 1862, 164, *N. Carolina.*—GERST. Archiv f. Nat. XXIX, II, 357;—In. Bericht, 1863, 43, *Alabama.*—SCUDD. Bost. Journ. Nat. Hist. VII, 450, *Alabama.*

See also GRYLLUS and LOCUSTA.

Copiophora.

cornuta SERV. Orthopt. 514, pl. x, fig. 3, *Amérique.*

mexicana SAUSS. Orthopt. nov. amer. I, 10;—In. Rev. et Mag. de Zool. 1859, 207, *Mexico.*—GERST. Archiv f. Nat. XXVI, II, 405;—In. Bericht, 1859–60, 49, *Mexico.*

Corydia.

azteca [Holocompsa] SAUSS. Orthopt. nov. amer. III, 13;—In. Rev. et Mag. de Zool. 1862, 230, *Mexico calida.*—[Holocompsa] GERST. Archiv f. Nat. XXIX, II, 354;—In. Bericht, 1862, 40, *Aus dem heissen Mexiko.*

colleris [Hokorompea] BURM. Handb. d. Entom. II, 492, *St. Thomas.*
cyanea [Hokorompea] BURM. Handb. d. Entom. II, 492, *St. Thomas.*

Creoxylus.

spinosus WESTW. Catal. Orthopt. 104, *In Indiis (Fabr. nec in Ind. orient.) Demerara.*

Cryptorremus.

punctulatus SCUDD. Bost. Journ. Nat. Hist. VII, 420, *Virginia, New York, Penn.*—GERST. Archiv f. Nat. XXIX, II, 355;—In. Bericht, 1862, 41, *Virginien und Pennsylvanien.*

Cyphoderris.

monstrosa UHLER, Proc. Entom. Soc. Philad. II, 552, *Oregon.*—DAL-LAS, Zool. Record, I, 573, *Oregon Territory.*

Cyphocrania.

angulata SERV. Ann. Sc. Nat. XXII, 61, *Ile Saint Vincent et Ile de la Guadeloupe.*
reticulata WESTW. Catal. Orthopt. 108, *St. Domingo.*

Cyrtophyllum.

.**concavus** SCUDD. Bost. Journ. Nat. Hist. VII, 441, *Mass. Conn. New York.*
perspicillatus BURM. Handb. d. Entom. II, 697, *Südkarolina.*—SCUDD. Bost. Journ. Nat. Hist. VII, 444, *Texas.* See also *Locusta perspicillata.*
See also LOCUSTA.

Dactylotum.

bicolor CHARP. Orthop. descr. tab. III, *Mexico.*—ENICUS. Archiv f. Nat. X, II, 999;—In. Bericht, 1843, 51, *Mexico.*

Dalhinia.

brevipes GIRARD, Marcy, Expl. Red River, 1853, 257, pl. xv, figs 9-13; 1854, 246, pl. xv, figs. 9-13, *Red River of Louisiana.*—SCUDD. Bost. Journ. Nat. Hist. VII, 443, *Nebraska.* See also *Phalangopsis brevipes.*
maxicana SAUSS. Orthopt. nov. amer. I, 15;—In. Rev. et Mag. de Zool. 1859, 212, *Mexico.*—GERST. Archiv f. Nat. XXVI, II, 605;—In. Bericht, 1859-60, 49.

robusta Girard, Marcy, Expl. Red River, 1853, 251; 1854, 246, *N. Mexico.*
See also Phalangopsis.

Dasyponexsa.

punctulata Burm. Diall. 389, *Virginie, New York, Pennsylvanie.*

Drelicus.

dorsalis Burm. Handb. d. Entom. II, 713, *Süd-Karolina.*
pachymerus Burm. Handb. d. Entom. II, 712, *Süd-Karolina.*

Diapheromera.

angulata Burm. Handb. d. Entom. II, 574, *Westindien.* See also
  Phasma angulatum.
Christophori Westw. Catal. Orthopt. 84, pl. xxiii, fig. 4, *St. Christopher.*
gigas Westw. Catal. Orthopt. 84, *Isles of Saint Vincent and Guadeloupe.* See also *Phasma gigas.*
spinipes Gray, Synops. Phasm. 34, *In India occidentali (St. Domingo).*
venustula Westw. Catal. Orthopt. 84, *Cuba.* See also *Phasma venustulum.*
  See also Phasma.

Diapheromera.

bivittata Harr. Treat. Ed. 1841-2, 119; Ed. 1852, 150; Ed. 1862,
  146, *America.*
calcarata Westw. Catal. Orthopt. 20, *Mexico.*
femorata ? Harr. Treat. Ed. 1841-2, 119; Ed. 1852, 150; Ed. 1862,
  146, fig. 67, *America.*—Scudd. Can. Nat. VII, 284, *Red River
  Settlements, British America.*—In. Bost. Journ. Nat. Hist. VII,
  433, *Mass. N. Hampshire, Illinois, Red River Settlements in
  British America, Nebraska.*—Pack. How to collect, 55;—In.
  Rep. Nat. Hist. Maine, 1862, 195, *N. England.*
Sayii Gray, Synops. Phasm. 18, *In America septentrionali.*—Fischl. W.
  Bull. Soc. Imp. Nat. Mosc. X, vi, 13, *Amérique septentrionale.*
  Serv. Orthopt. 247, *New York.*—Westw. Catal. Orthopt. 20,
  Amer. septentr.—Thomas, Trans. Ill. St. Agric. Soc. V, 441,
  Illinois.
Velii Walsh, Proc. Entom. Soc. Philad. III, 410, *Platte River, Nebraska.*—Dallas, Zool. Record, I, 572, *Illinois.*

Dictyophorum.

guttatus [Romaleu] BLANCH. Hist. Nat. Ins. III, 40, Amérique méridionale.

reticulatus THUNB. Mém. Acad. St. Petersb. V, 239, In America occidentali.

DIPLOPHYLLUS, see PHYLLOPTERA.

Ectobia.

flavocincta SCUDD. Bost. Journ. Nat. Hist. VII, 419, Mass. Western States, Lake Superior.—GERST. Archiv f. Nat. XXIX, II, 355; —In. Bericht, 1862, 41, Nord Amerika.—BLUNN. Blatt. 57, États occidentaux de l'Amérique du Nord, Lac Supérieur.

germanica SCUDD. Bost. Journ. Nat. Hist. VII, 418, Mass. Vermont, New York, Maryland.—GERST. Archiv f. Nat. XXIX, II, 355;—In. Bericht, 1862, 41, Nord Amerika.

lithophila SCUDD. Bost. Journ. Nat. Hist. VII, 418, Mass.—GERST. Archiv f. Nat. XXIX, II, 355;—In. Bericht, 1862, 41, Nord Amerika.

    See also BLATTA.

Empusa.

chlorophaea BLANCH. Hist. Nat. Ins. III, 2, pl. iii, fig. 1, New York.

fronticornis SERV. Orthopt. 144, Elle est très commune des Antilles, mais c'est sans doute par erreur ; je ne pense pas qu'il y ait d'Empuses en Amérique.

gongylodes WESTW. Drury, Ins. 1, 122, pl. l, fig. 2, Madras (and Philadelphia, sed ! Drury) Africa, Asia, E. Indies.

hyalina CHARP. Orthopt. descr. tab. II, In America meridionalis.

pectinicornis LAM. Hist. nat. Anim. sans Vert. IV, 251; 2e Ed. IV, 452; 3e Ed. II, 155, Jamaique.— SERV. Ann. Sc. Nat. XXII, 48, Jamaique.

pennicornis WESTW. Drury, Ins. 1, 121, pl. l, fig. 1, Jamaica.

spinifrons [Idolomorpha] SAUS. Orthopt. nov. amer. 1, 2;—In. Rev. et Mag. de Zool. 1859, 61, Am. mérid.

ENKOPTERA, see GRYLLUS.

Epaphrodita.

musarum SERV. Ann. Sc. Nat. XXII, 52;—In. Orthopt. 205, Saint Domingue. See also Mantis musarum.

    See also MANTIS.

Ephippigera.

tachivavensis HALD. Stansb. Expl. Utah. 371, pl. x, fig. 3, *Chihuahua.*—SCHAUM, Archiv f. Nat. XIX, II, 270;—In. Bericht, 1852, 130, *Utah.*
See also GRYLLUS and LOCUSTA.

Epilampra.

brasiliensis BRUNN. Blatt. 169, *Brésil, dans toute l'Amérique du Sud du versant oriental des Andes, Ile de Cuba, St. Domingue.*
mexicana (l'Isnez) SAUSS. Orthopt. nov. amer. III, 2; In. Rev. et Mag. de Zool. 1862, 228, *Mexico.*—In. Orthopt. Amér. moy. 30, pl. ii, fig. 26, *Terres chaudes du Mexique.*—BRUNN. Blatt. 188, *Mexique.*

Forcinella.

azteca DOHRN, Entom. Zeit. Stett. XXIII, 226, *Mexico!*—GERST. Archiv f. Nat. XXIX, II, 358;—In. Bericht, 1862, 44, *Mexico.*

Forficesila.

americana SERV. Orthopt. 22, *Saint Domingue, Cuba.*
gigantea SERV. Orthopt. 23, pl. i, fig. 2, *Europe, N. America.*
suturalis DOHRN, Entom. Zeit. Stett. XXIII, 226, *Cordova.*—GERST. Archiv f. Nat. XXIX, II, 358;—In. Bericht, 1862, 44, *Mexico.*
See also FORFICULA.

Forficula.

affinis [Forficesila] GUÉR. Sagra, Hist. nat. de Cuba. 330, pl. xii, fig. 2, *Cuba.*—[Forficesila] GERST. Archiv f. Nat. XXIV, II, 849;—In. Bericht, 1857, 157, *Cuba.*
albipes FABR. Mant. Ins. I, 224;—In. Entom. Syst. II, 3, *In America meridionalis Insulis.*—In. Nom. Entom. emend. Ed. 1797, 78; Ed. 1810, 78, *Am. m.*—GMEL. Linn. Syst. Nat. Ed. 13, IV, 2039, *In insulis America meridionali oppositis.*
americana PAL. DE BEAUV. Insectes, 165, pl. xiv, fig. 1, *Saint Domingue.*
annulata FABR. Entom. Syst. II, 4, *In America meridionalis Insulis.*—In. Nom. Entom. emend. Ed. 1797, 78; Ed. 1810, 78, *Am. m.*
auricularia JARO. N. Amer. Ins. 1854, 166; 1859, 118, *N. America.*
bimaculata PAL. DE BEAUV. Insectes, 165, pl. xiv, fig. 3, *Saint Domingue.*—SERV. Ann. Sc. Nat. XXII, 82;—In. Orthopt. 39, *Saint Domingue.*

bivittata Burm. Handb. d. Entom. II, 751, *St. Domingo, Portoriko, Columbia.*

californica Dohrn, Entom. Zeit. Stett. XXVI, 85, *California.*

distincta [Forficula] Guér. Sagra, Hist. nat. de Cuba, 329, pl. xli, fig. 1, *Cuba.*—[Forficula] Gerst. Archiv f. Nat. XXIV, II, 349;—In. Bericht, 1857, 157, *Cuba.*

elegans Burm. Handb. d. Entom. II, 753, *Insel St. Johanna in Westindien.*

elongata Fabr. Entom. Syst. II, 4, *In America meridionali Insulis.*—In. Nom. Entom. emend. Ed. 1797, 78; Ed. 1810, 78, *Am. ins.*

erythrocephala Fabr. Entom. Syst. II, 4, *In America meridionalis Insulis.*—In. Nom. Entom. emend. Ed. 1797, 78; Ed. 1810, 78, *Am. m.*

gagathina Burm. Handb. d. Entom. II, 753, *Portoriko.*

gigantea [Lapidura] Fisch. Orthopt. Eur. 52, 65, tab. vi, fig. 1*-1', *In Europâ meridionali, in insula Madera, in Africâ septentrionali, in Asiâ occidentali. In collectione D. Latreille duo specimina δ ex Americâ sept. allata aberrantur.*

lugubris Dohrn, Entom. Zeit. Stett. XXIII, 236, *Cordura.*—Gerst. Archiv f. Nat. XXIX, II, 359;—In. Bericht, 1862, 45, *Mexiko.*

minor Burm. Handb. d. Entom. II, 754, *Europa, Nordamerika.*—Serv. Orthopt. 44, *Europe, Amérique septentrionale.*—Fisch. Orthopt. Eur. 52, 70, tab. vi, fig. 7*-7', *In totâ Europâ, in insulâ Madera, in Americâ septentrionali?*

minuscula Latr. Humb. et Bonpl. Rec. d'Obs. zool. II, 119, pl. xl, figs. 8, 9, *L'Amérique équinoxiale.*

parallela Westw. Guér. Mag. de Zool. VII, Cl. ix, pl. clxxviii;—In. Introd. Class. Ins. I, 402, *Mexico.*—Gerst. Germ. Zeitschr. f. Entom. I, 319, *Mexico.*

procera Burm. Handb. d. Entom. II, 753, *Westindische Inseln.*

pulchella Serv. Orthopt. 42, *Amérique septentrionale, Niagara.*

ruficeps Burm. Handb. d. Entom. II, 755, *Mexiko.*

scabriuscula Serv. Orthopt. 38, *Amérique méridionale.*

taeniata Dohrn, Entom. Zeit. Stett. XXIII, 230, *Oaxaca, Miradoe, (Mexico).*—Gerst. Archiv f. Nat. XXIX, II, 359;—In. Bericht, 1862, 45, *Mexiko.*

unidentata Pal. de Beauv. Insectes, 165, pl. xiv, fig. 3, *Saint Domingue.*—Serv. Ann. Sc. Nat. XXII, 33;—In. Orthopt. 41, *Saint Domingue.*

GRATHOCLITA, see LOCUSTA.

Gomphocerus.

clavicornis Thunb. Mém. Acad. St. Petersb. V, 221, *In Indiâ.*

infuscatus Uhler, Harr. Treat. Ed. 1862, 161, *Mass.*

palidnus Burm. Handb. d. Entom. II, 650, *Pennsylvanica.*
radiatus Uhler, Harr. Treat. Ed. 1852, 181, *Mass.*
viridifasciatus Uhler, Harr. Treat. Ed. 1862, 181, *Mass.*

Gryllacris.

carolinensis Germ. Archiv f. Nat. XXVI, i, 276, *Carolina.*

Gryllotalpa.

americana Harr. Hitchc. Rep. 2d Ed. 576;—Ib. Catal. 56, *Mass.*—
Leidy, Proc. Acad. Nat. Sc. Philad. V, 204, *Newark, Delaware.*
azteca Saus. Orthopt. nov. amer. I, 15;—Ib. Rev. et Mag. de Zool.
1859, 315, *Mexico.*—Germ. Archiv f. Nat. XXVI, ii, 404;—
Ib. Bericht, 1859-60, 48, *Mexico.*
borealis Burm. Handb. d. Entom. ii, 740, *Nordamerika.*—Uhler,
Harr. Treat. Ed. 1862, 149, *Mass.*—Scudd. Bost. Journ. Nat.
Hist. VII, 426, *Mass. Nantucket, Vermont.*—Thomas, Trans.
Ill. St. Agric. Soc. V, 441, *Maryland.* See also *Gryllus borealis.*
brevipennis Serv. Orthopt. 368, *Amérique septentrionale, Caroline,
Philadelphie, Louisiane.*—Harr. Treat. Ed. 1841-2, 120; Ed.
1852, 131; Ed. 1862, 149, fig. 68, *Mass.*—Fitch, Amer. Journ.
Agric. and Sc. VI, 146, *New York.* See also *Gryllus brevipen-
nis.*
cultriger Uhler, Proc. Entom. Soc. Philad. II, 543, *El Paso.*—Dallas, Zool. Record, I, 573, *El Paso.*
didactyla Johnst. Trans. Entom. Soc. Lond. II, xxiv, *Saint Vincent.*
—Kirby and Spence, Introd. Entom. 7th Ed. 103, *St. Vincent.*
—Westw. Introd. Class. Ins. I, 447, *West Indies.* — Harr.
Treat. Ed. 1841-2, 121; Ed. 1852, 132; Ed. 1862, 149, *West
Indies.*—Westw. Cuv. Anim. Kingd. 560, *West Indies.*
hexadactyla Serv. Orthopt. 307, *Brésil, Guadeloupe.*—Guér. Sagra,
Hist. nat. de Cuba, 355, pl. xii, fig. 9, *Cuba, Brésil, Guadeloupe.*
longipennis Scudd. Bost. Journ. Nat. Hist. VII, 426, *Mass. Mary-
land.*—Germ. Archiv f. Nat. XXIX, ii, 356;—Ib. Bericht,
1862, 42, *Massachusetts.*—Thomas, Trans. Ill. St. Agric. Soc.
V, 441, *Arkansas.*
mexicana Burm. Handb. d. Entom. II, 740, *Alvarado in Mexiko.*
See also *Gryllus mexicanus.*
  See also GRYLLUS.

D

Gryllus.

abbreviatus Serv. Orthopt. 336, *Amérique septentrionale.*—Burm. Germ. Zeitschr. f. Entom. II, 74, *Nord America.*—De Haas, Bijdr. Kenn. Orthopt. 225, *Noord-Amerika.*—Scudd. Bost. Journ. Nat. Hist. VII, 427, *Mass. Cape Cod, Maryland.*

acuminatus [Tettigonia] Linn. Syst. Nat. 10th Ed. I, 429, *In Indiis.* —In. Syst. Nat. 12th Ed. II, 696; 13th Ed. I, 696, *America.*— [Tettigonia] In. Mus. Lud. Ulr. Reg. 130, *In Indiis.*—[Tettigonia] Müll. Linn. Natursyst. V, 450, *America.*—[Tettigonia] Goeze, Entom. Beytr. II, 60, *Der amerikanische Spitzwirbel.*— [Tettigonia] Gmel. Linn. Syst. Nat. I, IV, 2063, *In America meridionali.*—[Tettigonia] Burm. Gen. Ins. 13, tab. ix, fig. 1, *America.* — [Tettigonia] Stoll., Répr. de Spectres, Saut. & sabre, 18, 19. pl. viii*, fig. 27.-9, *Pennsylvanie.*

ægyptus Thunb. Mém. Acad. St. Pétersb. V, 241, *In insula Bartholomæi.*

æqualis Say. Journ. Acad. Nat. Sc. Philad. IV, 307;—In. Entom. of N. Amer. Ed. Leconte, II, 237, *United States.*

agilis [Tettigonia] Goeze, Entom. Beytr. II, 99, *Der pensylvanische Läufer.*—[Tettigonia] Gmel. Linn. Syst. Nat. I, IV, 2071, *Pennsylvania.*—[Locusta] Turt. Syst. Nat. Linn. II, 555, *Pennsylvania.*—[Pterophyllus] Harr. Hitchc. Rep. 583; 2d Ed. 576; —In. Catal. 56, *Mass.*

americanus Drury, Illustr. Nat. Hist. I, 128, pl. xlix, fig. 2; II, app. *Virginia, Antigua, New York, Madras, Sierra Leon.*

angustus Scudd. Bost. Journ. Nat. Hist. VII, 427, *Mass. Cape Cod.* —Gerst. Archiv f. Nat. XXIX, II, 356;—In. Berichte, 1862, 42, *Massachusetts.*

annulatus Herbst, Fuessly, Archiv d. Ins. 1786, 195, tab. liii, fig. 4, *Amerika.*—[Locusta] Gmel. Linn. Syst. Nat. I, IV, 2061, *America.*—Turt. Syst. Nat. Linn. II, 545, *America.*

annulipes [Phalangopsis] De Haan, Bijdr. Kenn. Orthopt. 226, *Port au Prince.*

æquilinus [Tettigonia] Linn. Syst. Nat. 10th Ed. I, 430; 12th Ed. II, 697; 13th Ed. I, 697;—[Tettigonia] In. Mus. Lud. Ulr. Reg. 133, *In Indiis.*—[Tettigonia] Müll. Linn. Naturyst. V, 431, *Indica.*—[Tettigonia] Goeze, Entom. Beytr. II, 61, *Der indianische Breitflügel.*

assimilis [Acheta] Goeze, Entom. Beytr. II, 67, *Die jamaische Hausgrille.*—[Acheta] Gmel. Linn. Syst. Nat. I, IV, 2060, *In insulis America meridionalis oppositis.*—Oliv. Encycl. méth. VI, 634, *Jamrique.*—[Acheta] Turt. Syst. Nat. Linn. II, 544, *Jamaica.*—Burm. Handb. d. Entom. II, 733, *Mittel und Süd-Amerika.*—De Haan, Bijdr. Kenn. Orthopt. 226, *Middel en Zuid-Amerika.*

arisons SAUSS. Orthopt. nov. amer. I, 16;—In. Rev. et Mag. de Zool.
1859, 316, *Tellus mexicana.*—GERST. Archiv f. Nat. XXVI,
II, 404;—In. Bericht. 1859-60, 48.

bicornis [Mantis] LINN. Syst. Nat. 10th Ed. I, 426;—[Mantis] In.
Mus. Lud. Ulr. Reg. 116, *In Indiis.*

bipunctatus DE GEER, Mém. III, 523, pl. xliii, fig. 7, *Pennsylvanie.*—
[Acheta] GOEZE, Entom. Beytr. II, 89, *Der pennsylvanische
Zweypunkt.*—In. De Geer, Gesch. Ins. III, 340, tab. xliii, fig.
7, *Pennsylvanica.*—OLIV. Encycl. méth. VI, 637, *Am. sept.
Pennsylvanie.*—BURM. Handb. d. Entom. II, 732, *Pennsylva-
nien.*—(Œcanthus) DE HAAN, Bijdr. Kenn. Orthopt. 225,
Noord-Amerika.

bivittatus SAY, Journ. Acad. Nat. Sc. Philad. IV, 308;—In. Entom.
of N. Amer. Ed. Leconte, II, 237, *Arkansas.*

borealis [Gryllotalpa] DE HAAN, Bijdr. Kenn. Orthopt. 225, *Noord-
Amerika.*

brevicornis [Acridium] LINN. Cent. Ins. rar. 15;—[Acridium] In.
Amœn. Acad. VI, 398;—[Acrida] In. Syst. Nat. 12th Ed. II,
699; 13th Ed. I, 692, *In America septentrionali.*—[Acrida]
MÜLL. Linn. Natursyst. V, 419, *In dem mitternächtlichen
America.*—[Acrida] GOEZE, Entom. Beytr. II, 43, *Das ameri-
konische Kurzhorn.*—[Acrida sive Truxalis] GMEL. Linn. Syst.
Nat. I, IV, 2056, *In America meridionali.*—[Truxalis] TURT.
Syst. Nat. Linn. II, 542, *America.*

brevipennis [Gryllotalpa] DE HAAN, Bijdr. Kenn. Orthopt. 225,
Noord-Amerika.

cœrulescens [Locusta] LINN. Syst. Nat. 10th Ed. I, 432; 12th Ed. II,
700; 13th Ed. I, 700, *In meridionalibus.*

camellifolius [Tettigonia] GOEZE, Entom. Beytr. II, 92, *Das amerikanische Kanälenblatt.*—[Tettigonia] GMEL. Linn. Syst. Nat.
I, IV, 2064, *America.*—[Locusta] TURT. Syst. Nat. Linn. II,
548, *America.*

campestris ?KALM, Travels, II, 10;—In. Pink. Voy. XIII, 506, *New
York, Canada.*—In. Travels, II, 69;—In. Pink. Voy. XIII, 524,
all parts of N. America where I have been.—In. Travels, II,
126;—In. Pink. Voy. XIII, 542, *New Jersey.*

carinatus [Dalla] LINN. Syst. Nat. 10th Ed. I, 427; 12th Ed. II, 693;
13th Ed. I, 693, *In Indiis.*—[Balla] MÜLL. Linn. Natursyst. V,
421, *Aus Indien.*—[Balla] GOEZE, Entom. Beytr. II, 46, *Der
indianische Glattschild.*—[Locusta] STOLL', Répr. d. Spectres,
Saut. de passage, 12, pl. v°, fig. 16, *L'Amérique.*

carolinus [Locusta] LINN. Syst. Nat. 10th Ed. I, 433; 12th Ed. II,
701; 13th Ed. I, 701, *America.*—[Mantis] In. Cent. Ins. rar. 13;
—[Mantis] In. Amœn. Acad. VI, 396, *Carolina.*—[Locusta]
MÜLL. Linn. Natursyst. V, 443, *Carolina.*—FABR. Syst. Entom.
291, *America.*—In. Spec. Ins. I, 368, *In America boreali.*—In.

Entom. Syst. II, 58, *America.*—[Locusta] GOEZE, Entom. Beytr. II, 76, *Der karolinische Gelbrand.*—[Locusta] GMEL. Linn. Syst. Nat. I, IV, 2078, *In America boreali.*—TURT. Syst. Nat. Linn. II, 562, *America.*—FITCH, Amer. Journ. Agric. and Sc. VI, 146, *New York.*—JAEG. N. Amer. Ins. 1854, 140, pl. v, fig. 22; 1859, 97, fig. 22, *United States.*

centurio [Locusta] DRURY, Illustr. Nat. Hist. II, 78, pl. xli, fig. 3, *Bay of Honduras.*—[Locusta] GOEZE, Entom. Beytr. II, 101, *Der amerikanische Hauptmann.*—[Locusta] STOLL', Répr. d. Spectres, Saut. de passage, 13, pl. vi*, fig. 19, *Nouvelle Géorgie.*

chrysomelas [Locusta] GMEL. Linn. Syst. Nat. I, IV, 2086, *Pennsylvania.*—TURT. Linn. Syst. Nat. II, 569, *Pennsylvania.*

citrifolius [Tettigonia] LINN. Syst. Nat. 10th Ed. I, 429; 12th Ed. II, 695; 13th Ed. I, 695;—[Tettigonia] In. Mus. Lud. Ulr. Reg. 125, *In Indiis.*—[Tettigonia] MÜLL. Linn. Natursyst. V, 427, *Aus den Indien.*—[Tettigonia] GOEZE, Entom. Beytr. II, 58, *Das indirmische Zitronblatt.*

columbinus THUNB. Mém. Acad. St. Petersb. IX, 399, 425, *In Bartholmi, ins. Americæ.*

concavus [Pterophylla] HARR. Hitch. Rep. 382; 2d. Ed. 576;—In. Catal. 56, *Mass.*

corallinus FITCH, Amer. Journ. Agric. and Sc. VI, 146, *New York.*

coriaceus [Tettigonia] LINN. Syst. Nat. 10th Ed. I, 430; 12th Ed. II, 697; 13th Ed. I, 697.—[Tettigonia] In. Mus. Lud. Ulr. Reg. 136, *In Indiis.*—[Tettigonia] MÜLL. Linn. Natursyst. V, 43, *Indien.*

coronatus [Tettigonia] LINN. Syst. Nat. 10th Ed. I, 430; 12th Ed. II, 697; 13th Ed. I, 697, *In Indiis.*—[Tettigonia] MÜLL. Linn. Naturyst. V, 430, *In Indien.*—[Tettigonia] GOEZE, Entom. Beytr. II, 61, *Die indianische Heuschrecke.*

cristatus [Locusta] LINN. Syst. Nat. 10th Ed. I, 431; 12th Ed. II, 699; 13th Ed. I, 699, *America, Arabia, Asia.*—[Locusta] In. Mus. Lud. Ulr. Reg. 137, *Asia, Africa, America.*—[Locusta] STOLL', Répr. d. Spectres, Saut. de passage, 21, pl. ix*, fig. 80, *Arabie et L'Amérique.*

crucis [Acheta] GMEL. Linn. Syst. Nat. I, IV, 2062, *In insula S. Crucis.*—OLIV. Encycl. méth. VI, 637, *Sainte Croix.*—[Acheta] TURT. Syst. Nat. Linn. II, 545, *Santa Cruz.*

cubensis SAUSS. Orthopt. nov. amer. I, 15;—In. Rev. et Mag. de Zool. 1859, 316, *Cuba.*—GERST. Archiv f. Nat. XXVI, II, 404;—In. Bericht, 1859-60, 48.

curvicaudus [Tettigonia] GOEZE, Entom. Beytr. II, 98, *Der pennsylvanische Krummschwanz.*—[Tettigonia] GMEL. Linn. Syst. Nat. I, IV, 2071, *In Pennsylvania prati.*—[Locusta] TURT. Syst. Nat. Linn. II, 555, *Pennsylvania.*—[Pterophylla] HARR. Hitche. Rep. 682; 2d Ed. 576;—In. Catal. 56, *Mass.*

cyaneus Thur. Syst. Nat. Linn. II, 563, *America.*

cyanipes Fabr. Syst. Entom. 293, *America.*—In. Spec. Ins. I, 370, *In Americæ meridionalis insulis.*—In. Entom. Syst. II, 60, *America.*—In. Nom. Entom. emend. Ed. 1797, 83; Ed. 1810, 83, *Am.*—[Locusta] Goeze, Entom. Beytr. II, 106, *Der amerikanische Blaufuss.*—[Locusta] Gmel. Linn. Syst. Nat. I, iv, 2080, *In insulis Americæ meridionali oppositis.*

dentatus [Locusta] Goeze, Entom. Beytr. II, 114, *Die indianische Heuschrekke.*

dux [Locusta] Daury, Illustr. Nat. Hist. II, 82, pl. xliv, *Bay of Honduras.*—[Locusta] Goeze, Entom. Beytr. II, 102, *Der amerikanische Fürst.*—Fabr. Spec. Ins. I, 362;—In. Entom. Syst. II, 41, *America meridionalis.*—In. Nom. Entom. emend. Ed. 1797, 61; Ed. 1810, 81, *Am. m.*—[Locusta] Gmel. Linn. Syst. Nat. I, iv, 2074, *In America meridionali.*

elongatus [Tetigonia] Linn. Mus. Lud. Ulr. Reg. 127, *In Indiis.*—[Tetigonia] Müll. Linn. Natursyst. V, 479, *Indien.*—[Tetigonia] Goeze, Entom. Beytr. II, 59, *Der indianische Lang-flügel.*

ensiger [Conocephalus] Harr. Hitchc. Rep. 2d Ed. 576;—In. Catal. 56, *Mass.*

erythropus [Locusta] Gmel. Linn. Syst. Nat. I, iv, 2086, *Pennsylvania.*—Thur. Syst. Nat. Linn. II, 568, *Pennsylvania.*

fasciatus De Geer, Mém. III, 522, pl. xliii, fig. 5, *Pensylvanie.*—[Acheta] Goeze, Entom. Beytr. II, 89, *Die pensylvanische Grille.*—[Tetigonia] In. Entom. Beytr. II, 89, *Die pensylvanische Sabelheuschrekke.*—In. De Geer, Gesch. Ins. III, 339, tab. xliii, fig. 5, *Pennsylvanien.*—[Acheta] Gmel. Linn. Syst. Nat. I, iv, 2063;—[Tetigonia] In. Linn. Syst. Nat. IV, 2072, *Pennsylvania.*—[Acheta] Thur. Syst. Nat. Linn. II, 547;—[Locusta] In. Syst. Nat. Linn. II, 555, *Pennsylvania.*—[Pterophylla] Harr. Hitchc. Rep. 582; 2d Ed. 576;—In. Catal. 56, *Mass.*—De Haan, Bijdr. Kenn. Orthopt. 225, *Noord-Amerika.*

fastigiatus [Tetigonia] Linn. Syst. Nat. 10th Ed. I, 430; 12th Ed. II, 697; 13th Ed. I, 697;—[Tetigonia] In. Mus. Lud. Ulr. Reg. 135, *In Indiis.*—[Tetigonia] Goeze, Entom. Beytr. II, 62, *Der indianische Langstachel.*

femur rubrum [Locusta] Goeze, Entom. Beytr. II, 115, *Die pensylvanische Rothhüfte.*

flavicornis Thunb. Mém. Acad. St. Petersb. IX, 406, *China, Indiis et Prom. bon. spei.*

flavipes [Acheta] Thur. Syst. Nat. Linn. II, 545, *St. Thomas Island.*

flavus Fabr. Entom. Syst. II, 53, *America.*—In. Nom. Entom. emend. Ed. 1797, 82; Ed. 1810, 82, *Am.*—Thur. Syst. Nat. Linn. II, 563, *America.*—Thunb. Mém. Acad. St. Petersb. V, 232; IX,

395, 410, *In America et in capite bonœ spei vulgaris.*—In. Hom. max. cap. 2, *In cap. bonæ spei et in America.*

formosus SAY, Amer. Entom. III, pl. xxxiv;—In. Entom. of N. Amer. Ed. Leconte, I, 78, pl. xxxiv, *Arkansas River.*

fuliginosus [Acheta] STOLL', Répr. d. Spectres, Grillons, 5, pl. iii*, fig. 10, *L'Amérique.*

fuscus THUNB. Mém. Acad. St. Petersb. V, 235; IX, 421, *Nova Cambria.*

giganteus [Acrida sive Truxalis] GMEL. Linn. Syst. Nat. I, IV, 2057, *America.*—[Truxalis] TURT. Syst. Nat. Linn. II, 512, *America.*

gigas [Mantis] LINN. Mus. Lud. Ulr. Reg. 109, *In India orientali et occidentali.*—[Acheta] GOEZE, Entom. Beytr. II, 86, *Die amerikanische Riesengrille.*—[Acheta] GMEL. Linn. Syst. Nat. I, IV, 2063,—TURT. Syst. Nat. Linn. II, 546, *America.*—[Acheta] ROEM. Gen. Ins. 13, tab. viii, fig. 8, *America.*

gongylodes [Mantis] LINN. Syst. Nat. 10th Ed. I, 426, *In Indiis.*—SULZ. Kenn. der Ins. Erkl. 30, tab. viii, fig. 56, *Indien.*

'gryllodes PALLAS, Spic. zool. I, 16, tab. i, fig. 10, *Jamaica.*—[Acheta] GMEL. Linn. Syst. Nat. I, IV, 2069.—TURT. Syst. Nat. Linn. II, 546, *Jamaica.*—OLIV. Encycl. méth. VI, 637, *Jamaique.*—[Enoptera] DE HAAN, Bijdr. Kenn. Orthopt. 229, 231, *Jamaica ? Java, Celebes.*

gryllotalpa [Acheta] LINN. Syst. Nat. 10th Ed. I, 428, *In Europa et America boreali herbosis et cultis.*—[Acheta] In. Syst. Nat. 12th Ed. II, 693; 13th Ed. I, 693, *In Europa et America borealis herbosis et cultis; in Java.*—[Acheta] In. Mus. Lud. Ulr. Reg. 123, *Europa, America, Asia.*—[Acheta] GMEL. Linn. Syst. Nat. I, IV, 2059, *In Europa, borealis America et Asia, ipsius Java cultis.*—[Acheta] VILL. Linn. Entom. Faun. Suec. I, 436, *In Europa et America borealis herbosis et cultis.*—[Acheta] TURT. Syst. Nat. Linn. II, 544, *Europa and America.*—OKEN, Allg. Naturg. V, C, 1528, *In ganz Europa, in Schweden nur bis Schonen ? in Nordamerica.*

guadaloupensis [Acheta] TURT. Syst. Nat. Linn. II, 546, *Guadeloupe.*

hæmatopus [Locusta] LINN. Syst. Nat. 10th Ed. I, 432; 12th Ed. II, 700; 13th Ed. I, 700;—[Locusta] In. Mus. Lud. Ulr. Reg. 143, *In Indiis.*—[Locusta] MÜLL. Linn. Natursyst. V, 439, *Indien.*—FABR. Syst. Entom. 289;—In. Spec. Ins. I, 365;—In. Entom. Syst. II, 52, *In Indiis.*—In. Nom. Entom. emend. Ed. 1797, 81; Ed. 1810, 81, *Ind.*—[Locusta] GOEZE, Entom. Beytr. II, 69, *Der indianische Blutschenkel.*

hirtipes SAY, Amer. Entom. III, pl. xxxiv;—In. Entom. of N. Amer. Ed. Leconte, I, 78, pl. xxxiv, *Arkansas River.*

hospes [Acheta] GOEZE, Entom. Beytr. II, 87, *Der amerikanische Gast.*—[Acheta] GMEL. Linn. Syst. Nat. I, IV, 2061, *America.*

—Oliv. Encycl. méth. VI, 636, *Am. sept. ex Pennsylvanie.*—
[Acheta] Turt. Syst. Nat. Linn. II, 545, *America.*

irroratus [Mantis] Linn. Cent. Ins. rar. 14;—[Mantis] In. Amœn.
Acad. VI, 397, *Carolina.*

lamellatus [Tettigonia] Linn. Syst. Nat. 10th Ed. I, 429, *In Indiis.*

lamellosus [Tettigonia] Linn. Mus. Lud. Ulr. Reg. 125;—[Tettigonia] In. Syst. Nat. 12th Ed. II, 696; 13th Ed. I, 696, *In Indiis.*—[Tettigonia] Gœze, Entom. Beytr. II, 60, *Das indianische Schenkelblatt.*—[Locusta] Turt. Syst. Nat. Linn. II, 550, *America.*

lateralis Fabr. Syst. Entom. 293, *America.*—In. Spec. Ins. I, 370, *In Americæ meridionalis insulis.*—In. Entom. Syst. II, 60, *America.*—In. Nom. Entom. emend. Ed. 1797, 82; Ed. 1810, 82, *Am.*—[Locusta] Gœze, Entom. Beytr. II, 107, *Der amerikanische Seitenpunkt.*—[Locusta] Gmel. Linn. Syst. Nat. I, iv, 2080, *In insulis America meridionali oppositis.*—Turt. Syst. Nat. Linn. II, 563, *America.*

laurifolius Linn. Mus. Adolph. Fred. 83, (*Fol. lauri) America.*—
[Tettigonia] In. Syst. Nat. 10th Ed. I, 429, *In Indiis.*—[Tettigonia] In. Syst. Nat. 12th Ed. II, 695; 13th Ed. I, 695, *In Indiis, Carolina.*—[Tettigonia] In. Mus. Lud. Ulr. Reg. 126, *In America meridionali.*—[Tettigonia] Müll. Linn. Naturyst. V, 428, *Carolina, Brasilia, Jamaica.*—[Tettigonia] Gœze, Entom. Beytr. II, 59, *Das karolinische Laubblatt.*—[Tettigonia] Gmel. Linn. Syst. Nat. I, iv, 2053, *America, Nova Hollandia.*—Shaw and Nodder, Nat. Misc. IV, pl. cxv, *America.*—[Locusta] Turt. Syst. Nat. Linn. II, 547, *America.*

lineaticeps Stål, Orthopt. Eug. Resa, 314, *California ad San Francisco.*—Gerst. Archiv f. Nat. XXVIII, ii, 313;—In. Bericht, 1861, 41, *California.*

luctuosus Burm. Germ. Zeitsch. f. Entom. II, 74, *Süd Karolina.*—Serv. Orthopt. 335, *Amérique septentrionale.*—De Haan, Bijdr. Kenn. Orthopt. 225, *Californie, Noord-Amerika.*—Scudd. Bost. Journ. Nat. Hist. VII, 427, *Mass. Cape Cod, N. Hampshire.*

lunus Fabr. Syst. Entom. 268;—In. Spec. Ins. I, 364;—In. Entom. Syst. II, 47, *In America meridionali.*

maculatus [Ephippiger] Harr. Hitch. Rep. 3d Ed. 576;—In. Catal. 56, *Mass.*

maxillosus [Tettigonia] Gœze, Entom. Beytr. II, 93, *Die amerikanische Kinnlade.*—[Tettigonia] Gmel. Linn. Syst. Nat. I, iv, 2061, *In insulis America oppositis.*—[Locusta] Turt. Syst. Nat. Linn. II, 549, *America.*

melanopterus [Tettigonia] Linn. Syst. Nat. 10th Ed. I, 430; 12th Ed. II, 697; 13th Ed. I, 697;—[Tettigonia] In. Mus. Lud. Ulr. Reg. 134, *In Indiis.*—[Tettigonia] Müll. Linn. Naturyst. V,

431, *Indica.*—[Tetigonia] GOEZE, Entom. Beytr. II, 62, *Der indianische Schwarzflügel.*

membranaceus [Acheta] DRURY, Illustr. Nat. Hist. II, 81, pl. xlii, fig. 2, *Bay of Honduras and Muskito Shore.*

mexicanus [Gryllotalpa] DE HAAN, Bijdr. Kenn. Orthopt. 326, *Mexica.*—SAUSS. Orthopt. nov. amer. I, 15;—In. Rev. et Mag. de Zool. 1859, 316, *Mexica.*—GERST. Archiv f. Nat. XXVI, II, 101;—In. Bericht, 1859–60, 48.

miles [Locusta] DRURY, Illustr. Nat. Hist. II, 79, pl. alli, fig. 3, *Bay of Honduras.* —[Locusta] GOEZE, Entom. Beytr. II, 102, *Der amerikanische Soldat.*—[Locusta] GMEL. Linn. Syst. Nat. I, IV, 2082, *America.*

militaris [Locusta] LINN. Syst. Nat. 10th Ed. I, 432; 12th Ed. II, 700; 13th Ed. I, 700, *America.*—[Locusta] In. Mus. Lud. Ulr. Reg. 142, *In Indiis.* —[Locusta] MÜLL. Linn. Natursyst. V, 432, *America.*—FABR. Syst. Entom. 288, *America.*—In. Spec. Ins. I, 361, *In America meridionali.*—In. Entom. Syst. II, 59, *America.*—In. Nom. Entom. emend. Ed. 1787, 81; Ed. 1810, 81, *Am.*—[Locusta] GOEZE, Entom. Beytr. II, 69, *Der amerikanische Feierflügel.*—[Locusta] GMEL. Linn. Syst. Nat. I, IV, 2075, *In America meridionali.*—TURT. Syst. Nat. Linn. II, 558, *America.*

minutus [Acheta] LINN. Syst. Nat. 12th Ed. II, 694; 13th Ed. I, 694, *America.*—[Acheta] MÜLL. Linn. Natursyst. V, 424, *America.*—[Acheta] GOEZE, Entom. Beytr. II, 53, *Die jamaikanische Grille.*—[Acheta] GMEL. Linn. Syst. Nat. I, IV, 2060, *In America meridionali.*—[Acheta] TURT. Syst. Nat. Linn. II, 546, *America.*

monstrosus [Acheta] GOEZE, Entom. Beytr. II, 86, *Der isländische Drachenschwanz.*—OLIV. Encycl. meth. VI, 633, pl. cxxvlii, fig. 15, *Am. mérid.*

morbillosus [Locusta] LINN. Syst. Nat. 10th Ed. I, 431, *In Indiis.*

myrtifolius [Locusta] DRURY, Illustr. Nat. Hist. II, 78, pl. xli, fig. 3, *New York.*—[Tetigonia] GMEL. Linn. Syst. Nat. I, IV, 2064, *In America meridimali.* —[Phyllopterus] WESTW. Drury, Ins. II, 88, pl. xli, fig. 3, *N. York, America.*

neglectus SCUDD. Bost. Journ. Nat. Hist. VII, 426, *Mass. Cape Cod.*—PACK. How to collect 55;—In. Rep. Nat. Hist. Maine, 1862, 195, *Maine.*—GERST. Archiv f. Nat. XXIX, II, 356;—In. Bericht, 1862, 42, *Massachusetts.*

niger SCUDD. Bost. Journ. Nat. Hist. VII, 428, *Mass.*—GERST. Archiv f. Nat. XXIX, II, 356;—In. Bericht, 1862, 42, *Massachusetts.*

niveus DE GEER, Mém. III, 522, pl. xliii, fig. 6, *Pensylvanie.*—[Acheta] GOEZE, Entom. Beytr. II, 59, *Die pensylvanische Grille.*—In. De Geer, Gesch. Ins. III, 339, tab. xliii, fig. 6, *Pensylvanien.*—[Acheta] GMEL. Linn. Syst. Nat. I, IV, 2063,

Pennsylvanica.—OLIV. Encycl. méth. VI, 63?, *Am. sept.*—
TURT. Syst. Nat. Linn. II, 547, *Pennsylvanica.*—(*Fcanthus*)
DE HAAN, Bijdr. Kenn. Orthopt. 225, *Noord-Amerika.*

nubilus SAY, Journ. Acad. Nat. Sc. Philad. IV, 308;—In. Entom. of
N. Amer. Ed. LeConte, II, 237, *Arkansas.*

oblongifolius [Tettigonia] GOEZE, Entom. Beytr. II, 98, *Das pennsylvanische Blatt.*—[Pterophyllus] HARR. Hitche. Rep. 582;
2d Ed. 576;—In. Catal. 56, *Mass.*

obscuratus [Tettigonia] STOLL', Répr. d. Spectres, Saut. à sabre, 20,
pl. viii°, fig. 33, *L'Amérique méridionale.*

obscurus FABR. Suppl. Entom. Syst. 194, *America borealis.*

occidentalis THUNB. Mém. Acad. St. Petersb. IX, 400, 429, *In
America meridionalis, insula Barthelemi.*

ocellatus LINN. Mus. Adolph. Fred. 82, *America.*—[Tettigonia] In.
Syst. Nat. 10th Ed. I, 429; 12th Ed. II, 696; 13th Ed. I, 696;—
[Tettigonia] In. Mus. Lud. Ulr. Reg. 129, *In Indiis.*—[Tettigonia] MÜLL. Naturayst. V, 429, *In den Indien.*—[Tettigonia]
GOEZE, Entom. Beytr. II, 60, *Das indianische Flügelauge.*

oxycephalus [Tettigonia] STOLL', Répr. d. Spectres, Saut. à sabre,
19, pl. viii°, figs. 20–2, *Vraisemblement l'Amérique.*

permonatus UHLER, Proc. Entom. Soc. Philad. II, 547, *Kansas.*—
DALLAS, Zool. Record, I, 573, *Kansas.*

perspicillatus LINN. Cent. Ins. rar. 15;—[Locusta] In. Amoen.
Acad. VI, 398;—[Locusta] In. Syst. Nat. 12th Ed. II, 703;
13th Ed. I, 702, *In Indiis.*—[Locusta] MÜLL. Linn. Naturayst.
V, 446, *Aus den Indien.*—FABR. Syst. Entom. 293;—In. Spec.
Ins. I, 371, *In Indiis.*—In. Nom. Entom. emend. Ed. 1797,
82; Fd. 1810, 82, *Ind.*—[Locusta] GOEZE, Entom. Beytr.
II, 82, *Der indianische Brillenträger.*—[Tettigonia] In. Entom. Beytr. II, 93, *Der amerikanische Brillenträger.*—[Locusta]
TURT. Syst. Nat. Linn. II, 548, *America.*

phthisicus [Mantis] LINN. Syst. Nat. 10th Ed. I, 425;—[Mantis] In.
Mus. Lud. Ulr. Reg. 110, *In Indiis.*

precarius [Mantis] LINN. Syst. Nat. 10th Ed. I, 426;—[Mantis] In.
Mus. Lud. Ulr. Reg. 114, *America, Asia.*

pulicarius BURM. Handb. d. Entom. II, 732, *Jamaica.*—[Nemobius]
DE HAAN, Bijdr. Kenn. Orthopt. 226, *Jamaica.*

pumilus BURM. Handb. d. Entom. II, 732, *St. Jean und St. Thomas.*
—[Nemobius] DE HAAN, Bijdr. Kenn. Orthopt. 226, *St.
Jean.*

punctulatus [Acheta] GMEL. Linn. Syst. Nat. I, IV, 2058.—TURT.
Syst. Nat. Linn. II, 547, *Pennsylvania.*

purpurascens [Locusta] STOLL', Répr. d. Spectres, Saut. de passage,
17, pl. viii°, fig. 22, *L'Amérique.*

reticularis [Locusta] TURT. Syst. Nat. Linn. II, 551, *Guadeloupe.*

ruber LINN. Mus. Adolph. Fred. 83, *In Indiis.*

rugosus [Tettigonia] LINN. Syst. Nat. 10th Ed. 1, 150; 12th Ed. II, 697; 13th Ed. 1, 697;—[Tettigonia] In. Mus. Lud. Ulr. Reg. 132, *In Indiis.*—[Tettigonia] MÜLL. Linn. Natursyst. V, 436, *In Indien.*—(Tettigonia) GOEZE, Entom. Beytr. II, 61, *Der indianische Runzelbalg.*

rusticus FABR. Syst. Entom. 292, *America.*—In. Spec. Ins. 1, 370, *In America meridionalis insulis.* — In. Entom. Syst. II, 60, *America.*—In. Nom. Entom. emend. Ed. 1797, 82; Ed. 1810, 82, *Am.*—[Locusta] GOEZE, Entom. Beytr. II, 107, *Der amerikanische Bauer.*—[Locusta] GMEL. Linn. Syst. Nat. 1, IV, 2080, *In insulis America meridionali oppositis.* — TURT. Syst. Nat. Linn. II, 563, *America.*

sanguinipes FABR. Suppl. Entom. Syst. 193, *America borealis.*

serialis THUNB. Mém. Acad. St. Petersb. V, 241; IX, 399, 434, *In insula Bartholemi.*

serratus [Bulla] LINN. Syst. Nat. 10th Ed. 1, 427.—SULZ. Kennz. der Ins. Erkl. 21, tab. vili, fig. 58, *Indien.* —[Bulla] LINN. Mus. Lud. Ulr. Reg. 131, *In Indiis.*

serripes FABR. Mant. Ins. 1, 236;—In. Entom. Syst. II, 48, *In Indiis.*—In. Nom. Entom. emend. Ed. 1797, 81; Ed. 1810, 81, *Ind.*—TURT. Syst. Nat. Linn. II, 558, *America and Indien.*

siccifolius [Mantis] LINN. Syst. Nat. 10th Ed. 1, 425;—[Mantis] In. Mus. Ulr. Reg. 111, *In Indiis.*

specularis [Tettigonia] GOEZE. Entom. Beytr. II, 93, *Die amerikanische Spiegelträger.*—[Tettigonia] GMEL. Linn. Syst. Nat. 1, IV, 2064, *America.*—[Locusta] TURT. Syst. Nat. Linn. II, 349, *America.*

spinulosus [Locusta] LINN. Amœn. Acad. VI, 398;—(Locusta) In. Syst. Nat. 12th Ed. II, 703; 13th Ed. 1, 703, *In Indiis.*—[Locusta] MÜLL. Linn. Natursyst. V, 445, *Aus Indien.*—[Locusta] GOEZE, Entom. Beytr. II, 81, *Der indianische Dornträger.*

squarrosus [Locusta] STOLL', Repr. d. Spectres, Saut. de passage, 15, pl. vIII', fig. 25, *L'Amérique méridionale.*

strumarius [Mantis] LINN. Syst. Nat. 10th Ed. 1, 436, *In Indiis.*

succinctus [Locusta] LINN. Syst. Nat. 12th Ed. II, 699; 13th Ed. 1, 699, *Jara, Carolina.*—[Locusta] MÜLL. Linn. Natursyst. V, 436, *Jara, Carolina.* — FABR. Syst. Entom. 287;—In. Spec. Ins. 1, 362;—In. Entom. Syst. II, 46, *In Indiis.*—In. Nom. Entom. emend. Ed. 1797, 81; Ed. 1810, 81, *Ind.*

sulphureus FABR. Spec. Ins. 1, 369, *In America boreali.*—In. Entom. Syst. II, 59, *America.*—In. Nom. Entom. emend. Ed. 1797, 82; Ed. 1810, 82, *Am.*—[Locusta] GMEL. Linn. Syst. Nat. 1, IV, 2079, *In America boreali.*—TURT. Syst. Nat. Linn. II, 563, *America.*

surinamensis FABR. Syst. Entom. 291;—In. Spec. Ins. 1, 367;—In. Entom. Syst. II, 57, *In America meridionali.*

talpa OLIV. Encycl. méth. VI, 633, pl. cxxviii, figs. 10–14, *Europe,*
 Am. sept.

tartaricus PANZ. Drury, Ins. 200, tab. xlix, fig. 2, *Virginien, Antigua.
 New York, Madras in Ostindien,* so wie auf *Sierra Leon* in
 Afrika zu Hause.

tessulatus [Acheta] GMEL. Linn. Syst. Nat. I, IV, 2063, *In insula S.
 Johannis.*—[Acheta] TURT. Syst. Nat. Linn. II, 546, *St. John
 Island.*

tricolor [Mantis] LINN. Mus. Lud. Ulr. Reg. 117, *In Indiis.*

trifasciatus SAY, Amer. Entom. III, pl. xxxiv;—Ins. Entom. of N.
 Amer. Ed. LeConte, I, 76, pl. xxxiv, *Arkansas River.*

triops [Tettigonia] LINN. Syst. Nat. 10th Ed. I, 430; 12th Ed. II, 697,
 13th Ed. I, 697;—[Tettigonia] In. Mus. Lud. Ulr. Reg. 131, *In
 Indiis.*—[Tettigonia] MÜLL Linn. Natursyst. V, 430, *Aus den
 Indien.*—[Tettigonia] GOEZE, Entom. Beytr. II, 60, *Das indianische Dreyauge.*

tuberculatus [Conocephalus] HARR. Ittsche. Rep. 582; 2d Ed. 876;
 —In. Catal. 56, *Mass.*

turcicus FABR. Nom. Entom. emend. Ed. 1797, 81; Ed. 1810, 81, *Ind.*

unicolor [Bulla] LINN. Syst. Nat. 10th Ed. I, 427; 12th Ed. II, 692;
 13th Ed. I, 692. *In Indiis*—[Bulla] MÜLL. Linn. Natursyst.
 V, 410, *Aus den Indica.*—[Bulla] GOEZE, Entom. Beytr. II,
 43, *Die indianische Grille.*—OLIV. Encycl. méth. VI, 635,
 Guadeloupe.

variegatus [Locusta] LINN. Syst. Nat. 10th Ed. I, 432; 12th Ed. II,
 700; 13th Ed. I. 700;—[Locusta] In. Mus. Lud. Ulr. Reg.
 144. *America.*—[Locusta] MÜLL. Linn. Natursyst. V, 441,
 America.—FABR. Syst. Entom. 290;—In. Spec. Ins. I, 366;
 —In. Entom. Syst. II, 54;—In. Nom. Entom. emend. Ed.
 1797, 81; Ed. 1810, 81, *America.*—[Locusta] GOEZE, Entom.
 Beytr. II, 72, *Die amerikanische Buntscheckr.*—HERBST, Fu-
 essly, Archiv d. Entom. 1786, 184, tab. liii, fig. 8, *America.*
 —[Locusta] GMEL. Linn. Syst. Nat. I, IV, 2076, *America.*—
 TURT. Syst. Nat. Linn. II, 560, *America.*

variolosus [Bulla] LINN. Syst. Nat. 12th Ed. II, 693; 13th Ed. I, 693,
 In Indiis.—[Bulla] MÜLL. Linn. Natursyst. V, 420, *In Indien.*

vicinus [Platydactylus] DE HAAN, Bijdr. Kenn. Orthopt. 226, *Buenos
 Ayres, Cuba.*

virens THUNB. Mém. Acad. St. Petersb. V, 250; IX, 398, 419, *In insula Americes Barthelemi.*

virginianus FABR. Syst. Entom. 291;—In. Spec. Ins. I, 368;—In.
 Entom. Syst. II, 57, *America borealis.* — [Locusta] GOEZE,
 Entom. Beytr. II, 108, *Die virginische Grünader.* — [Locusta]
 GMEL. Linn. Syst. Nat. I, IV, 2078, *In America boreali.*—
 TURT. Syst. Nat. Linn. II, 562, *N. America.*

viridifasciatus [Locusta] GOLM, Entom. Beytr. II, 116, *Die grasgrünische Graubinde.*

viridimaculatus [Bulla] GOLM, Entom. Beytr. II, 84, *Der indimirche Grasfleck.* •

vitreipennis MARSCH. Annal. Wien. Mus. I, 214, tab. xviii, fig. 6. • *Georgia America.* — EMCHR. Archiv f. Nat. III, ii, 808, *Georgia in Nord-America.* •

vorax [Acheta] STOLL', Répr. d. Spectres, Grillons, 8, pl. iv°, figs. 19, 20, *L'Amérique.* — ? EMM. Agric. of N. Y. V, pl. ix, fig. 1, *New York.*

Hadroserum.

subterraneus SCUDD. Bost. Journ. Nat. Hist. VII, 441, *Mammoth Cave, Kentucky.*

Hapithus.

agitator UOLER, Proc. Entom. Soc. Philad. II, 548, *Maryland.* — DAL-LAS, Zool. Record, I, 673, *Baltimore.*

Haplopus.

angulatus BURM. Handb. d. Entom. II, 571, *St. Thomas and St. John.*

bispinosus WESTW. Catal. Orthopt. 87, *America, Brasilia.*

Cytherea WESTW. Catal. Orthopt. 86, pl. xviii, fig. 5, *St. Domingo.*

Evadne WESTW. Catal. Orthopt. 85, pl. xviii, fig. 6, *St. Domingo.*

jamaicensis WESTW. Catal. Orthopt. 86, *India occidentalis, Jamaica.*

Ligia WESTW. Catal. Orthopt. 89, pl. xl, figs. 1, 2, *St. Domingo.*

micropterus WESTW. Catal. Orthopt. 87, *India occidental. insulis St. Thomas et St. John; nec Amboyna. See also Phasma micropterum.*

spinipes WESTW. Catal. Orthopt. 87, *Ind. occident. See also Phasma spinipes.*

See also PHASMA.

HARPAX, see MANTIS.

Heterogamia.

• **mexicana** BURM. Handb. d. Entom. II, 490, *Mexico.*

Heteronemia.

mexicana GRAY, Synops. Phasm. 19, *Mexico.*

Hetrodes.

spinulosus PICT. W. Bull. Soc. Imp. Nat. Mosc. 1839, 110, *In India*.

Hippiscus, see ŒDIPODA.

Hippopedon.

saltator SAUSS. Orthopt. nov. amer. II, 35;— In. Rev. et Mag. de
    Zool. 1861, 323, *Mexico*.—GERST. Archiv f. Nat. XXVIII, II,
    317;—In. Bericht, 1861, 43, *Mexico*.

Holocompsa.

azteca SAUSS. Orthopt. Amér. moy. 151, *La côte du Mexique; pro-
    vince de Vera Cruz.*—BRUNN. Blatt. 347, *Mexique.* See also
    Corydia azteca.
collaris SAUSS. Orthopt. Amér. moy. 151, *Antilles et l'île Maurice.*—
    BRUNN. Blatt. 347, tab. x, fig. 50, *St. Thomas, Bresil, Cuba.*
    See also *Blatta collaris* and *Corydia collaris.*
cyanea SAUSS. Orthopt. Amér. moy. 150, *l'île Maurice et Cuba.*—
    BRUNN. Blatt. 346, *St. Thomas.* See also *Corydia cyanea.*
See also BLATTA and CORYDIA.

Hololampra, see BLATTA.

Homœogamia.

mexicana BRUNN. Blatt. 360, tab. xi, fig. 53, *Mexique, Oaxaca.* See
    also *Polyphaga mexicana.*
See also POLYPHAGA.

Hymenotes.

rhombea WESTW. Proc. Zool. Soc. Lond. V, 130, *Jamaica.*—GUÉR.
    Sagra, Hist. nat. de Cuba, 358, pl. xii, fig. 11, *Jamaique.*
    See also *Acridium rhombeum.*
Sagrai WESTW. Mag. Nat. Hist. [n. s.] III, 493, fig. 67*, on p. 492,
    Cuba.—GUÉR. Sagra, Hist. nat. de Cuba, 357, 358, pl. xii,
    fig. 10, *Cuba.*
See also ACRIDIUM.

Ichthydion.

mexicanum Saus. Rev. et Mag. de Zool. 1859, 380, *Mexico calida.* — Gerst. Archiv f. Nat. XXVI, ii, 406;—Jn. Bericht,
1859—60, 50, *Mexico.*

Idolomorpha, sie Empusa.

Ischnoptera.

azteca Saus. Orthopt. nov. amer. III, 9;—Jn. Rev. et Mag. de Zool.
1862, 170, *Mexico calida.*—Jn. Orthopt. Amér. moy. 88, *Mexique, sur la côte du golfe.* — Gerst. Archiv f. Nat. XXIX, ii.
354;—Jn. Bericht, 1862, 40, *Aus den heissen Gegenden Mexiko's.*—Brunn. Blatt. 141, *Mexique.*
bicolor Saus. Orthopt. Amér. moy. 90, *St. Domingue.* — ? Brunn.
Blatt. 139, *St. Domingue.*
borealis Brunn. Blatt. 133, *Amérique du Nord.*
buprostoides Brunn. Blatt. 140, *Cuba.*
consobrina Saus. Orthopt. Amér. moy. 88. *Les parties chaudes de
Mexique, Cordova.*
capitata Brunn. Blatt. 140, *Cuba.*
Couloniana Saus. Orthopt. nov. amer. III, 9; — Jn. Rev. et Mag.
de Zool. 1862, 169, *America borealis.*—Jn. Orthopt. Amér. moy.
83, *États unis.*—Gerst. Archiv f. Nat. XXIX, ii, 354;—Jn.
Bericht. 1862, 40, *Nord Amerika.*
elongata Saus. Orthopt. Amér. moy. 89, *Les Antilles, St. Domingue.*
lata Brunn. Blatt. 135, *Amérique du Nord ?, St. Domingue.*
mexicana Saus. Orthopt. nov. amer. III, 9;—Jn. Rev. et Mag. de
Zool. 1862, 170, *Mexico calida.*—Jn. Orthopt. Amér. moy. 86,
Les régions chaudes du Mexique, Turtla, Alvarado et Cordova.
—Gerst. Archiv f. Nat. XXIX. ii, 354;—Jn. Bericht, 1862,
40, *Aus den heissen Gegenden Mexiko's.*—Brunn. Blatt. 141,
Mexique.
Nortoniana Saus. Orthopt. nov. amer. III, 9; — Jn. Rev. et Mag.
de Zool. 1862, 169, *America borealis.*—Gerst. Archiv f. Nat.
XXIX, ii, 354;—Jn. Bericht, 1862, 40, *Nord Amerika.*
occidentalis Saus. Orthopt. Amér. moy. 87, *L'Amérique septentrionale, Nouvelle Orléans.*
pennsylvanica Saus. Orthopt. Amér. moy. 84, *États unis.*—Brunn.
Blatt. 135, *Columbie, Amérique du Nord, Indiana, Maryland.*
punctulata Saus. Orthopt. Amér. moy. 91, *Saint Domingue.*
rufa Brunn. Blatt. 131, tab. iii, fig. 13, *Brésil, Portorico.*
rufescens Saus. Orthopt. Amér. moy. 91, *Saint Domingue.* —
? Brunn. Blatt. 139, *St. Domingue.*

translucida Saus. Orthopt. Amér. moy. 85, *L'Amérique septen-*
trionale.

Uhleriana Saus. Orthopt. nov. amer. III, 8;—In. Rev. et Mag. de
Zool. 1862, 169, *Pennsylvania.*—In. Orthopt. Amér. moy. 83,
États unis Pennsylvanie.—Gerst. Archiv f. Nat. XXIX, II,
354;—In. Bericht, 1863, 40, *Pennsylvanien.*

unicolor Brunn. Blatt. 134, *Massachusetts, Amérique du Nord.*

Makkierina.

americana Serv. Ann. Sc. Nat. XXII, 39, *Afrique, Amérique et Eu-*
rope.—In. Orthopt. 64, *Amérique méridionale, les autres parties*
du monde.—Macq. Catal. Mus. Lille, 324, *Amér. mérid.* See
also *Blatta americana.*

fuliginosa Serv. Orthopt. 70, *Amérique du Nord.*

orientalis Skuse, Trans. Entom. Soc. Lond. III, 104, *Jamaica.*
See also Blatta.

Labia.

minor Dours. Entom. Mag. V, 372, *Wanborough, New York.*—
Dohrn, Entom. Zeit. Stett. XXV, 426, *Europa, Sibirien,*
Amerika, Vereinigten Staaten.

minuta Scudd. Bost. Journ. Nat. Hist. VII, 413, *Mass. Virginia.*—
Gerst. Archiv f. Nat. XXIX, II, 358;—In. Bericht, 1863, 44,
Mass. Virginien.

Labidura.

americana Dohrn, Entom. Zeit. Stett. XXIV, 319, *In insulis Haiti,*
Cuba, in Amer. centrali (Costarica, Columbia occidentali, Ven-
ezuela).

gagatina Dohrn, Entom. Zeit. Stett. XXIV, 320, *In insula Portorica.*

riparia Dohrn, Entom. Zeit. Stett. XXIV, 313, *Mittel und Süd*
Europa, Madeira, Ost und Süd Afrika, Sibirien, Japan, Per-
sien, Ostindien, Neuholland, Westindien und Süd Amerika;
(among the special localities given are) Cuba, Mexico.
See also Forficula.

Lefeur, see Œdipoda.
Leucophora, see Panchlora.
Lophophyllus, see Phylloptera.

Loboptera.

indica Brunn. Blatt. 62, *India.*

Locusta.

abortiva [Chloealtis] HARR. Treat. Ed. 1841-2, 149; Ed. 1852,
160; Ed. 1862, 184, *Mass. N. Hampshir.* — [Chloealtis]
ERICHS. Archiv f. Nat. IX, II, 231; — In. Bericht, 1842, 87,
Mass.

acuminata DE GEER, Mém. III, 442, pl. xxxvii, fig. 8, *Indes.*—
FABR. Syst. Entom. 284, *America*—In. Spec. Ins. I, 358, *In
America meridionali.*—In. Nom. Entom. emend. Ed. 1797, 80;
Ed. 1810, 80, *Ind. Eur.*—OKEN, Lehrb. d. Nat. III, I, 451,
Indien.

aequalis HARR. Hitchc. Rep. 585; 2d Ed. 576 ;—In. Catal. 56;—In.
Treat. Ed. 1841-2. 144; Ed. 1852, 155; Ed. 1862, 175, *Mass.*

affinis PAL. DE BEAUV. Insectes, 219, pl. xii. fig. 5, *Saint Domingue.*

agilis DE GEER, Mém. III, 457, pl. xl, fig. 3, *Pensylvanie.*—GOEZE,
De Geer, Gesch. Ins. III, 296, tab. xl, fig. 3, *Pennsylvanien.*—
HARR. Treat. Ed. 1841-2, 130; Ed. 1852, 141; Ed. 1862, 162,
Pennsylvania, Southern States.—[Xiphidium] DE HAAN, Bijdr.
Kenn. Orthopt. 178, *S. Carolina.*

annulipes [Rhaphidophorus] DE HAAN, Bijdr. Kenn. Orthopt. 178,
St. Domingo.

apiculata HARR. Hitchc. Rep. 2d Ed. 576;—In. Catal. 56, *Mass.*

aquilina DE GEER, Mém. III, 450, pl. xxxviii, fig. 6, pl. xxxix, fig.
1, *Indes.*

camellifolia FABR. Syst. Entom. 283;—In. Spec. Ins. I, 356;—In.
Entom. Syst. II, 35;—In. Nom. Entom. emend. Ed. 1797, 80;
Ed. 1810, 80, *America.* See also *Gryllus camellifolius.*

carolina CAT. Carol. II, 89, pl. lxxxix (caroliniana), *Carolina.*—MORT.
Phil. Trans. XLIV, 603 (caroliniana), *Carolina.* — HARR.
Hitchc. Rep. 563; 2d Ed. 576;—In. Catal. 56;—In. Encycl.
Amer. VIII, 41, *America.*—In. Treat. Ed. 1841-2, 142; Ed.
1852, 153; Ed. 1862, 175, pl. ili, fig. 3, *Mass.*—EMM. Agric. of
N. Y. V, 145, pl. ix, fig. 9, *New York.*—PACK. How to collect,
57;—In. Rep. Nat. Hist. Maine, 1862, 198, *Maine.* See also
Gryllus carolinus and *Œdipoda carolina.*

centurio [Rutiokeva] WESTW. Drury, Ins. II, 88, pl. xli, fig. 8. *Bay
of Honduras, America.* See also *Gryllus centurio.*

corincipennis HARR. Hitchc. Rep. 563; 2d Ed. 576;—In. Catal. 56,
Mass.

citrifolia FABR. Syst. Entom. 242;—In. Spec. Ins. I, 356;—In. Entom.
Syst. II, 33, *In Indiis.*—In. Nom. Entom. emend. Ed. 1797, 80;
Ed. 1810, 80, *Ind.*—BILLB. Enum. Ins. 84, *Ind.*

consperса [Chloealtis] HARR. Treat. Ed. 1841-2, 149; Ed. 1852,
160; Ed. 1862, 184, *Mass.*—[Chloealtis] ERICHS. Archiv f.
Nat. IX, II, 230;—In. Bericht, 1842, 86, *Mass.*

corallina HARR. Treat. Ed. 1841-2, 142; Ed. 1852, 153; Ed. 1862,
176, *Mass.*—EMM. Agric. of N. Y. V, 146, *New York.*—PACK.
How to collect, 57;—Id. Rep. Nat. Hist. Maine, 1861, 106,
Maine.

coriacea FABR. Spec. Ins. I, 358;—Id. Entom. Syst. II, 40, *In Indiis.*
—Id. Nom. Entom. emend. Ed. 1797, 81; Ed. 1810, 81, *Ind.*
—(Acantbolls) DE HAAN, Bijdr. Kenn. Orthopt. 178, *Marti-
nique.*

cornuta BLANCH. Hist. Nat. Ins. III, 26, *Amérique méridionale.*

coronata DE GEER, Mém. III, 448, pl. xxxviii, fig. 5, *Elle doit être
venue de l'une des deux Indes, ou bien de l'Afrique.*—FABR.
Syst. Entum. 285;—Id. Spec. Ins. I, 358;—Id. Entom. Syst. II,
40, *In Indiis.*—Id. Nom. Entom. emend. Ed. 1797, 80; Ed.
1810, 80, *Ind.*

cubaensis (Rhaphidophorus) DE HAAN, Bijdr. Kenn. Orthopt. 178,
218, *Cuba.*

curtipennis HARR. Hitchc. Rep. 2d Ed. 576;—Id. Catal. 56.—(Chloealtis) in Treat. Ed. 1841-2, 149; Ed. 1852, 160; Ed. 1862,
184, pl. ill, fig. 1, *Mass.*—(Chloealtis) ENICHS. Archiv f. Nat.
IX, II, 231;—Id. Berichi, 1842, 87, *Mass.*

curvicauda DE GEER, Mém. III, 446, pl. xxxviii, fig. 3, *Pensylvanie.*—
GOEZE, De Geer, Gesch. Ins. III, 289, tab. xxxviii, fig. 3, *Pen-
sylvanica.*—(Phaneroptera) DE HAAN, Bijdr. Kenn. Orthopt.
178, *Vereenigde Staaten.* See also *Gryllus curvicaudus.*

dissimilis (Conocephalus) DE HAAN, Bijdr. Kenn. Orthopt. 178,
Vereenigde Staaten.

dorsalis [Ephippigera] DE HAAN, Bijdr. Kenn. Orthopt. 178, *S. Carolina.*

dux [Rutioloves] WESTW. Drury, Ins. II, 22, pl. xlv, *Bay of Honduras, Brazil.*—DUNC. Introd. Entom. 257, pl. xv, fig. 2, *Tropical
America.* See also *Gryllus dux.*

elongata FABR. Nom. Entom. emend. Ed. 1797, 80; Ed. 1810, 80, *Ind.*

enumerata HARR. Hitchc. Rep. 583; 2d Ed. 576;—Id. Catal. 56;—Id.
Treat. Ed. 1841-2, 145; Ed. 1852, 156; Ed. 1862, 180, *Mass.*

fasciata DE GEER, Mém. III, 458, pl. xl, fig. 4, *Pensylvanie.*

flavovittata PACK. Rep. Nat. Hist. Maine, 1861, 375, *Webster Lake.*

fusca [Xiphidium] DE HAAN, Bijdr. Kenn. Orthopt. 189, *Europa
media, Tripoli, Java, Porto-Rico, America media.*

glaberrima (Xiphidium) DE HAAN, Bijdr. Kenn. Orthopt. 178, *S.
Carolina.*

glauca [Xiphidium] DE HAAN, Bijdr. Kenn. Orthopt. 178, *S. Carolina.*

guttata [Conocephalus] DE HAAN, Bijdr. Kenn. Orthopt. 178, *Cuba.*

infuscata [Tragocephala] HARR. Treat. Ed. 1841-2, 147; Ed. 1852,
158; Ed. 1862, 181, *Mass.*

40 CATALOGUE OF DESCRIBED

lanceolata PAL. DE BEAUV. Insectes, 219, pl. xii, fig. 4, *Saint Domingue.*

lapidicola [Rhaphidophorus] DE HAAN, Bijdr. Kenn. Orthopt. 178, *Cuba.*

latipennis HARR. Treat. Ed. 1841-2, 144; Ed. 1852, 153; Ed. 1862, 179, *Mass.*—PACK. Rep. Nat. Hist. Maine, 1861, 374, *Mt. Katahdin.*

laurifolia FABR. Syst. Entom. 282;—In. Spec. Ins. I, 356, *America, Nova Hollandia.*—In. Entom. Syst. II, 34, *America meridionalis, Nova Hollandia.*—In. Nom. Entom. emend. Ed. 1797, 80; Ed. 1810, 80, *Amer. m.*—PAL. DE BEAUV. Insectes, 219, pl. xii, fig. 3, *Saint Domingue.*—[Phyllophora] DE HAAN, Bijdr. Kenn. Orthopt. 178, *St. Domingo.* See also *Gryllus laurifolius.*

leucostoma KIRBY, Faun. bor. amer. IV, 250, *N. America, Lat. 65°.* See also *Acridium leucostomum.*

maritima HARR. Treat. Ed. 1841-2, 143; Ed. 1852, 154; Ed. 1862, 179, *Sandwich, Mass.*

marmorata HARR. Treat. Ed. 1841-2, 145; Ed. 1852, 156; Ed. 1862, 179, *Mass.*

maxillosa FABR. Syst. Entom. 284, *America.*—In. Spec. Ins. I, 357, *In America insulis.*—In. Entom. Syst. II, 37;—In. Nom. Entom. emend. Ed. 1797, 80; Ed. 1810, 80, *America.* See also *Gryllus maxillosus.*

melanoptera FABR. Syst. Entom. 283;—In. Spec. Ins. I, 358;—In. Entom. Syst. II, 40, *In Indiis.*—In. Nom. Entom. emend. Ed. 1797, 81; Ed. 1810, 81, *Ind.*

miles [Eutheleres] WESTW. Drury, Ins. II, 89, pl. xlii, fig. 2, *Bay of Honduras, America.* See also *Gryllus miles.*

musarum PAL. DE BEAUV. Insectes, 218, pl. xii, fig. 1, *Saint Domingue.*—[Acantholis] DE HAAN, Bijdr. Kenn. Orthopt. 178, *St. Domingo.*

myrtifolia FABR. Syst. Entom. 282, *America.*—In. Spec. Ins. I, 356, *In America meridionali.*—In. Entom. Syst. II, 34, *America.*

nebulosa HARR. Treat. Ed. 1841-2, 148; Ed. 1852, 157; Ed. 1862, 181, *Mass.*—?EMM. Agric. of N. Y. V, 148, pl. ix, fig. 7, *New York, Western Massachusetts.*

nodifrons [Conocephalus] DE HAAN, Bijdr. Kenn. Orthopt. 178, *St. Domingo.*

oblongifolia DE GEER, Mém. III, 445, pl. xxxviii, fig. 2, *Pensylvanie.*—GOEZE, De Geer, Geschh. Ins. III, 288, tab. xxxviii, fig. 2, *Pennsylvanien.*—[Phyllophora] DE HAAN, Bijdr. Kenn. Orthopt. 178, *Vereenigde Staaten.*

obtusa [Conocephalus] DE HAAN, Bijdr. Kenn. Orthopt. 178, *Vereenigde Staaten.*

ocellata FABR. Syst. Entom. 284;—In. Spec. Ins. I, 357;—In. Entom.

Syst. II, 39, *In Indiis.*—In. Nom. Entom. emend. Ed. 1797, 80; Ed. 1810, 80, *Ind.*

pachymera [Ephippigera] De Haan, Bijdr. Kenn. Orthopt. 178, *S. Carolina.*

pariscelidis Harr. Hitchc. Rep. 2d Ed. 576;—In. Catal. 56, *Mass.*

perspicillata Fabr. Syst. Entom. 283;—In. Spec. Ins. I, 357;—In. Entom. Syst. II, 36;—In. Nom. Entom. emend. Ed. 1797, 80; Ed. 1810, 80, *America.*—[Acanthodis] De Haan, Bijdr. Kenn. Orthopt. 178, *Mexico.*—[Cyrtophyllus] De Haan, Bijdr. Kenn. Orthopt. 178, *S. Carolina.* See also *Gryllus perspicillatus.*

radiata Harr. Hitchc. Rep. 2d Ed. 576;—In. Catal. 56, *Mass.*—[Tragocephala] In. Treat. Ed. 1841-2, 148; Ed. 1852, 159; Ed. 1862, 183, *Mass. N. Carolina.*

roticulata Fabr. Entom. Syst. II, 40;—In. Nom. Entom. emend. Ed. 1797, 81; Ed. 1810, 81, *Guadeloupe.*

retinervis [Phylloptera] De Haan, Bijdr. Kenn. Orthopt. 178, *Vereenigde Staaten.*

ambricollis [Acanthodis] De Haan, Bijdr. Kenn. Orthopt. 178, *Martinique.*

septentrionalis [Phaneroptera] De Haan, Bijdr. Kenn. Orthopt. 178, *Vereenigde Staaten.*

serrulata Pal. de Beauv. Insectes, 218, pl. xii, fig. 2, *Saint Domingue.*—[Polyancistrus] De Haan, Bijdr. Kenn. Orthopt. 178, *St. Domingo.*

specularis Fabr. Syst. Entom. 281;—In. Spec. Ins. I, 357;—In. Entom. Syst. II, 36;—In. Nom. Entom. emend. Ed. 1797, 80; Ed. 1810, 80, *America.* See also *Gryllus specularis.*

spinulosa Fabr. Spec. Ins. I, 361;—In. Entom. Syst. II, 44, *In Indiis.*—In. Nom. Entom. emend. Ed. 1797, 81; Ed. 1810, 81, *Ind.* See also *Gryllus spinulosus.*

sulphurea Harr. Hitchc. Rep. 583; 2d Ed. 576;—In. Catal. 56;—In. Treat. Ed. 1841-2, 113; Ed. 1852, 151; Ed. 1862, 177, *Mass.*—Emm. Agric. of N. Y. V, 146, *New York.*—Pack. How to collect, 57;—In. Rep. Nat. Hist. Maine, 1862, 136, *Maine.* See also *Gryllus sulphureus.*

talpa [Anastostoma] De Haan, Bijdr. Kenn. Orthopt. 178, *Mexico.*

tartarica ? Westw. Drury, Ins. I, 121, pl. xlix, fig. 3, *Virginia, Antigua, New York, Madras, Sierra Leone, Tartaria and Africa.*

triops Fabr. Syst. Entom. 283;—In. Spec. Ins. I, 358;—In. Entom. Syst. II, 40, *In Indiis.*—In. Nom. Entom. emend. Ed. 1797, 80; Ed. 1810, 80, *Ind.*

tuberculata Harr. Hitchc. Rep. 583; 2d Ed. 576;—In. Catal. 55, *Mass.*—White, Rich. Arc. Search Exp. II, 360, *Borders of Mackenzie and Slave Rivers, Fort Simpson.*

verruculata Kirby, Faun. bor. amer. IV, 250, *N. America, Lat. 57°.* See also *Acridium verruculatum.*

46 CATALOGUE OF DESCRIBED

viridifasciata HANS. Hitch. Rep. 383; 2d Ed. 576;—In. Catal. 56 ;—
[Tragacephala] In. Treat. Ed. 1841-2. 147; Ed. 1852, 158;
Ed. 1862, 182, MILL.—THOMAS, Trans. Ill. St. Agric. Soc. V,
451, *Illinois.* See also *Gryllus viridifasciatus.*

vorax [Gnathoclita] DE HAAN, Bijdr. Kenn. Orthopt. 203, *America.*
—— GOSSE, Can. Nat. 278, *Canada.*

See also ACRIDIUM, GRYLLUS and ŒDIPODA.

Machærocera.

mexicana SAUSS. Rev. et Mag. de Zool. 1859, 391, *Mexico calida.*—
GERST. Archiv f. Nat. XXVI, II, 406;—In. Bericht, 1859-60,
50.

Mantis.

angulata FABR. Entom. Syst. II, 13;—In. Nom. Entom. emend. Ed.
1797, 79; Ed. 1810, 79, *Guadeloupe.*—TURT. Syst. Nat. Linn.
II, 533, *Guadeloupe.*

angusta GMEL. Linn. Syst. Nat. I, IV, 2055, *Antigua.*—TURT. Syst.
Nat. Linn. II, 541, *Antigua.*

antillarum [Stigmatoptera] SAUSS. Orthopt. nov. amer. I, 1;—In.
Rev. et Mag. de Zool. 1859, 60, *St. Thomas.*—GERST. Archiv
f. Nat. XXVI, II, 407;—In. Bericht, 1859-60, 46, *St. Thomas.*

azteca [Stigmatoptera] SAUSS. Orthopt. nov. amer. I, 1;—In. Rev. et
Mag. de Zool. 1859, 60, *Mexico.*—GERST. Archiv f. Nat.
XXVI, II, 407;—In. Bericht, 1859-60, 46, *Mexico.*

bicornis LINN. Syst. Nat. 12th Ed. II, 691; 13th Ed. I, 691, *In India.*
See also *Gryllus bicornis.*

bidens FABR. Syst. Entom. 277;—In. Spec. Ins. I, 350;—In. Entom.
Syst. II, 22;—In. Nom. Entom. emend. Ed. 1797, 78; Ed.
1810, 79, *America.*—GOEZE, Entom. Beytr. II, 91, *Die
amerikanische Fangheuschrekke.*—GMEL. Linn. Syst. Nat. I,
IV, 2051, *America*—OLIV. Encycl. méth. VII, 629, *Amérique.*
—TURT. Syst. Nat. Linn. II, 538, *America.*—LICHT. Trans.
Linn. Soc. Lond. VI, 24, *America.*—DE HAAN, Bijdr. Kenn.
Orthopt. 79, *Brasilia, Mexico, Antilles.*

bicornis GOEZE, Entom. Beytr. II, 97, *Die indianische Fangheuschrekke.*

bifasciata DE HAAN, Bijdr. Kenn. Orthopt. 60, 78, *Cuba.*

bispinosa FABR. Syst. Entom. 274;—In. Spec. Ins. I, 346;—In.
Entom. Syst. II, 15;—In. Nom. Entom. emend. Ed. 1797,
78; Ed. 1810, 79, *America.*—GOEZE, Entom. Beytr. II, 30, *Die
amerikanische Fangheuschrekke.*—GMEL. Linn. Syst. Nat. IV,
2051, *America*—OLIV. Encycl. méth. VII, 633, *Amérique.*—

Shaw and Nodder, Nat. Misc. IX, 1797, pl. ccccxiii, America.—Turt. Syst. Nat. Linn. II, 534, America.

calamus Fabr. Entom. Syst. II, 13;—Id. Nom. Entom. emend. Ed.
1797, 79; Ed. 1810, 79, Ins. St. Cruz.—Turt. Syst. Nat.
Linn. II, 533, Santa Cruz.

cancellata Fabr. Syst. Entom. 274.—Id. Spec. Ins. I, 347, In Indiis.
—Id. Nom. Entom. emend. Ed. 1797, 79; Ed. 1810, 79, Ind.
Goeze, Entom. Beytr. II, 30, Die indianische Fangheuschrekke.

carolina Linn. Syst. Nat. 12th Ed. II, 691; 13th Ed. I, 691, Carolina.
—Müll. Linn. Naturyst. V, 414, Carolina.—Goeze, Entom.
Beytr. II, 26, Die karolinische Fangheuschrekke.—Gmel. Linn.
Syst. Nat. I, iv, 2053, Carolina.—Oliv. Encycl. méth. VII,
637, Caroline.—Stoll', Répr. des Spectr. Spectres, 70, pl.
xxiv, figs. 91, 92, Nouvelle Géorgie ou Virginie.—Turt. Syst.
Nat. Linn. II, 540 (carolina), Carolina.—[Stagmatoptera]
Burm. Handb. d. Entom. II, 538, Nordamerika, Südkarolina.—
De Haan, Bijdr. Kenn. Orthopt. 60, Tennessee.—Zimm. Archiv
f. Nat. IX, 390, Rockingham, N. Carolina.—Thomas, Trans.
Ill. St. Agric. Soc. V, 441, Illinois. See also Gryllus carolinus.

cellularis [Phasma] Burm. Handb. d. Entom. II, 552, Mexico.

chlorophaea De Haan. Bijdr. Kenn. Orthopt. 60, 79, New York.—
Blanch. Guér. Mag. de Zool. V, 133, Watertown, N. York.

cingulata Goeze, Entom. Beytr. II, 29, Die jamaische Fangheuschrekke.
—Drury, Illustr. Nat. Hist. II, 89, pl. xlix, fig. 2, Jamaica.—
Gmel. Linn. Syst. Nat. I, iv, 2055, Jamaica.—Oliv. Encycl.
méth. VII, 633, Jamaïque.—Turt. Syst. Nat. Linn. II, 540,
Jamaica.—Serv. Ann. Sc. Nat. XXII, 51, Jamaïque.—
Westw. Drury, Ins. II, 99, pl. xlix, fig. 2, Jamaica.—[Acanthi-
tes] Burm. Handb. d. Entom. II, 542, Jamaica.—Serv. Or-
thopt. 197, Brésil, Mexique, Antilles.—De Haan, Bijdr. Kenn.
Orthopt. 60, Jamaica.—Gués. Sagra, Hist. nat. du Cuba, 349,
Jamaïque, St. Domingue. Cuba.

conspurcata Serv. Orthopt. 190, Amérique septentrionale.

cordata Fabr. Suppl. Entom. Syst. 190, In Indiis.

cubaensis De Haan, Bijdr. Kenn. Orthopt. 60, 73, Cuba.

domingensis Pal. de Beauv. Insectes, 51, pl. xii, fig. 2, Saint Domingue.—Gués. Sagra, Hist. nat. de Cuba, 348, Antilles.

ferox [Stagmatoptera] Saur. Orthopt. nov. amer. I, 2;—Id. Rev. et
Mag. de Zool. 1859, 50, Carolina.—Gerst. Archiv f. Nat.
XXVII, ii, 402;—Id. Bericht, 1859-60, 46.

ferula Fabr. Entom. Syst. II, 12;—Id. Nom. Entom. emend. Ed.
1797, 79; Ed. 1810, 79, Guadeloupe.—Turt. Syst. Nat. Linn.
II, 533, Guadeloupe.

filiformis Fabr. Mant. Ins. I, 227;—Id. Entom. Syst. II, 12;—Id.
Nom. Entom. emend. Ed. 1797, 79; Ed. 1810, 79, Amer.
merid.—Gmel. Linn. Syst. Nat. I, iv, 2048, America, India,

Italia.—OLIV. Encycl. méth. VII, 625, *Amérique méridionale, et dans l'Inde, et peut être dans l'Italie.*

flabellicornis LICHT. Trans. Linn. Soc. Lond. VI, 22, *In Indiis.*

fuscata WIEDE. Obs. Entom. 97, *America.*

fuscifolia [Acanthops] BLANCH. Hist. nat. Ins. III, 12, *Cayenne, Am. mérid.*

gemmata STOLL', Répr. des Spectr. Spectres, 71, pl. xxlv, fig. 93, *Nouvelle Georgie ou Virginie.*

gigas GOEZE, Entom. Beytr. II, 29, *Der riesenähnliche Riese.*—DRURY, Illustr. Nat. Hist. II, 89, pl. 1, *Island of St. Vincent.* See also *Gryllus gigas.*

gongylodes DRURY, Illustr. Nat. Hist. I, 129, pl. 1, fig. 3; II, app. *Mantras, Philadelphia.*—PANZER, Drury, Ins. 202, tab. 1, fig. 3, *Mantras, Virginia.*—LICHT. Trans. Linn. Soc. Lond. VI, 31, *In Indiis.* (See Charp. Germ. Zeitsch. f. Entom. V, 291.) See also *Gryllus gongylodes.*

hyalina DE GEER, Mém. III. 410, pl. xxxvii, fig. 1, *Amérique.*—FABR. Syst. Entom. 277;—In. Spec. Ins. I, 349;—In. Entom. Syst. II, 21;—In. Nom. Entom. emend. Ed. 1797, 79; Ed. 1810, 79, *America.*—GOEZE, Entom. Beytr. II, 30, 31, *Der amerikanische Glasflügel.*—In. De Geer, Gesch. Ins. III, 266, tab. xxxvii, fig. 1, *America.*—GMEL. Linn. Syst. Nat. I, IV, 2051, *America.* — STOLL', Répr. des Spectr. Spectres, 60, pl. xx, fig. 75, *Amérique.*—OLIV. Encycl. méth. VII, 629, *Amérique.*—LICHT. Trans. Linn. Soc. Lond. VI, 30, *America.*—TURT. Syst. Nat. Linn. II, 538, *America.*—BULL. Enum. Ins. 61, *Amer.*—[Phoaina] BURM. Handb. d. Entom. II, 537, *Mittelamerika.*—DE HAAN, Bijdr. Kenn. Orthopt. 60, *Centraal America.*

inquinata SERV. Orthopt. 191, *Caroline du Sud.*

irrorata LINN. Syst. Nat. 12th Ed. II, 690; 13th Ed. I, 690, *Carolina.*—MÜLL. Linn. Natursyst. V, 413, *Carolina.*—FABR. Syst. Entom. 276, *America*—In. Spec. Ins. I, 348, *In America meridionali*—In. Entom. Syst. II, 19, *America*—In. Nom. Entom. emend. Ed. 1797, 79; Ed. 1810, 79, *Amer.*—GOEZE, Entom. Beytr. II, 25, *Die karolinische Fangheuschrecke.* — GMEL. Linn. Syst. Nat. I, IV, 2050, *In America meridionali.*—OLIV. Encycl. méth. VII, 628, *Amérique méridionale.*—TURT. Syst. Nat. Linn. II, 537, *America.* See also *Gryllus irroratus.*

jamaicensis DRURY, Illustr. Nat. Hist. II, 80, pl. xlix, fig. 1, *Jamaica.*—GOEZE, Entom. Beytr. II, 29, *Die jamaische Fangheuschrecke.*—FABR. Spec. Ins. I, 346;—In. Entom. Syst. II, 15, *Jamaica.*—GMEL. Linn. Syst. Nat. I, IV, 2054, *Jamaica.*—OLIV. Encycl. méth. VII, 634, *Jamaïque.*—TURT. Syst. Nat. Linn. II, 634, *Jamaica.*

latipennis [Stagmatoptera] BURM. Handb. d. Entom. II, 538, *Mexico.*—DE HAAN, Bijdr. Kenn. Orthopt. 60, *Mexico.*

umbata HAAN, Icon. Orthopt. tab. A. Gen. Mantis, fig. 2, *Mexico.*—
De HAAN, Bijdr. Kenn. Orthopt. 60, *Mexico.*

linearis DRURY, Illustr. Nat. Hist. I, 134, pl. 1, fig. 3; II, app. *Antigua.*
—GOEZE, Entom. Beytr. II, 29, *Die antiguaische Fangheu-
schrecke.*—PANZER, Drury, Ins. 203, tab. 1, fig. 3, *Antigua.*
—FABR. Nom. Entom. emend. Ed. 1797, 79; Ed. 1810, 79,
Ind.

luna SERV. Orthopt. 183, *Carolina.*

marginata PAL. DE BEAUV. Insectes, 62, pl. xii. fig. 3, *Saint Domingue.*—BILLB. Enum. Ins. 64, *Ind. occ.*—GUÉR. Sagra, Hist.
nat. de Cuba, 349, *Saint Domingue, Cuba.*

mexicana [Cardioptera] SAUSS. Orthopt. nov. amer. II, 2;—In. Rev.
et Mag. de Zool. 1861, 127, *Mexico calida.*—[Cardioptera]
GERST. Archiv f. Nat. XXVIII, 11, 311;—In. Bericht, 1861,
39, *Mexiko.*

minuta DRURY, Illustr. Nat. Hist. II, 75, pl. xxxix, fig. 5, *America.*
—GOEZE, Entom. Beytr. II, 26, *Die amerikanische Fangheu-
schrecke.*—FABR. Spec. Ins. 1, 350, *In America meridionali.*—
In. Entom. Syst. II, 24, *Am. merid.*—In. Nom. Entom. emend.
Ed. 1797, 79; Ed. 1810, 79, *Am. m.*—GMEL. Linn. Syst. Nat.
I, iv, 2052, *In America meridionali.*—OLIV. Encycl. méth. VII,
631, *Amérique méridionale aux environs d'Antigua.*

musarum PAL. DE BEAUV. Insectes, 111, pl. xiii, fig. 3, *Saint Domin-
gue.*—[Stagmatoptera] BURM. Handb. d. Entom. II, 537,
Angeblich von St. Domingo, aber wahrscheinlich aus Afrika.—
[Harpax] De HAAN, Bijdr. Kenn. Orthopt. 60, *St. Domingo.*—
[Epaphrodita] GUÉR. Sagra, Hist. nat. de Cuba, 347, *Cuba,
Martinique.*

oratoria LICHT. Trans. Linn. Soc. Lond. VI, 29, *Ubique in zona torrida
et temperata.*

pagana GOEZE, Entom. Beytr. II, 31, *Orleans.*

parva [Thespis] WESTW. Drury, Ins. II, 81, pl. xxxix, fig. 5, *America.*
—GMEL. Linn. Syst. Nat. I, iv, 2055, *America.* — OLIV. Encycl. méth. VII, 634, *Amérique.* — TURT. Syst. Nat. Linn. II,
540, *America.*

pectinata DRURY, Illustr. Nat. Hist. I, 128, pl. 1, fig. 1; II, app. *Jamaica.*

pectinicornis FABR. Spec. Ins. I, 347, *In Indiis, Jamaica.*—In. Entom. Syst. II, 18;—In. Nom. Entom. emend. Ed. 1797, 79;
Ed. 1810, 79, *Jamaica.*—PANZER, Drury, Ins. 201, tab. 1, fig.
1, *Jamaica.*—HERBST, Fuessly, Archiv d. Ins. 1786, 187, tab.
1, fig. 2, *Jamaica.*— GMEL. Linn. Syst. Nat. I, iv, 2053, *In
India, Australi, America, Jamaica.*—OLIV. Encycl. méth. VII,
632, pl. cxxxiii, fig. 3, *Jamaique.*—TURT. Syst. Nat. Linn. II,
533, *Jamaica.*

phryganoides Serv. Orthopt. 198, *Amérique septentrionale.* — De Haan, Bijdr. Kenn. Orthopt. 60, *New York, Cuba.* — In. Dijdr. Kenn. Orthopt. 80, *Cuba.*

phthisica Linn. Syst. Nat. 12th Ed. II, 689; 13th Ed. I, 689, *In Indiis.*—Goeze, Entom. Beytr. II, 20, *Die indianische Fangheuschrecke. See also Gryllus phthisicus.*

precaria Linn. Syst. Nat. 12th Ed. II, 691; 13th Ed. I, 691, *America, Africa.*—De Geer, Mém. III, 407, pl. xxxvi, fig. 4–8, *L'Amérique méridionale et particulièrement à Surinam.*—Fabr. Syst. Entom. 277;—In. Spec. Ins. I, 349;—In. Entom. Syst. II, 20, *America, Africa*—In. Nom. Entom. emend. Ed. 1797, 79; Ed. 1810, 79, *Am.* —Herbst, Fuessly, Archiv d. Ins. 1786, 166, tab. I, fig. 1, *America*—Gmel. Linn. Syst. Nat. IV, 2050, *America, Africa.*—Oliv. Encycl. méth. VII, 628, *Amérique, Afrique, Asie.*—Licht. Trans. Linn. Soc. Lond. VI, 26, *In America* (See Charp. Germ. Zeitsch. Entom. V, 503).—Lam. Hist. nat. Anim. sans Vert. IV, 250; 2º Ed. IV, 451; 2ª Ed. II, 155, *L'Amérique méridionale, l'Afrique.*—Dillb. Enum. Ins. 64, *Amer. Afr.*—Serv. Ann. Sc. Nat. XXII, 53, *Amérique et l'Afrique.*—Hahn, Icon. Orthopt. tab. A, Gen. Mantis, fig. 1, *America, Africa. See also Gryllus precarius.*

religiosa Browne, Nat. Hist. Jamaica, 433, Mantis, 2, Index, III, iv, *Jamaica.*

reticulata Thunb. Mém. Acad. St. Petersb. V, 285, *In Ins. Bartholemi.*

rhombica Latr. Humb. et Bonpl. Rec. d'Obs. Zool. II, 103, pl. xxxix, fig. 2, 3, *L'Amérique équinoxiale.*

siccifolia Linn. Syst. Nat. 13th Ed. I, 689, *In Indiis.*—Fabr. Syst. Entom. 274;—In. Spec. Ins. I, 347;—In. Entom. Syst. II, 18, *In Indiis.*—In. Nom. Entom. emend. Ed. 1797, 79; Ed. 1810, 79, *Ind.*—Goeze, Entom. Beytr. II, 21, *Das indianische Zitterblatt. See also Gryllus siccifolius.*

simulacrum Fabr. Entom. Syst. II, 21;—In. Nom. Entom. emend. Ed. 1797, 79; Ed. 1810, 79, *America.*—Thunb. Syst. Nat. Linn. II, 538, *America.*—Licht. Trans. Linn. Soc. Lond. VI, 28, *In Indiis.*—Dillb. Enum. Ins. 64, *Amer.*

spinosa Fabr. Syst. Entom. 274;—In. Entom. Syst. II, 14, *In Indiis.*—In. Nom. Entom. emend. Ed. 1797, 79; Ed. 1810; 79, *Ind.*—Goeze, Entom. Beytr. II, 30, *Die indianische Fangheuschrecke.*

strumaria Linn. Syst. Nat. 12th Ed. II, 691; 13th Ed. I, 691, *In Indiis.*—Müll. Linn. Natursyst. V, 414, *Aus den Indien.*—Fabr. Syst. Entom. 274;—In. Spec. Ins. I, 347;—In. Entom. Syst. II, 18, *In Indiis*—In. Nom. Entom. emend. Ed. 1797, 79; Ed. 1810, 79, *Ind.*—Goeze, Entom. Beytr. II, 27, *Der indianische Kropfträger*—Licht. Trans. Linn. Soc. Lond. VI, 26, *In*

Indiis.—LAM. Hist. nat. Anim. sans Vert. IV, 250; 2ᵉ Ed.
IV, 451; 3ᵉ Ed. II, 155, *Les Indes.* See also *Gryllus strumarius.*
Sumichrasti [Cardioptera] SAUSS. Orthopt. nov. amer. II, 1;—In.
Rev. et Mag. de Zool. 1864, 178, *Cordova, Mexico calida.*—
[Cardioptera] GERST. Archiv f. Nat. XXVIII, II, 311.—In.
Bericht, 1861, 39, *Mexiko.*
toltoca [Stigmatoptera] SAUSS. Orthopt. nov. amer. II, 1;—In. Rev.
et Mag. de Zool. 1861, 137, *Mexico calida.*—[Stigmatoptera]
GERST. Archiv f. Nat. XXVIII, II, 311;— In. Bericht, 1861,
39, *Mexika.*
tricolor LINN. Syst. Nat. 12th Ed. II, 691; 13th Ed. I, 691, *In Indiis.*
— GOEZE, Entom. Beytr. II, 27, *Die indianische Fanghen-*
schrike. — FABR. Nom. Entom. emend. Ed. 1797, 79; Ed.
1810, 79, *Ind.* See also *Gryllus tricolor.*
urbana FABR. Syst. Entom. 278;—In. Spec. Ins. I, 350;—In. Entom.
Syst. II, 23, *In Indiis.*—In. Nom. Entom. emend. Ed. 1797,
79; Ed. 1810, 79, *Ind.*—GOEZE, Entom. Beytr. II, 31, *Die*
indianische Reutstreife.—LICHT. Trans. Linn. Soc. Lond. VI,
27, *In Indiis.*
venusta [Oxypilus] DE HAAN, Bijdr. Kenn. Orthopt. 60, *St. Domingo.*
viridana OLIV. Encycl. méth. VII, 636, *Ternate, Amboine, Bande,*
côte de Guinée en Afrique et dans l'Amérique espagnole.
viridimargo [Photina] BURM. Handb. d. Entom. II, 538, *Mexiko.*—
DE HAAN, Bijdr. Kenn. Orthopt. 60, *Mexico.*
See also GRYLLUS.

Merometidium.

De Geeri STÅL, Orthopt. Eug. Resa, 322, *Insula St. Joseph in sinu*
Panamensi.—GERST. Archiv f. Nat. XXVIII, II, 816;—In.
Bericht, 1861, 44, *Insel St. Joseph bei Panama.*

Metrioten.

acuticornis WESTW. Catal. Orthopt. 162, *In America aequinoctiali.*
Blanchardi WESTW. Catal. Orthopt. 159, *In provincia de Chiquitos.*
Stollii WESTW. Catal. Orthopt. 159, *Am. merid.*

Microcentrum.

affiliatum SCUDD. Bost. Journ. Nat. Hist. VII, 447, *Mass. Maryland,*
Key West, Florida, Texas, Nebraska.
retinervis SCUDD. Bost. Journ. Nat. Hist. VII, 446, *North Carolina,*
District of Columbia.
thoracicum SCUDD. Bost. Journ. Nat. Hist. VII, 447, *Tortugas,*

Florida.—GERST. Archiv f. Nat. XXIX, II, 357;—In. Bericht. 1862, 43, *Florida.*

Monachidium.

superbum STÅL, Öfr. Kongl. Vet. Akad. Förhandl. 1855, 352, *Honduras.*

Monachoda.

Thunbergii GERST. Archiv f. Nat. XXIV, II, 318;—In. Bericht, 1857, 156, *Cuba.*—? BRUNN. Blatt. 368, *Ile de Cuba.* See also *Blatta Thunbergii.*
 See also BLATTA.

Monastria.

biguttata SAUSS. Orthopt. Amér. moy. 256, *L'Amérique méridionale, Brésil.*
semialata SAUSS. Orthopt. Amér. moy. 258, *L'Amérique méridionale.*
similis SAUSS. Orthopt. Amér. moy. 257, *L'Amérique méridionale.*

Myrmecophila.

——— ? ILARR. Treat. Ed. 1841-2, 125, *Mass.*—FITCH. 6-9 Rep. 186; —In. Trans. N. Y. St. Agric. Soc. XXII, 669, *Mass.*

Nauphoeta.

cinerea SAUSS. Orthopt. Amér. moy. 204, *Cuba, Ile de France, cosmopolite.*
laevigata BRUNN. Blatt. 285, tab. vii, fig. 33, *Brésil, Ile de Cuba, St. Domingue, Ténériffe, Madère.*
pallida BRUNN. Blatt. 286, *Cuba.*

Necroscia.

Cyllarus WESTW. Catal. Orthopt. 155, pl. xiii, fig. 2, pl. xiv, fig. 5, *Jamaica.*

Nemobius.

exiguus SCUDD. Bost. Journ. Nat. Hist. VII, 429, *Missouri, Minnesota.*

fasciatus Scudd. Bost. Journ. Nat. Hist. VII, 430, *Mass. Indiana, S. Carolina.*

toltecus Sauss. Orthopt. nov. amer. I, 16;—In. Rev. et Mag. de Zool. 1859, 316, *Mexico.*—Gerst. Archiv f. Nat. XXVI, II, 404;—In. Bericht, 1859–60, 48.

vittatus Scudd. Bost. Journ. Nat. Hist. VII, 430, *Mass. Maine, Connecticut.*—Pack. Rep. Nat. Hist. Maine, 1861, 376, *Chamberlain Farm, Maine.*—Gerst. Archiv f. Nat. XXIX, II, 356;—In. Bericht, 1862, 42, *Massachusetts.*—Thomas, Trans. Ill. St. Agric. Soc. V, 413, *Illinois.* See also *Acheta vittata.*

See also Acheta and Gryllus.

Nyctibora.

mexicana Sauss. Orthopt. nov. amer. III, 10;—In. Rev. et Mag. de Zool. 1862, 227, *Mexico culida.*—In. Orthopt. Amér. moy. 66, *Les parties chaudes du Mexique, Cordova.*—Brunn. Blatt. 147, *Mexique.*

Oecanthus.

angustipennis Fitch, 3d–5th Rep. 3d Rep. 95;—In. Trans. N. Y. St. Agric. Soc. XVI, 411, *New York.*

bipunctatus Serv. Ann. Sc. Nat. XXII, 135, *Pennsylvanie.* See also *Gryllus bipunctatus.*

discoloratus Fitch, 3d–5th Rep. 3d Rep. 95;—In. Trans. N. Y. St. Agric. Soc. XVI, 411, *New York.*

fasciatus Fitch, 3d–5th Rep. 3d Rep. 96;—In. Trans. N. Y. St. Agric. Soc. XVI, 412, *New York.*

fuscipes Fitch, 3d–5th Rep. 3d Rep. 95;—In. Trans. N. Y. St. Agric. Soc. XVI, 411, *New York.*

niveus Serv. Ann. Sc. Nat. XXII, 135, *Pennsylvanie.*—In. Orthopt. 361, *Amérique septentrionale.*—Harr. Treat. Ed. 1841–2, 124; Ed. 1852, 135; Ed. 1862, 151, figs. 71, 72, *Mass.*—Fitch, 3d–5th Rep. 3d Rep. 86;—In. Trans. N. Y. St. Agric. Soc. XVI, 404, *New York.*—Scudd. Bost. Journ. Nat. Hist. VII, 431, *Mass. Connecticut.*—Thomas, Trans. Ill. St. Agric. Soc. V, 414, *Illinois.* See also *Acheta nivea* and *Gryllus niveus.*

punctulatus Fitch, 3d–5th Rep. 3d Rep. 97;—In. Trans. N. Y. St. Agric. Soc. XVI, 413, *Southern States.*

See also Acheta and Gryllus.

Oedipoda.

aequalis Erich. Archiv f. Nat. IX, II, 230;—In. Bericht, 1842, 86, *Mass.*—Uhler, Harr. Treat. Ed. 1862, 178, *Mass.*—Scudd.

Can. Nat. VII, 287, *Southern shore of Lake Winnipeg.*—In.
Ibat. Journ. Nat. Hist. VII, 470, *Mass. Conn. Minnesota, Red
River, British America.*

azteca SAUSS. Orthopt. nov. amer. II, 28;—In. Rev. et Mag. de Zool.
1861, 397, *Mexico.*—GERST. Archiv f. Nat. XXVIII, II, 317;
—In. Bericht, 1861, 43, *Mexiko.*

carolina BURM. Handb. d. Entom. II, 643, *Nordamerika.*—SERV.
Orthopt. 723, *Amérique septentrionale, Caroline, Pennsylvanie.*
—[Locusta] ERICHS. Archiv f. Nat. XIII, II, 140;—In.
Bericht, 1846, 76.—UHLER, Harr. Treat. Ed. 1862, 176, *Mass.*
—SCUDD. Bost. Journ. Nat. Hist. VII, 468, *Mass. Maine,
Connecticut.*—PACK. Rep. Nat. Hist. Maine, 1861, 373, *Mana-
miscontis, Maine.* See also *Acridium carolinum.*

corallina ERICHS. Archiv f. Nat. IX, II, 229;—In. Bericht, 1842, 83,
Mass.

corallipes HALD. Stansb. Expl. Utah, 371, pl. x, fig. 2, *Utah.*—
SCHAUM, Archiv f. Nat. XVIII, II, 271;—In. Bericht, 1852,
131, *Utah.*—TAYLOR, Report Smiths. Inst. 1858, 206, *Salt
Lake country.*

costalis SCUDD. Bost. Journ. Nat. Hist. VII, 473, *Texas.*—GERST.
Archiv f. Nat. XXIX, II, 358;—In. Bericht, 1863, 44, *Texas.*

discoidea SERV. Orthopt. 724, *Brésil, Amérique septentrionale, Cayenne,
Philadelphie.*—SCUDD. Bost. Journ. Nat. Hist. VII, 469, *N.
Carolina, Southern States.* See also *Acridium discoideum.*

elophas [Leprus] SAUSS. Orthopt. nov. amer. II, 28;—In. Rev. et
Mag. de Zool. 1861, 398, *Mexico.*—[Leprus] GERST. Archiv f.
Nat. XXVIII, II, 317;—In. Bericht, 1861, 43, *Merida.*

euccrata ERICHS. Archiv f. Nat. IX, II, 230;—In. Bericht, 1842, 86,
Mass.—UHLER, Harr. Treat. Ed. 1862, 180, *Mass.*—SCUDD.
Bost. Journ. Nat. Hist. VII, 472. *Mass. Connecticut.*

fenestralis BURM. Germ. Zeitsch. f. Entom. II, 54, *Nord Amerika.*
—SERV. Orthopt. 726, *Amérique septentrionale.*

haltenais [Sphingonotus] SAUSS. Orthopt. nov. amer. II, 26;—In. Rev.
et Mag. de Zool. 1861, 893, *Haïti.*—GERST. Archiv f. Nat.
XXVIII, II, 317;—In. Bericht, 1861, 43, *Merida.*

latipennis ERICHS. Archiv f. Nat. IX, II, 230;—In. Bericht, 1842, 86,
Mass.—UHLER, Harr. Treat. Ed. 1862, 178, *Mass.*—PACK.
Rep. Nat. Hist. Maine, 1861, 373, *Mattamiscontis, Maine.*

maritima ERICHS. Archiv f. Nat. IX, II, 229;—In. Bericht, 1842, 83,
Mass.—UHLER, Harr. Treat. Ed. 1862, 178, *Sandwich, Mass.*
—SCUDD. Bost. Journ. Nat. Hist. VII, 472, *Seashore of
Mass. Connecticut.*

marmorata ERICHS. Archiv f. Nat. IX, II, 230;—In. Bericht, 1842, 86,
Mass.—UHLER, Harr. Treat. Ed. 1862, 179, *Mass.*—SCUDD.
Bost. Journ. Nat. Hist. VII, 472, *Mass.*

mexicana Sauss. Orthopt. nov. amer. II, 27;—Rov. et Mag. de Zool. 1861, 397, *Mexiko.*—Gerst. Archiv f. Nat. XXVIII, II, 317; —In. Bericht, 1861, 45, *Mexiko.*

musica Serv. Orthopt. 730, *Nouvelle Hollande, Iules, Cap de Bonne Espérance.*

nebulosa Erichs. Archiv f. Nat. IX, II, 230;—In. Bericht, 1842, 86, *Mass.*—Uhler, Harr. Treat. Ed. 1869, 181, *Mass.*

obliterata Germ. Burm. Handb. d. Entom. II, 643, *Nordamerika.*

ocelote [Hippiscus] Sauss. Orthopt. nov. amer. II, 29;—In. Rev. et Mag. de Zool. 1861, 398, *Mexiko.*—[Hippiscus] Gerst. Archiv f. Nat. XXVIII, II, 317;—In. Bericht, 1861, 45, *Mexiko.*

pallidipennis Burm. Handb. d. Entom. II, 641, *Mexiko, aus der Gegend bei Zimapan.*

pardalina Sauss. Orthopt. nov. amer. II, 27;—In. Rev. et Mag. de Zool. 1861, 324, *Mexico.*—Gerst. Archiv f. Nat. XXVIII, II, 317;—In. Bericht, 1861, 45, *Mexiko.*

pellucida Scudd. Bost. Journ. Nat. Hist. VII, 472, *Mass. Conn. Vermont, Maine.*—Gerst. Archiv f. Nat. XXIX, II, 358;—In. Bericht, 1862, 44, *Nord Amerika.*

phoenicoptera Germ. Burm. Handb. d. Entom. II, 643, *Nordamerika.* —Scudd. Bost. Journ. Nat. Hist. VII, 466, *Mass. Maine, Connecticut. See also Acridium phoenicopterum.*

rugosa Scudd. Bost. Journ. Nat. Hist. VII, 469, *Mass. Maine.*— Gerst. Archiv f. Nat. XXIX, II, 358;—In. Bericht, 1862, 44, *Nord Amerika.*

sordida Burm. Handb. d. Entom. II, 643, *Pennsylvania.*—Scudd. Bost. Journ. Nat. Hist. VII, 473, *Mass. Conn. Maine. See also Acridium sordidum.*

sulphurea Burm. Handb. d. Entom. II, 643, *Carolina.*— Uhler, Harr. Treat. Ed. 1862, 177, *Mass.*—Scudd. Bost. Journ. Nat. Hist. VII, 470, *Mass. Maine, Conn. See also Acridium sulphureum.* •

Sumichrasti [Sphingonotus] Sauss. Orthopt. nov. amer. II, 26;— In. Rev. et Mag. de Zool. 1861, 324, *Mexico calida.* — Gerst. Archiv f. Nat. XXVIII, II, 317;— In. Bericht, 1861, 45, *Mexico.*

toltecs Sauss. Orthopt. nov. amer. II, 28;—In. Rev. et Mag. de Zool. 1861, 397, *Mexico.*—Gerst. Archiv f. Nat. XXVIII, 317;— In. Bericht, 1861, 45, *Mexiko.*

venusta Stål. Orthopt. Eug. Resa, 344, *San Francisco, California.* — Gerst. Archiv f. Nat. XXVIII, II, 319;—In. Bericht, 1861, 47, *San Francisco.*

verruculata Scudd. Can. Nat. VII, 287, *Point Wigwam, Lake Winnipeg.* — In. Bost. Journ. Nat. Hist. VII, 471, *Mass. New Hampshire, White Mts. of N. Hampshire, Maine, Lake Winnipeg, Saguenay River, Canada East.*

virginiana Burm. Handb. d. Entom. II, 645, *Nordamerika.* See also
          Acridium virginianum.
xanthoptera Germ. Burm. Handb. d. Entom. II, 643, *Carolina.—*
          Scudd. Bost. Journ. Nat. Hist. VII, 469, *Mass. Missouri.*
          See also *Acridium xanthopterum.*
     See also Acridium.

Ommatolampis.

mexicana Saussure. Rev. et Mag. de Zool. 1859, 393, *Mexico frigida,*
          Tabasco.
Yersinii Saussure. Rev. et Mag. de Zool. 1859, 394, *America meridi-*
          onalis ?

Opomala.

bivittata Serv. Orthopt. 589, *Amérique septentrionale.—*Thomas,
          Trans. Ill. St. Agric. Soc. V, 447, *Illinois.* See also *Acridium*
          bivittatum.
brachyptera Scudd. Bost. Journ. Nat. Hist. VII, 454, *Massachusetts.*
          —Germ. Archiv f. Nat. XXIX, II, 858;—In. Bericht, 1862,
          44, *Massachusetts.*
brevipennis Thomas, Trans. Ill. St. Agric. Soc. V, 451, *Illinois.*
marginicollis Serv. Orthopt. 591, *Amérique septentrionale.* See also
          Acridium marginicolle.
mexicana Saussure. Orthopt. nov. amer. II, 6;—In. Rev. et Mag. de
          Zool. 1861, 156, *Mexico.—*Germ. Archiv f. Nat. XXVIII, II,
          316;—In. Bericht, 1861, 44, *Mexito.*
punctipennis Serv. Orthopt. 590, *Amérique septentrionale.—*Thomas,
          Trans. Ill. St. Agric. Soc. V, 417, *Illinois.* See also *Acridium*
          punctipenne.
varipes Serv. Orthopt. 588, *Amérique septentrionale.* See also *Acri-*
          dium varipes.
     See also Acridium.

Orphulina.

agile Scudd. Bost. Journ. Nat. Hist. VII, 453, *Maryland, Illinois.*
concinnum Scudd. Bost. Journ. Nat. Hist. VII, 452, *Cape Cod.*
          —Germ. Archiv f. Nat. XXIX, II, 857;—In. Bericht, 1862,
          43, *Cape Cod.*
glaberrimum Scudd. Bost. Journ. Nat. Hist. VII, 453, *Conn. Geor-*
          gia.
glaucum Serv. Orthopt. 524, *Amérique septentrionale.*
gracile Harr. Treat. Ed. 1841-2, 151; Ed. 1852, 142; Ed. 1862, 163,
          fig. 78, *Mass.—*Ericus. Archiv f. Nat. IX, II, 227;—In. Be-

richt, 1842, 83, *Mass.*—FITCH, Amer. Journ. Agric. and Sc.
VI, 146, *New York.*—PACK. Rep. Nat. Hist. Maine, 1861, 376,
Chamberlain Farm, Maine.
berbaceum SERV. Orthopt. 524, *Amérique septentrionale.*
longipennis SCUDD. Bost. Journ. Nat. Hist. VII, 453, *Texas.*—
GERST. Archiv f. Nat. XXIX, II, 357;—IN. Bericht, 1862,
43, *Texas.*
vulgare HARR. Treat. Ed. 1841-2, 130; Ed. 1852, 112; Ed. 1862,
162, fig. 77, *Mass.*—EMICOR. Archiv f. Nat. IX, II, 227;—IN.
Bericht, 1842, 83, *Mass.* — FITCH, Amer. Journ. Agric. and
Sc. VI, 146, *New York.*—SCUDD. Bost. Journ. Nat. Hist. VII,
452, *Mass. Conn. Cape Cod.*—GERST. Archiv f. Nat. XXIX,
II, 357;—IN. Bericht, 1862, 43, *Cape Cod.*

Orchesticum.

americanus SAUSS. Orthopt. nov. amer. I, 5;—IN. Rev. et Mag. de
Zool. 1859, 201, *America borealis, Tennessee.*—GERST. Archiv
f. Nat. XXVI. II, 405;—IN. Bericht, 1859-60, 49, *Tennessee.*

Orocharis.

saltator UHLER, Proc. Entom. Soc. Philad. II, 545, *Maryland.*—DAL-
LAS, Zool. Record, I, 579, *Baltimore.*

OROPUS, see PHYLLOPTERA.
OXYA, see ACRIDIUM.

Oxycoryphus.

astecus SAUSS. Orthopt. nov. amer. II, 17;—IN. Rev. et Mag. de
Zool. 1861, 815, *Mexico.*—GERST. Archiv f. Nat. XXVIII,
II, 317;—IN. Bericht, 1861, 45, *Mexiko.*
Burkhartianus SAUSS. Orthopt. nov. amer. II, 16;—IN. Rev. et
Mag. de Zool. 1861, 811, *Mexico.* —GERST. Archiv f. Nat.
XXVIII, II, 317;—IN. Bericht, 1861, 45, *Mexiko.*
mexicanus SAUSS. Orthopt. nov. amer. II, 17;—IN. Rev. et Mag. de
Zool. 1861, 814, *Mexico.* — GERST. Archiv f. Nat. XXVIII,
II, 317;—IN. Bericht, 1861, 45, *Mexiko.*
Montezuma SAUSS. Orthopt. nov. amer. II, 18;— IN. Rev. et Mag.
de Zool. 1861, 818, *Mexico.*—GERST. Archiv f. Nat. XXVIII,
II, 517;—IN. Bericht, 1861, 45, *Mexiko.*
toltecus SAUSS. Orthopt. nov. amer. II, 16;—IN. Rev. et Mag. de
Zool. 1861, 814, *Mexico altier.* — GERST. Archiv f. Nat.
XXVIII, II, 317;—IN. Bericht, 1861, 45, *Mexiko.*

totonacus SAUSS. Orthopt. nov. amer. II, 17;—Id. Rev. et Mag. de
    Zool. 1861, 313; Mexico.—GERST. Archiv f. Nat. XXVIII, II,
    317;—Id. Bericht, 1861, 45, Mexiko.
zapotecus SAUSS. Orthopt. nov. amer. II, 18;—Id. Rev. et Mag. de
    Zool. 1861, 316, Mexico.—GERST. Archiv f. Nat. XXVIII, II,
    317;—Id. Bericht, 1861, 45, Mexiko.

Oxyphyum.

Jurinei SAUSS. Orthopt. nov. amer. II, 7;—Id. Rev. et Mag. de
    Zool. 1861, 157, America meridionalis !

OXYPILUS, see MANTIS.

Pamphagus.

lateralis THUNB. Mém. Acad. St. Petersb. V, 260, In India.

Panchlora.

antillarum SAUSS. Orthopt. nov. amer. III, 14;—Id. Rev. et Mag. de
    Zool. 1862, 230, Cuba.—Id. Orthopt. Amér. moy. 193, Cuba.
    —GERST. Archiv f. Nat. XXIX, II, 354;—Id. Bericht, 1862,
    40, Cuba.—BRUNN. Blatt. 273, Cuba.
azteca SAUSS. Orthopt. nov. amer. III, 13;—Id. Rev. et Mag. de
    Zool. 1862, 230, Mexico calida.—Id. Orthopt. Amér. moy. 198,
    pl. II, fig. 31, Les terres chaudes du Mexique ; dans la Cordillière
    de Cordova.—GERST. Archiv f. Nat. XXIX, II, 354;—Id.
    Bericht, 1862, 40, Aus dem heissen Mexiko.
cubensis SAUSS. Orthopt. nov. amer. III, 13;—Id. Rev. et Mag. de
    Zool. 1862, 230;—Id. Orthopt. Amér. moy. 192, Cuba.—
    GERST. Archiv f. Nat. XXIX, II, 354;—Id. Bericht, 1862, 40,
    Cuba.
exoleta BRUNN. Blatt. 272, Brésil, Jamaïque, Venezuela, l'era Cruz,
    Surinam.
hyalina SAUSS. Orthopt. nov. amer. III, 14;—Id. Rev. et Mag. de
    Zool. 1862, 231, Guatemala.—GERST. Archiv f. Nat. XXIX,
    II, 354;—Id. Bericht, 1862, 40, Guatemala.—BRUNN. Blatt.
    275, Guatemala.
indica SAUSS. Orthopt. Amér. moy. 88, Cosmopolite ; Antilles, Cuba,
    Haïti, Etats unis et Mexique (Orizaba), Brésil, Ile de France et
    Ceylan.
lactea BRUNN. Blatt. 277, Oaxaca, Mexique.
Lanceadon SAUSS. Blatt. nov. 21;—Id. Rev. et Mag. de Zool. 1864,
    312;—Id. Orthopt. Amér. moy. 194, pl. II, fig. 29, Guatemala.

maderæ Saurs. Orthopt. Amér. moy. 201, *Les Antilles, le Mexique, presque cosmopolite; Brésil, Sénégal, Madère, Indes, probablement originaire de l'Afrique.* See also *Blatta maderæ.*

mexicana Saurs. Orthopt. nov. amer. III, 14;—In. Rev. et Mag. de Zool. 1862, 231, *Mexico temperata.*—In. Orthopt. Amér. moy. 197, *Les régions tempérées du Mexique; dans les vallées du versant orientale de la Cordillière.*

nivea Brunn. Blatt. 274, *Cuba, Venezuela.*

Pooyi Saurs. Orthopt. nov. amer. III, 14;—In. Rev. et Mag. de Zool. 1862, 230, *Cuba.*—In. Orthopt. Amér. moy. 194, *Cuba et les terres tempérées du Mexique.*—Gerst. Archiv f. Nat. XXIX, II, 354;—In. Bericht, 1863, 40, *Cuba.*

surinamensis Saurs. Orthopt. Amér. moy. 168, *La nouvelle Orléans, les Antilles, l'île de Cuba, à ce qu'il paraît, tous les continents aux Indes orientales et l'île Maurice; dans les serres du Jardin des Plantes à Paris; nous la croyons d'origine asiatique.*—[Leucophæa] Brunn. Blatt. 278, tab. vii, fig. 82, *Brésil, Cayenne, Martinique, Mexique, Sénégal, Amoy, Java, îles Philippines, Paris.* See also *Blatta surinamensis.*

virescens Saurs. Orthopt. Amér. moy. 180, *Les Antilles; versant orientale du Mexique; Cuba et Brésil, Surinam.* See also *Blatta virescens.*

viridis Burm. Handb. d. Entom. II, 506, *Westindien.*— Saurs. Orthopt. Amér. moy. 193, *Les Indes occidentales.*—Brunn. Blatt. 273, *Amérique méridionale.*

zendala Saurs. Orthopt. nov. amer. III, 14;— In. Rev. et Mag. de Zool. 1862, 231, *Guatemala.*—In. Orthopt. Amér. moy. 196, pl. II, fig. 30, *Guatemala, Izabel.*—Gerst. Archiv f. Nat. XXIX, II, 354;— In. Bericht, 1863, 40, *Guatemala.* — Brunn. Blatt. 276, *Guatemala.*

See also BLATTA.

Paragryllus.

Martinii Guér. Iconogr. Règne Anim. Ins. 329, *Pointe-à-Pitre.*—In. Sagra, Illust. nat. de Cuba, 354, *Point à Pitre.*—Erichs. Archiv f. Nat. XIII, II, 138;—In. Bericht, 1846, 74, *Pointe à Pitre.*

Parairopex.

æquatorialis Saurs. Orthopt. Amér. moy. 61, *Amérique méridionale; les plateaux de la République de l'Equateur.*

histrio Saurs. Orthopt. nov. amer. III, 13;— In. Rev. et Mag. de Zool. 1862, 339, *America borealis.* — In. Orthopt. Amér. moy.

58, pl. 1, fig. 5, *Amérique méridionale.* — BURM. Blatt. 162,
Amérique méridionale.

mexicana BURM. Blatt. 151, tab. iv, fig. 15, *Oaxaca, Mexique.*

Paroccanthus.

mexicanus SAUSS. Orthopt. nov. amer. I, 16;—In. Rev. et Mag. de
Zool. 1859, 317, *Mexico.*—GERST. Archiv f. Nat. XXVI, II,
404;—In. Bericht, 1859–60, 48, *Mexiko.*

Pediza.

virescens SAUSS. Orthopt. nov. amer. II, 8;—In. Rev. et Mag. de
Zool. 1861, 137, *Mexico.*—GERST. Archiv f. Nat. XXVIII, II,
317;—In. Bericht, 1861, 45, *Mexiko.*

Pegasidion.

volitans SAUSS. Orthopt. nov. amer. II, 22;—In. Rev. et Mag. de
Zool. 1861, 319, *Mexico orientalis.* — GERST. Archiv f. Nat.
XXVIII, II, 317;—In. Bericht, 1861, 45, *Mexiko.*

Periplaneta.

americana BURM. Handb. d. Entom. II, 503, *Ursprünglich in wärme-
ren Amerika, jetzt durch den Handel überall zwischen den Tro-
pen.*—FISCH. Orthopt. Europ. 116, *Hoce species e suo patria
genuina h. e. ex America regionibus tepidioribus, cum mercibus,
non solum in omnes urbis partes, quæ tropica vocnata, adrecta
est, serum in Europa quoque urbibus.*—SCUDD. Boat. Journ.
Nat. Hist. VII, 416, *Mass. Indiana, Mexico, Texas.*—GERST.
Peters, Handb. d. Zool. Arthr. 43, *Ursprünglich in Mittel und
Süd Amerika.*—[Caeriaca] SAUSS. Orthopt. Amér. moy. 71,
*Toutes les contrées du monde, quoique d'origine américaine.   Au
Mexique, cette espèce est peut-être la plus commune, et elle habite
à toutes les altitudes. Je l'ai prise sur la côte à Tampico et à
Tuxpan, dans la Cordillère à Mexillon, sur le plâteau à Texit-
lan, etc.   J'al aussi pris nombre d'individus à Cuba et à Haiti.
Cette Blatte s'étend dans l'Amérique du Nord jusque près du
Canada ; elle a aussi envahi les ports de Mer de l'Europe.—*
BURM. Blatt. 232, tab. v, fig. 24, *Dans le monde entier.* See also
Blatta americana.

australasiae [Cucurlacs] Sauss. Orthopt. Amér. moy. 12, *L'Amérique. Commune aux Antilles, à Cuba, d'où elle arrive souvent avec des boîtes de cigares. J'ai pris ce katériac au Mexique dans le Cordillère orientale, et je possède des individus qui ont été pris au Pérou.* — Brunn. Blatt. 233, *Ile de Madère, Ile St. Thomé sur la côte occidentale de l'Afrique et des Indes occidentales, Colombie, Batavia, Padang, Banjermassing, Suède, Belgique.* See also *Blatta australasiae.*

decorata [Stylopyga] Brunn. Blatt. 224, *Mexique, Acapulco, Vénézuela, Buenos Ayres, côte orientale d'Afrique, Zanzibar, Madagascar, Madras.*

fuliginosa Brunn. Blatt. 236, *Amérique du Nord.*

mysteca Sauss. Orthopt. nov. amer. III, 9;—In. Rev. et Mag. de Zool. 1862, 171, *Mexico temperata.*—In. Orthopt. Amér. moy. 77, *Les terres tempérées du Mexique, Oaxaca.*—Gerst. Archiv f. Nat. XXIX, ii, 854;—In. Bericht, 1862, 40, *Aus den gemässigten Strichen Mexiko's.*

occidentalis [Stylopyga] Sauss. Blatt. nov. 14;—In. Rev. et Mag. de Zool. 1864, 818, *Antille.*—In. Orthopt. Amér. moy. 4, *Les Antilles, la Martinique.* — [Stylopyga] Gerst. Archiv f. Nat. XXX, ii, 430;—In. Bericht, 1863–4, 124, *Antillen.*—Dallas, Zool. Record, I, 871, *W. Indies.*

orientalis Gerst. Peters, Handb. d. Zool. II, 45, *Ueber Europa allgemein verbreitet, wohin sie aus Vorderasien eingewandert sein soll; auch in Nord Amerika.*—[Stylopyga] Sauss. Orthopt. Amér. moy. 78, *Cette espèce a déjà fait invasion aux États unis. J'en ai reçu des individus de New York.*—[Stylopyga] Brunn. Blatt. 226, *Principalement l'Asie et l'Europe. Elle abonde dans les Indes orientales, ainsi que dans l'Asie mineure, rare sur les côtes de la Méditerranée; également rare en Italie et dans l'Espagne méridionale. Algérie, toute l'Europe centrale, l'Amérique du Nord, Chile, Buenos Ayres, Nouvelle Hollande.*

See also **Blatta.**

Petaloptera, see **Phylloptera.**

Petasodes.

dominica Sauss. Orthopt. Amér. moy. 261, *Amérique méridionale, Brésil.*

Pezotettix.

borealis Scudd. Can. Nat. VII, 284, *Pas ou Saskatchewan River, Lake Winnipeg, Anticosti.*—In. Bost. Journ. Nat. Hist. VII, 464, *Minnesota, Saskatchewan River, Lake Winnipeg, Anticosti—*

64

CATALOGUE OF DESCRIBED

GERST. Archiv f. Nat. XXIX, II, 358;—In. Bericht, 1862, 41, *Nord Amerika.*

edax SAUSS. Orthopt. nov. amer. II, 11;—In. Rev. et Mag. de Zool. 1861, 161, *Mexico temperata.*—GERST. Archiv f. Nat. XXVIII, II, 817;—In. Bericht, 1861, 43, *Carolina.*

glacialis SCUDD. Bost. Journ. Nat. Hist. VII, 650, *White Mts. N. Hampshire.*—GERST. Archiv f. Nat. XXX, II, 437; —In. Bericht, 1863–4, 181, *White Mountains.*

longicornis SAUSS. Orthopt. nov. amer. II, 9;—In. Rev. et Mag. de Zool. 1861, 159, *Carolina.*—GERST. Archiv f. Nat. XXVIII, II, 317;—In. Bericht, 1861, 43, *Carolina.*

mexicana SAUSS. Orthopt. nov. amer. II, 10;—In. Rev. et Mag. de Zool. 1861, 160, *Mexico temperata.*—GERST. Archiv f. Nat. XXVIII, II, 317;—In. Bericht, 1861, 43, *Mexiko.*

Scudderi UHLER, Proc. Entom. Soc. Philad. II, 553, *Maryland, Southern Illinois.*—DALLAS, Zool. Record, I, 374, *Baltimore.*

septentrionalis SAUSS. Orthopt. nov. amer. II, 10;—In. Rev. et Mag. de Zool. 1861, 159, *Labrador.*—GERST. Archiv f. Nat. XXVIII, II, 317;—In. Bericht, 1861, 43, *Labrador.*

Sumichrasti SAUSS. Orthopt. nov. amer. II, 11;—In. Rev. et Mag. de Zool. 1861, 160, *Mexico.*—GERST. Archiv f. Nat. XXVIII, II, 317;—In. Bericht, 1861, 43, *Mexiko.*

Zimmermanni SAUSS. Orthopt. nov. amer. II, 9;—In. Rev. et Mag. de Zool. 1861, 159, *Carolina.*—GERST. Archiv f. Nat. XXVIII, II, 317;—In. 1861, 43, *Carolina.*

Platanagropsis.

annulipes SERV. Ann. Sc. Nat. XXII, 167, *Port au Prince.*—In. Orthopt. 369, *Port au Prince.*—OKEN, Isis, 1835, 174, *Prinzenhaven.*—BLANCH. Hist. nat. Ins. III, 82, *Port au Prince.*—GUÉR. Sagra, Hist. nat. de Cuba, 353, pl. xii, fig. 9, *Cuba.* See also *Gryllus anaulipes.*

astoca SAUSS. Orthopt. nov. amer. I, 15;—In. Rev. et Mag. de Zool. 1859, 209, *Mexico.*—GERST. Archiv f. Nat. XXVI, II, 403;—In. Bericht, 1859–60, 48, *Mexiko.*

brevipes [Daihinia] HALD. Proc. Amer. Ass. Adv. Sc. II, 316, *River Platte.*—SCHAUM, Archiv f. Nat. XVIII, II, 211;—In. Bericht, 1851, 137, *Amerika.*

gracilipes [Daihinia] HALD. Proc. Amer. Ass. Adv. Sc. II, 346, *Pennsylvania.*—SCHAUM, Archiv f. Nat. XVIII, II, 211;—In. Bericht, 1851, 137, *Amerika.*

lapidicola BURM. Handb. d. Entom. II, 733, *Virginia und Süd Karolina.*—UHLER, Harr. Treat. Ed. 1862, 155, *Mass.*

longipes SERV. Ann. Sc. Nat. XXII, 167, *Amérique méridionale.*—In.

Orthopt. 369, pl. xil, fig. 1, *Amérique méridionale.*—Burm., Handb. d. Entom. II, 722, *Mittel America*—Blanch. Hist. nat. Ins. III, 31, *Amérique méridionale.*

maculata Harr. Treat. Ed. 1852, 137; Ed. 1862, 155, fig. 73, *Mass.*

robustus [Dulhinia] Hald. Proc. Amer. Ass. Adv. Sc. II, 346, *N. America*—Schaum, Archiv f. Nat. XVIII, ii, 241;—In. Bericht, 1851, 137, *America.*

scabripes Hald. Proc. Acad. Nat. Sc. Philad. VI, 361, *Selma, Alabama*—Gerst. Archiv f. Nat. XX, ii, 246;—In. Bericht, 1855, 58, *Alabama.*

—— Thomps. Ann. Mag. Nat. Hist. XIII, 113, *Mammoth Cave in Kentucky.*—Hald. Stansb. Expl. Utah, 373, *Utah.*

See also Gryllus.

Phaneropterа.

alipes Westw. Arc. Entom. II, 87, pl. lxx, fig. 1, *Colombia, Mexico.*—Erichs. Archiv f. Nat. XI, ii, 137;—In. Bericht, 1844, 63, *Colombien, Mexiko.*

angustifolia Harr. Treat. Ed. 1841-2, 179; Ed. 1852, 140; Ed. 1862, 161, fig. 76, *Mass.*—Erichs. Archiv f. Nat. IX, ii, 327; —In. Bericht, 1847, 83, *Mass.*—Emm. Agric. of N. Y. V, 145, pl. ix, fig. 2, *New York.*—Jaeg. N. Amer. Ins. 1854, 154; 1859, 109, *N. America.*—Pack. How to collect, 56;—In. Rep. Nat. Hist. Maine, 1862, 156, *Maine.* — Thomas, Trans. Ill. St. Agric. Soc. V, 415, *Illinois.*

curvicauda Burm. Handb. d. Entom. II, 690, *Carolina.*—Serv. Ann. Sc. Nat. XXII, 159, *Pennsylvanie.*—Uhler, Harr. Treat. Ed. 1862, 161, *Middle and Southern States.* — Scudd. Can. Nat. VII, 283, *Red River Settlements, British America.*—In. Bost. Journ. Nat. Hist. VII, 446, *Mass. Conn. Maine, Red River Settlements.* See also *Locusta curvicauda.*

hystrix Westw. Arc. Entom. II, 88, pl. lxx, fig. 2, *Colombia.*—Erichs. Archiv f. Nat. XI, ii, 137;—In. Bericht, 1844, 63, *Columbien.*

mexicana Saus. Orthopt. nov. amer. II, 4;—In. Rev. et Mag. de Zool. 1861, 139, *Mexico.*—Gerst. Archiv f. Nat. XXVIII, ii, 316;—In. Bericht, 1861, 44, *Mexiko* (erroneously quoted under the genus Phylloptera).

septentrionalis Serv. Orthopt. 416, *Amérique septentrionale.* See also *Locusta septentrionalis.*

toltaca Saus. Orthopt. nov. amer. I, 5;—In. Rev. et Mag. de Zool. 1859, 201, *Mexico.*—Gerst. Archiv f. Nat. XXVI, 405;—In. Bericht, 1859-60, 49, *Mexiko.*

See also Locusta.

Phasma.

acuticorne GRAY, Synops. Phasm. 26, *In America æquinoctiali.*

angulatum FABR. Suppl. Entom. Syst. 187, *Guadeloupe.*—PAL. DE BEAUV. Insectes, 166, pl. xiv, fig. 4, *Saint Domingue.*—[Diapherodes] DE HAAN, Bijdr. Kenn. Orthopt. 102, *Porto Rico, St. Thomas, St. Jean, St. Croix, Antigua.*

baculum LATR. Hist. nat. Crust. et Ins. XII, 104, *Antilles.*

bispinosum FABR. Suppl. Entom. Syst. 188, *America.*—SERV. Ann. Sc. Nat. XXII, 58, *Amérique.*

buprestoides STOLL', Répr. des Spectr. Spectres, 68, pl. xxiii, fig. 81, *Nouvelle Georgie ou l'Amérique septentrionale.*—[Anisomorpha] DE HAAN, Bijdr. Kenn. Orthopt. 101, *Carolina, Virginia, Georgia.*

calamus FABR. Suppl. Entom. Syst. 187, *Insula St. Croix.*—LICHT. Trans. Linn. Soc. Lond. VI, 10, *In Insula St. Croix.*—[Bacteria] DE HAAN, Bijdr. Kenn. Orthopt. 102, *Porto Rico, St. Thomas, St. Jean, St. Croix, Antigua.*

calcaratum [Bacteria] DE HAAN, Bijdr. Kenn. Orthopt. 101, 134, *Mexico.*

citrifolium LICHT. Trans. Linn. Soc. Lond. VI, 17, *In India* (San Charp. Germ. Zeitsch. f. Entom. V, 289).

cornutum GUILD. Trans. Linn. Soc. Lond. XIV, 137, tab. vii, figs. 1-10, *In America media insularumque oppositarum dumetis.*—SERV. Ferr. Bull. Sc. nat. I, 1824,296, *Amérique équinoxiale.*—OKEN, Lis, 1829, 1212, *In America media insularumque oppositarum dumetis.*—PERTY, De Ins. in Del. Anim. Art. 19, *In America media, insularumque objacentium dumetis.* — WESTW. Introd. Class. Ins. I, 434, *West Indies.*—[Acanthoderus] DE HAAN, Bijdr. Kenn. Orthopt. 102, *Porto Rico, St. Thomas, St. Jean, St. Croix, Antigua.*

cubaense [Bacteria] DE HAAN, Bijdr. Kenn. Orthopt. 101, *Cuba.*

dracunculus LICHT. Trans. Linn. Soc. Lond. VI, 16, *In India* (neo Charp. Germ. Zeitsch. f. Entom. V, 247).

femoratum [Bacteria] DE HAAN, Bijdr. Kenn. Orthopt. 101, 134, *Pensylvania, Tennesse, Zuid-Caroline.*

ferrugineum PAL. DE BEAUV. Insectes, 166, pl. xiv, figs. 6, 7, *Etats unis d'Amérique, Caroline du Sud, Virginie.*—[Anisomorpha] DE HAAN, Bijdr. Kenn. Orthopt. 101, *Caroline, Virginie, Georgie.*

ferula FABR. Suppl. Entom. Syst. 187, *Guadeloupe.*

filiforme FABR. Suppl. Entom. Syst. 186, *America meridionalis.*—DILLE. Enam. Ins. 63, *Amer.*—OKEN. Allg. Naturg. V, C, 1507, *In Westindien.*

gigas [Diapherodes] WESTW. Drury, Ins. II, 100, pl. 1, *St. Vincent.*

havaniense WESTW. Catal. Orthopt. 34, pl. xxii, fig. 7, *In Insula Havannah.*

jamalcense FABR. Suppl. Entom. Syst. 188, *Jamaica.*—STOLL', Répr. des Spectr. Spectres, 15, 17, pl. vi, figs. 20, 21, *Isles Moluques, Ternate, Amboine et Banda; à la côte de Guinée en Afrique et dans l'Amérique espagnole.*—[Platycrana] WESTW. Drury, Ins. II, 99, pl. xlix, fig. 1, *Jamaica.*

laterale LICHT. Trans. Linn. Soc. Lond. VI, 16, *In Indiis* (Sec Charp. Germ. Zeitsch. f. Entom. V, 286).

lineare [Bacteria] DE HAAN, Bijdr. Kenn. Orthopt. 102, *Porto Rico, St. Thomas, St. Jean, St. Croix, Antigoa.*

mexicanum [Bacteria] DE HAAN, Bijdr. Kenn. Orthopt. 101, *Mexico.*

micropterum [Haplopus] DE HAAN, Bijdr. Kenn. Orthopt. 102, 128, *Porto Rico, St. Thomas, St. Jean, St. Croix, Antigoa.*

Ohrtmanni LICHT. Trans. Linn. Soc. Lond. VI, 17, tab. ii, fig. 1, *In Indiis.*

planulum WESTW. Catal. Orthopt. 34, pl. i, fig. 2, *St. Domingo.*

reticulatum STOLL', Répr. du Spectr. Spectres, 67, pl. xxiii, fig. 85, *Spectre américain.*—PAL. DE BEAUV. Insectes, 166, pl. xiv, fig. 3, *Saint Domingue.*

spinicolle BURM. Handb. d. Entom. II, 563, *St. Domingo bei Port au Prince*—DE HAAN, Bijdr. Kenn. Orthopt. 101, *St. Domingo.*—GUÉR. Sagra, Hist. nat. de Cuba, 332, *Cuba.*

spinipes [Haplopus] DE HAAN, Bijdr. Kenn. Orthopt. 102, *St. Domingo.*

spinosum FABR. Suppl. Entom. Syst. 188, *In Indiis.*—SERV. Ann. Sc. Nat. XXII, 58, *Des Indes.*—[Bacteria] DE HAAN, Bijdr. Kenn. Orthopt. 102, 131, *St. Domingo.*

striatum [Bacteria] DE HAAN, Bijdr. Kenn. Orthopt. 101, *Mexica.*

tridens [Bacteria] DE HAAN, Bijdr. Kenn. Orthopt. 101, 131, *Mexica.*

venustulum [Diapherodes] DE HAAN, Bijdr. Kenn. Orthopt. 101, 103, *Cuba.*

Phibalosoma.

ploiaria WESTW. Catal. Orthopt. 79, pl. xiii, fig. 4, *In plagis occidentalis America septentrionalis.*

Phllochora.

consperga BURM. Blatt. 203, tab. vii, fig. 85, *Cuba, Brésil.*

Phoraspis.

atomaria BLANCH. Ann. Soc. Entom. France, [1] VI, 287, pl. x, fig. 2, *Guadeloupe.*—SERV. Orthopt. 126, *Guadeloupe.*—SAUSS. Orthopt. Amér. moy. 144, *Guadeloupe.*—BURM. Blatt. 159, *Guadeloupe, Brésil.*

mexicana Saus. Orthopt. nov. amer. III, 11;—In. Rev. et Mag. de
    Zool. 1862, 228, *Mexico.*—In. Orthopt. Amér. moy. 143,
    Mexique.—Burm. Blatt. 153, *Mexique.*
pantherina Blanch. Ann. Soc. Entom. France, [1] VI, 292, pl. x,
    fig. 9, *St. Domingo.*—Serv. Orthopt. 127, *Saint Domingue.*—
    Saus. Orthopt. Amér. moy. 144, *Guadeloupe.*—Burm. Blatt.
    140, *Saint Domingue.*

PHORTICCA, see ZETOBORA.
PHOTINA, see MANTIS.

Phyllodromia.

adspersicollis Burm. Blatt. 107, *Mexique, Rio Janeiro.*
bivittata Burm. Blatt. 92, *Cap de Bonne Espérance, Ile de France,
    Cuba, Pérou, Brésil.*   See also *Blatta bivittata.*
borealis Burm. Blatt. 101, *Amérique du Nord.*
Burmeisteri Gerst. Archiv f. Nat. XXIV, 11, 345;—In. Bericht,
    1857, 156, *Cuba.*   See also *Blatta Burmeisteri.*
cubensis Burm. Blatt. 109, *Cuba.*   See also *Blatta cubensis.*
delicatula Gerst. Archiv f. Nat. XXIV, 11, 318;—In. Bericht, 1857,
    156, *Cuba.*   See also *Blatta delicatula.*
germanica Burm. Blatt. 90, tab. II, fig. 7, *Nouvelle Hollande, Ram-
    boldie sur l'île de Ceylon, nord de l'Afrique, Guinée supérieure,
    Martinique, Chili, Amérique du Nord, l'Europe, Kirguises, Si-
    bérie, Sicile, Algérie.*
punctulata Burm. Blatt. 108, *St. Domingue.*
totonaca Burm. Blatt. 94, *Mexique.*
vitrea Burm. Blatt. 109, tab. II, fig. 6, *Verasruz, Iles de Fidji.*
    See also BLATTA.

Phyllopsipena.

pulchellus Uhler, Proc. Entom. Soc. Philad. II, 544, *Maryland, New
    York.*—Dallas, Zool. Record. I, 572, *Maryland, N. York.*

Phylloptera.

azteca Saus. Orthopt. nov. amer. I, 7;—In. Rev. et Mag. de Zool.
    1859, 202, *Cordova, Mexico.*—Gerst. Archiv f. Nat. XXVI,
    11, 405;—In. Bericht, 1859-60, 49, *Mexiko.*
caudata Scudd. Bost. Journ. Nat. Hist. VII, 445, *Texas.*
couloniana Saus. Orthopt. nov. amer. II, 4;—In. Rev. et Mag. de
    Zool. 1861, 128, *Cuba.*—Gerst. Archiv f. Nat. XXVIII, 11,
    316;—In. Bericht, 1861, 44, *Cuba.*

curvicauda HARR. Treat. E.I. 1841-2, 123; Ed. 1852, 140; Ed. 1862, 161, *Middle and Southern States.*

huastecs [Orophus] SAUSS. Orthopt. nov. amer. I, 8;—In. Rev. et Mag. de Zool. 1859, 203, *Mexico*—GERST. Archiv f. Nat. XXVI, II, 403;—In. Bericht, 1859–60, 49, *Mexico.*

laurifolia SERV. Orthopt. 404, *Martinique, Cap de Bonne Espérance !* —MACQ. Catal. Mus. Lille, 323, *Martinien.* — GUER. Sagra, Hist. nat. de Cuba, 351, *Surinam, Brésil, Martinique, Cuba.* See also *Locusta laurifolia.*

leguman [Lobophyllus] SAUSS. Orthopt. nov. amer. I, 8;—In. Rev. et Mag. de Zool. 1859, 203, *America*—GERST. Archiv f. Nat. XXVI, II, 403;—In. Bericht, 1859–60, 49, *America.*

mexicana [Orophus] SAUSS. Orthopt. nov. amer. I, 7;—In. Rev. et Mag. de Zool. 1859, 204, *Mexico*—GERST. Archiv f. Nat. XXVI, II, 403;—In. Bericht, 1859–60, 49, *Mexico.*

myrtifolia SERV. Ann. Sc. Nat. XXII, 143, *Amérique.*—? GOSSE, Can. Nat. 278, *Canada.*

oblongifolia BURM. Handb. d. Entom. II, 693, *Nordamerika.*—HARR. Treat. Ed. 1841-2, 128; Ed. 1852, 139; Ed. 1862, 159, fig. 75, *Mass. Penn.* — EMM. Agric. of N. Y. V, 145, *New York.*— JAEG. N. Amer. Ins. 1851, 154; 1859, 109, *N. America.*—SCUDD. Bost. Journ. Nat. Hist. VII, 444, *Mass.*—THOMAS, Trans. Ill. St. Agric. Soc. V, 445, *Illinois.* See also *Locusta oblongifolia.*

otomaria [Orophus] SAUSS. Orthopt. nov. amer. I, 7;—In. Rev. et Mag. de Zool. 1859, 204, *Mexico*—GERST. Archiv f. Nat. XXVI, II, 403;—In. Bericht, 1859–60, 49, *Mexico.*

pisifolia [Diplophyllus] SAUSS. Orthopt. nov. amer. I, 6;—In. Rev. et Mag. de Zool. 1859, 202, *Mexico.*—GERST. Archiv f. Nat. XXVI, II, 403;—In. Bericht, 1859–60, 49, *Mexico.*

retinervis BURM. Handb. d. Entom. II, 692, *Nordamerika.* See also *Locusta retinervis.*

rhombifolia [Orophus] SAUSS. Orthopt. nov. amer. I, 8;—Rev. et Mag. de Zool. 1859, 204, *Carolina.*—GERST. Archiv f. Nat. XXVI, II, 403;—In. Bericht, 1859–60, 49, *Carolina.*

rotundifolia SCUDD. Bost. Journ. Nat. Hist. VII, 445, *Mass. Vermont, Conn. Rhode Island, Illinois.*

salicifolia [Orophus] SAUSS. Orthopt. nov. amer. I, 7;—In. Rev. et Mag. de Zool. 1859, 204, *Carolina.*—GERST. Archiv f. Nat. XXVI, II, 403;—In. Bericht, 1859–60, 49, *Carolina.*

tarasca SAUSS. Orthopt. nov. amer. I, 7;—In. Rev. et Mag. de Zool. 1859, 203, *Mechoacan, Mexico.*—GERST. Archiv f. Nat. XXVI, II, 403;—In. Bericht, 1859–60, 49, *Mexico.*

tomollata [Orophus] SAUSS. Orthopt. nov. amer. II, 4;—In. Rev. et Mag. de Zool. 1861, 129, *Mexico.*—[Orophus] GERST. Archiv f. Nat. XXVIII, II, 316;—In. Bericht, 1861, 44, *Mexico.*

toltoca SAUSS. Orthopt. nov. amer. I, 7;—In. Rev. et Mag. de Zool

1859, 203, *Mexico*—GERST. Archiv f. Nat. XXVI, II, 405;—
    In. Bericht, 1859–60, 49, *Mexico*.

totonacus [Urophus] SAUSS. Orthopt. nov. amer. I, 8;—In. Rev. et
    Mag. de Zool. 1859, 204, *Mexico*—GERST. Archiv f. Nat.
    XXVI, II, 405;—In. Bericht, 1859–60, 49, *Mexico*.

zendala [Petaloptera] SAUSS. Orthopt. nov. amer. I, 9;—In. Rev. et
    Mag. de Zool. 1859, 203, *Mexico*—GERST. Archiv f. Nat.
    XXVI, II, 405;—In. Bericht, 1859–60, 49, *Mexico*.

    See also LOCUSTA.

Phyllocirtus.

elegans GUÉR. Iconogr. Règne Anim. Ins. 333, *Mexique*—ERICHS.
    Archiv f. Nat. XIII, II, 138;—In. Bericht, 1846, 74, *Mexico*.—
    GERST. Entom. Zeit. Stett. XXIV, 427, *Columbia, Mexico*.

Phymateus.

miliaris SERV. Ann. Sc. Nat. XXII, 278, *Amérique méridionale ?*

    PLANES, see EPILAMPRA.

Platamodes.

pennsylvanica SCUDD. Bost. Journ. Nat. Hist. VII, 417, *Indiana,
    Maryland*.

unicolor SCUDD. Bost. Journ. Nat. Hist. VII, 417, *Massachusetts*.—
    GERST. Archiv f. Nat. XXIX, II, 255;—In. Bericht, 1863, 41,
    Massachusetts.

Platycrana.

jamaicensis GRAY, Synops. Phasm. 36, *In India occidentali*. See
    also *Phasma jamaicensis*.

Stollii BRM. Handb. d. Entom. II, 582, *America*.

venustula BRM. Germ. Zeitschr. f. Entom. II, 38, *Cuba*.—SERV.
    Orthopt. 242, *Cuba*—GUÉR. Sagra, Hist. nat. de Cuba, 851,
    Cuba.

viridana SERV. Orthopt. 241, *Amérique ?*

    See also PHASMA.

Platydactylum.

Sauloyi GUÉR. Iconogr. Règne Anim. Ins. 330, *Martinique*.—ERICHS.
    Archiv f. Nat. XIII, II, 139;—In. Bericht, 1846, 75, *Martinique*.
    —GUÉR. Sagra, Hist. nat. de Cuba, 854, *Guadeloupe*.

surinamensis Serv. Orthopt. 365, pl. ix, fig. 1, *Amérique méridionale, Brésil.*—Blanch. Hist. nat. Ins. III, 32, *Amérique méridionale*. See also Gryllus.

Platyphyllum.

concavum Harr. Treat. Ed. 1841–2, 178; Ed. 1852, 139; Ed. 1862, 158, fig. 74, *Mass. Penn.*—Erichs. Archiv f. Nat. IX, ii, 237;—In. Bericht, 1842, 83, *Mass.*—Fitch, Amer. Journ. Agric. and Sc. VI, 146, *New York.*—Emm. Agric. of N. Y. V, 144, pl. ix, fig. 8, *New York.*—Jaeg. N. Amer. Ins. 1854, 150, tab. v, fig. 23–25; 1859, 105, fig. 23 (on p. 106), 24 (on p. 107), *America.*—Thomas, Trans. Ill. St. Agric. Soc. V, 445, *Illinois.*
coriaceum Serv. Orthopt. 446, *Martinique.*—Blanch. Hist. nat. Ins. III, 22, *Martinique.*
perspicillatum Serv. Orthopt. 445, *Mexique.* — Uhler, Harr. Treat. Ed. 1862, 138, *N. England.*
Zimmermanni Sauss. Orthopt. nov. amer. I, 5;—In. Rev. et Mag. de Zool. 1859, 206, *Carolina meridionalis.*—Gerst. Archiv f. Nat. XXVI, ii, 405; — In. Bericht, 1859–60, 49, *Süd Carolina.*

Platyphyum.

aztecum Sauss. Orthopt. nov. amer. II, 12;— In. Rev. et Mag. de Zool. 1861, 161, *Mexico temperata.*— Gerst. Archiv f. Nat. XXVIII, ii, 317;—In. Bericht, 1861, 45, *Mexico.*
mexicanum Bruns. Orthopt. Stud. 4;—In. Verhandl. zool. bot. Gesellsch. Wien, 1861, 224, *Au pied de la nüge sur le volcan d'Orizaba, Mexico.*—Gerst. Archiv f. Nat. XXVIII, ii, 319; —In. Bericht, 1861, 47, *Orizaba.*

Platyzosteria, see Polyzosteria.

Plectoptera.

Pooyi Sauss. Orthopt. Amér. moy. 177, *Cuba.*
porcellana Sauss. Orthopt. Amér. moy. 176, figs. on pp. 158–151, 161, 175, *Cuba.*

Podisma, see Acridium.

Poroplotcra.

corallinus Sauss. Orthopt. nov. amer. II, 8;— In. Rev. et Mag. de Zool. 1861, 158, *Mexico temperata.* — Gerst. Archiv f. Nat.

XXVIII, 11, 317;—In. Bericht, 1861, 45, *Aus dem gemässigten Mexiko.*

Polyzosterine.

serrulatus SERV. Ann. Sc. Nat. XXII, 154;— In. Orthopt. 833, *St. Domingue.*—BLANCH. Hist. nat. Ins. III, 22, *St. Domingue.*—CHARP. Orthopt. descr.-tab. 1, *St. Domingo.*—ERICHS. Archiv f. Nat. X, 11, 298;—In. Bericht, 1843, 50, *St. Domingo.*—In. Archiv f. Nat. XIII, 11, 139;—In. Bericht, 1846, 75, *Haiti.*—GUÉR. Sagra, Hist. nat. de Cuba, 355, *Cuba, St. Domingue.* See also *Lacesta serrulata.*

   See also LACESTA.

Polyphaga.

mexicana [Homœogamia] SAUSS. Orthopt. Amér. moy. 226, pl. II, figs. 36, 37, *Mexique; terres chaudes de la Cordillière orientale, Orizaba.*

   See also BLATTA.

Polyzosteria.

azteca SAUSS. Orthopt. nov. amer. III, 2;—In. Rev. et Mag. de Zool. 1862, 163, *Mexico alta.*—In. Orthopt. Amér. moy. 55, *Les terres froides du Mexique, le plateau.*—GERST. Archiv f. Nat. XXIX, 11, 354;—In. Bericht, 1862, 40, *Hoch Mexiko.*

mexicana SAUSS. Orthopt. nov. amer. III, 1;—In. Rev. et Mag. de Zool. 1862, 163, *Mexico alta.*—In. Orthopt. Amér. moy. 54, *Les terres froides du Mexique, le plateau.*—GERST. Archiv f. Nat. XXIX, 11, 354;—In. Bericht, 1862, 40, *Hoch Mexiko.*— [Platyzosteria] BRUNN. Blatt. 216, *Haut Mexique.*

opaca [Platyzosteria] BRUNN. Blatt. 216, *Ile de Cuba.*

orientalis SAUSS. Orthopt. Amér. moy. 54, *Originaire de l'hémisphère oriental s'est répandue dans l'Amérique au Brésil.*

rufovittata [Platyzosteria] BRUNN. Blatt. 215, *Oaxaca, Mexique.*

Prisopus.

berosus WESTW. Catal. Orthopt. 168, pl. xx, fig. 7, *Litt. orcid. Americ. septentrionalis, Panama.*

mexicanus SAUSS. Orthopt. nov. amer. I, 4;—In. Rev. et Mag. de Zool. 1852, 63, *Mexico.*—GERST. Archiv f. Nat. XXVI, 11, 404;—In. Bericht, 1859-60, 46, *Mexiko.*

Proscratara.

conspersa [Tribonium] SAUSS. Orthopt. cor. amer. III, 15;—Is. Rev. et Mag. de Zool. 1862, 232, Cuba.—[Tribonium] Orthopt. Amér. mny. 208, Cuba; probablement importée du Brésil.

Psalidophora.

bipunctata Donax, Entom. Zeit. Stett. XXV, 419, Mass.

brunneipennis SERV. Orthopt. 30, Amérique boréale, Philadelphie.— BURM. Germ. Zeitsch. f. Entom. II, 80, Nord-Amerika.— Donax, Entom. Zeit. Stett. XXV, 418, In America boreali, Pennsylvania, Virginia.

parallela Donax, Entom. Zeit. Stett. XXIII, 227, taf. 1, fig. 8, Cordova.—Is. Entom. Zeit. Stett. XXV, 418, Mexiko? — GERST. Archiv f. Nat. XXIX, 11, 339;—Is. Bericht. 1862, 45, Mexiko.

Lherminieri SERV. Orthopt. 29, Guadeloupe, Brésil.

Psalis.

americana SERV. Ann. Sc. Nat. XXII, 35, Saint Domingue.

Pterimoxylus.

difformipes SERV. Orthopt. 227, Amérique méridionale. — WESTW. Catal. Orthopt. 90, pl. xxxvi, fig. 1, America meridionalis.

Pterophyllum.

concavum HARR. Encycl. Amer. VIII, 42, America.—GERMAR, Alab. 182, Alabama. See also Gryllus concavus.

See also GRYLLUS?

Pycnoscelus.

obscurus SCUDD. Bost. Journ. Nat. Hist. VII, 422, Mass. — GERST. Archiv f. Nat. XXIX, 11, 350;—Is. Bericht. 1862, 42, Massachusetts.

Pygidicrana.

Saussurei Donax, Entom. Zeit. Stett. XXIII, 225, taf. 1, fig. 2, Cordova, Veracruz.—Is. Entom. Zeit. Stett. 1863, 63, Mexico!— GERST. Archiv f. Nat. XXIX, 11, 358; — Is. Bericht. 1862, 44, Mexiko.

Pyrgomorpha.

coronatus Serv. Orthopt. 261, *Probablement de l'Amérique méridionale.*—Westw. Catal. Orthopt. 58, *America meridionalis.*

Rhammatocerus, see Stenobothrus.

Rhaphidophora.

Agassizii Scudd. Gen. Rhaph. 6;— In. Proc. Bost. Soc. Nat. Hist. VIII, 11, *Islands in Gulf of Georgia, Washington Territory.*— Gerst. Archiv f. Nat. XXVIII, II, 316;— In. Bericht, 1861, 44, *Inseln im Golf von Georgia.*

cavernarum Saus. Ann. Soc. Entom. France, [iv] I, 492, *La grotte du Mammouth, aux États unis.* — Gerst. Archiv f. Nat. XXVIII, II, 315;—In. Bericht, 1861, 43. *Mammuth-Höhle.*

gracilipes Scudd. Gen. Rhaph. 2;—In. Proc. Bost. Soc. Nat. Hist. VIII, 7, *Pennsylvania.*

lapidicola Scudd. Gen. Rhaph. 2;—In. Proc. Bost. Soc. Nat. Hist. VIII, 7, *United States.* See also *Locusta lapidicola.*

maculata Harr. Treat. Ed. 1841-2, 126, *Mass.* — Erichs. Archiv f. Nat. IX, II, 227;— In. Bericht, 1842, 83, *Mass.* — Fitch. Amer. Journ. Agric. and Sc. VI, 146, *N. York.*—Pack. Rep. Nat. Hist. Maine, 1861, 375, *Grand Falls, Maine.* — Thomas. Trans. Ill. St. Agric. Soc. V, 444, *Illinois.*

scabripes Scudd. Gen. Rhaph. 2;— In. Proc. Bost. Soc. Nat. Hist. VIII, 7, *Alabama.*

stygia Scudd. Gen. Rhaph. 4;—In. Proc. Bost. Soc. Nat. Hist. VIII, 8, *Hickman's Cave, Kentucky.*—Gerst. Archiv f. Nat. XXVIII, II, 316;—In. Bericht, 1861, 44, *Höhle in Kentucky.*

subterranea Scudd. Gen. Rhaph. 3;—In. Proc. Bost. Soc. Nat. Hist. VIII, 8, *Mammoth Cave, Kentucky.* — Gerst. Archiv f. Nat. XXVIII, II, 316;—In. Bericht, 1861, 44, *Mammuth-Höhle.*

xanthostoma Scudd. Gen. Rhaph. 7;—In. Proc. Bost. Soc. Nat. Hist. VIII, 12, *Crescent City, California.*—Gerst. Archiv f. Nat. XXVIII, II, 316;—In. Bericht, 1861, 44, *Küste des Stillen Oceans.*

See also Locusta.

Rhipipteryx.

mexicanus Saus. Orthopt. nov. amer. I, 15;—In. Rev. et Mag. de Zool. 1859, 316, *Mexico culida.*—Gerst. Archiv f. Nat. XXVI, II, 404;—In. Bericht, 1859-60, 48, *Mexico.*

Rhombea.

cicada FELT. Phil. Trans. LIV, 55, pl. vi, *Jamaica.*—WESTW. Mag.
Nat. Hist. [n. s.] III, 490, fig. 6:¹ (on p. 492), *Jamaica.*

Romalea.

centurio BURM. Handb. d. Entom. II, 620, *Georgien.*—SAUSS. Rev.
et Mag. de Zool. 1859, 392, *Mexico calida.* See also *Acridium
centurio.*

eques BURM. Handb. d. Entom. II, 620, *Aus Mexico von Zimapan.*—
SAUSS. Rev. et Mag. de Zool. 1859, 392, *Mexico calida.*

gigantea BURM. Handb. d. Entom. II, 619, *Südkarolina.* See also
Acridium giganteum.

Marci SERV. Orthopt. 623, *D'une partie de l'Amérique voisine de la
Caroline du Sud.*

microptera SERV. Ann. Sc. Nat. XXII, 280, *Amérique septentrionale.*
—OKEN, Isis, 1835, 176, *N. Amerика.*—SERV. Orthopt. 632,
Amérique septentrionale, Caroline.—CHARP. Orthopt. descr. tab.
xlix, *America media et septentrionalis.*—ERICHS. Archiv f. Nat.
X, II, 299;—ID. Bericht, 1843, 51, *Nordamerika.*

miles GERST. Handb. d. Zool. II, 55, *Von Brasilien bis Mexiko.*

pedes GERST. Archiv f. Nat. XXVI, II, 407;—ID. Bericht, 1859–60,
51, *Mexico.*—SAUSS. Rev. et Mag. de Zool. 1859, 392, *Mexico
calida.*

See also ACRIDIUM and DICTYOPHORUS.

RUTIODERES, see LOCUSTA.

Schizobranca.

mexicanus SAUSS. Orthopt. nov. amer. I, 12;—ID. Rev. et Mag. de
Zool. 1859, 209, *Mexico.*—GERST. Archiv f. Nat. XXVI, II,
405;—ID. Bericht, 1859–60, 49, *Mexico.*

Spectrum.

baculus LAM. Hist. nat. Anim. sans Vert. IV, 255; 2ᵉ Ed. IV, 456;
3ᵉ Ed. II, 157, *Antilles.*

bivittatum SAY, Amer. Entom. III, pl. xxxviii;—ID. Entom. of N.
Amer. Ed. LeConte, I, 62, pl. xxxviii, *Cumberland Island,
Florida.*

calamus LAM. Hist. nat. Anim. sans Vert. IV, 255; 2ᵉ Ed. IV, 456;
3ᵉ Ed. II, 156, *L'Isle de Saint Croix d'Amérique.*

femoratum SAY, Exp. Long. II, 297;—ID. Entom. of N. Amer. Ed.

Le Conte, I, 192, *Falls of Niagara, Missouri River.*—Id. Amer. Entom. III, pl. xxxvii;—Id. Entom. of N. Amer. Ed. Leconte, I, 63, pl. xxxvii, *Niagara, Missouri, N. Jersey, Mass.*—Harr. Mitch. Rep. 582; 2d Ed. 576;—Id. Catal. 56, *Mass.*—Leidy, Proc. Acad. Nat. Sc. Philad. III, 80, *In most parts of the United States; abundant in Iowa.*—Erichs. Archiv f. Nat. XIII, II, 139;—Id. Bericht, 1846, 74.—Hald. Amer. Journ. Sc. [II] V, 435, *Chihuahua, Santa Fé.*—Exx. Agric. of N. Y. V, 142, pl. vii, figs. 1, 2, *Albany, Western Massachusetts.*—Jaeg. N. Amer. Ins. 1854, 173; 1859, 123, *N. America.*—Thomas, Trans. Ill. St. Agric. Soc. V, 441, *Illinois.*

ferula Lam. Hist. nat. Anim. sans Vert. IV, 255; 2° Ed. IV, 455; 3° Ed. II, 156, *Guadeloupe.*

filiforme Lam. Hist. nat. Anim. sans Vert. IV, 255; 2° Ed. IV, 455; 3° Ed. II, 156, *Amérique méridionale.*

vittatum Jaeg. N. Amer. Ins. 1854, 173; 1859, 123, *N. America.*

Sphærarium.

mexicanum Sauss. Rev. et Mag. de Zool. 1859, 390, *Mexico calida.*—Gerst. Archiv f. Nat. XXVI, II, 407;—Id. Bericht, 1859-60, 51, *Mexico.*

purpurascens Charp. Orthopt. descr. tab. xxxi, *Mexico.*—Erichs. Archiv f. Nat. IX, II, 223;—Id. Bericht, 1848, 24, *Mexico.*

Sphingonotus, see Œdipoda.

Spongophora.

bipunctata Scudd. Bost. Journ. Nat. Hist. VII, 415, *Mass.*—Gerst. Archiv f. Nat. XXIX, II, 356;—Id. Bericht, 1862, 44, *Massachusetts.*

Stetrodea.

thoracicum Serv. Ann. Sc. Nat. XXII, 141;—Id. Orthopt. 402, *Amérique méridionale.*

Stenobothrus.

admirabilis Uhler, Proc. Entom. Soc. Philad. II, 553, *Maryland.*—Dallas, Zool. Record, I, 574, *Baltimore.*

æqualis Scudd. Bost. Journ. Nat. Hist. VII, 459, *Mass. Maine, New York, Minnesota.*—Gerst. Archiv f. Nat. XXIX, II, 358;—Id. Bericht, 1862, 44, *Massachusetts und Connecticut.*

bilineatus Scudd. Bost. Journ. Nat. Hist. VII, 460, *Mass.*—Gerst. Archiv f. Nat. XXIX, ii, 358 ; — In. Bericht, 1862, 41, *Massachusetts und Connecticut.*

curtipennis Scudd. Can. Nat. VII, 283, *Red River Settlements.*—In. Bost. Journ. Nat. Hist. VII, 456, *Mass. Maine, Conn. Red River Settlements.*—Gerst. Archiv f. Nat. XXIX, ii, 358;— In. Bericht, 1862, 41, *Massachusetts und Connecticut.*

gregarius [Rhammatocerus] Sauss. Orthopt. nov. amer. II, 20;—In. Rev. et Mag. de Zool. 1861, 318, *St. Thomas, Haiti.*—Gerst. Archiv f. Nat. XXVIII, ii, 317;—In. Bericht, 1861, 45, *St. Thomas und Taiti (sic !).*

longipennis Scudd. Bost. Journ. Nat. Hist. VII, 457, *Mass.*—Gerst. Archiv f. Nat. XXIX, ii, 358;—In. Bericht, 1862, 41, *Massachusetts und Connecticut.*

maculipennis Scudd. Bost. Journ. Nat. Hist. VII, 458, *Mass.*—Gerst. Archiv f. Nat. XXIX, ii, 358;—In. Bericht, 1862, 41, *Massachusetts und Connecticut.*

melanoplourus Scudd. Bost. Journ. Nat. Hist. VII, 456, *Mass. Maine.*—Gerst. Archiv f. Nat. XXIX, ii, 358;—In. Bericht, 1862, 44, *Massachusetts und Connecticut.*

mystecus [Rhammatocerus] Sauss. Orthopt. nov. amer. II, 19;—In. Rev. et Mag. de Zool. 1861, 317, *Mexico.*—Gerst. Archiv f. Nat. XXVIII, ii, 317;—In. Bericht, 1861, 45, *Mexico.*

occidentalis [Rhammatocerus] Sauss. Orthopt. nov. amer. II, 19;— In. Rev. et Mag. de Zool. 1861, 317, *Tennessee.*—Gerst. Archiv f. Nat. XXVIII, ii, 317;—In. Bericht, 1861, 45. *Tennessee.*

propinquans Scudd. Bost. Journ. Nat. Hist. VII, 46, *Conn. Minnesota.*—Gerst. Archiv f. Nat. XXIX, ii, 358;—In. Bericht, 1862, 44, *Massachusetts und Connecticut.*

speciosus Scudd. Bost. Journ. Nat. Hist. VII,458, *Minnesota.*—Gerst. Archiv f. Nat. XXIX, ii, 358 ; — In. Bericht, 1862, 41, *Massachusetts und Connecticut.*

tepaneous [Rhammatocerus] Sauss. Orthopt. nov. amer. II, 21;—In. Rev. et Mag. de Zool. 1861, 319, *Mexico.*—Gerst. Archiv f. Nat. XXVIII, ii, 317;—In. Bericht, 1861, 45, *Mexico.*

viatorius [Rhammatocerus] Sauss. Orthopt. nov. amer. II, 20;—In. Rev. et Mag. de Zool. 1861, 317, *In tota Mexico.*—Gerst. Archiv f. Nat. XXVIII, ii, 317;—In. Bericht, 1861, 45, *Mexico.*

Stenopelmatus.

fuscus Hald. Stansb. Expl. Utah, 372, *Santa Fé, Chihuahua.* — Schaum, Archiv f. Nat. XIX, ii, 270;—In. Bericht, 1852, 139, *Utah.*

histrio Saus. Orthopt. nov. amer. I, 14;—In. Rev. et Mag. de Zool. 1859, 210, *Mexico.*—Gerst. Archiv f. Nat. XXVI, ii, 405;—In. Bericht, 1859–60, 49, *Mexiko.*

mexicanus Saus. Orthopt. nov. amer. I, 13;—In. Rev. et Mag. de Zool. 1859, 210, *Mexico.*—Gerst. Archiv f. Nat. XXVI, ii, 405;—In. Bericht, 1859–60, 49, *Mexiko.*

minor Saus. Orthopt. nov. amer. I, 13;—In. Rev. et Mag. de Zool. 1859, 210, *Mexico.*—Gerst. Archiv f. Nat. XXVI, ii, 405;—In. Bericht, 1859–60, 49, *Mexiko.*

Nietti Saus. Orthopt. nov. amer. I, 13;—In. Rev. et Mag. de Zool. 1859, 210, *Mexico.*—Gerst. Archiv f. Nat. XXVI, ii, 405;—In. Bericht, 1859–60, 49, *Mexiko.*

Salléi Saus. Orthopt. nov. amer. I, 13;—In. Rev. et Mag. du Zool. 1859, 210, *Mexico.*—Gerst. Archiv f. Nat. XXVI, ii, 405;—In. Bericht, 1859–60, 49, *Mexiko.*

sartorianus Saus. Orthopt. nov. amer. I, 14;—In. Rev. et Mag. de Zool. 1859, 211, *Mexico.*—Gerst. Archiv f. Nat. XXVI, ii, 405;—In. Bericht, 1859–60, 49, *Mexiko.*

sumiohrasti Saus. Orthopt. nov. amer. I, 13;—In. Rev. et Mag. de Zool. 1859, 210, *Mexico.*—Gerst. Archiv f. Nat. XXVI, ii, 405;—In. Bericht, 1859–60, 49, *Mexiko.*

talpa Dunn. Handb. d. Entom. II, 721, *Von Zimapan in Mexiko.*—Hald. Stansb. Expl. Utah, 372, *Jalapa.*

Stigmatoptera, see Mantis.

.

Hyleopyga.

orientalis Scudd. Bost. Journ. Nat. Hist. VII, 416, *Mass. New York, Maryland.* See also *Periplaneta orientalis.*
See also Periplaneta.

Temnopteryx.

doropeltiformis Brunn. Blatt. 87, *Amérique du Nord.*
tarasca Brunn. Blatt. 86, *Mexico.*
virginica Brunn. Blatt. 86, *Draper's Valley en Virginia.*

Teratodes.

monticollis Serv. Orthopt. 631, *Des Indes.*— Blanch. Hist. nat. Ins. III, 41, *Amérique méridionale.*

Tettigidea.

lateralis Scudd. Bost. Journ. Nat. Hist. VII, 477, *Mass. Maine, New Hampshire, Connecticut, Southern Illinois.*

polymorpha Scudd. Bost. Journ. Nat. Hist. VII, 477, *Mass. Maine, New Hampshire, Missouri, Conn. Southern Illinois, Alabama.*

Tettigonia, seu Gryllus.

Tettix.

arenosa Burm. Handb. d. Entom. II, 659, *Südkarolina.* See also *Acridium arenosum.*

azteca Saus. Orthopt. nov. amer. II, 31;—In. Rev. et Mag. de Zool. 1861, 400, *Mexico calida.*—Gerst. Archiv f. Nat. XXVIII, ii, 317;—In. Bericht, 1861, 45, *Mexico.*

bilineata Harr. Treat. Ed. 1841-2, 151; Ed. 1852, 162; Ed. 1862, 186, *Mass.*—Erichs. Archiv f. Nat. IX, ii, 231;—In. Bericht, 1842, 87, *Mass.*

chichimeca Saus. Orthopt. nov. amer. II, 31;—In. Rev. et Mag. de Zool. 1861, 400, *Mexico calida.*—Gerst. Archiv f. Nat. XXVIII, ii, 317;—In. Bericht, 1861, 45, *Mexico.*

cristata Pack. Rep. Nat. Hist. Maine, 1861, 375, *Grand Falls, Maine.*

cucullata Burm. Handb. d. Entom. II, 658, *Südkarolina.*—Scudd. Bost. Journ. Nat. Hist. VII, 475, *Mass. Missouri.* See also *Acridium cucullatum.*

dorsalis Harr. Treat. Ed. 1841-2, 151; Ed. 1852, 162; Ed. 1862, 186, *Mass.*—Erichs. Archiv f. Nat. IX, ii, 231;—In. Bericht, 1842, 87, *Mass.*—Fitch, Amer. Journ. Agric. and Sc. VI, 116, *New York.*

granulata Scudd. Can. Nat. VII, 288, *Northern Minnesota.*—In. Bost. Journ. Nat. Hist. VII, 474, *Mass. Maine, N. Hampshire, Minnesota.* See also *Acridium granulatum.*

Harrisii Pack. Rep. Nat. Hist. Maine, 1861, 376, *Fish River Lakes, Maine.*

lateralis Harr. Hitchc. Rep. 583; 2d Ed. 577;—In. Catal. 57;—In. Treat. Ed. 1841-2, 151; Ed. 1852, 162; Ed. 1862, 187, *Mass.*—Erichs. Archiv f. Nat. IX, ii, 231;—In. Bericht, 1842, 87, *Mass.*

mexicana Saus. Orthopt. nov. amer. II, 30;—In. Rev. et Mag. de Zool. 1861, 399, *Mexico calida.*—Gerst. Archiv f. Nat. XXVIII, ii, 317;—In. Bericht, 1861, 45, *Mexico.*

ornata Harr. Hitchc. Rep. 2d Ed. 577;—In. Catal. 57;—In. Treat. Ed. 1841-2, 150; Ed. 1852, 162; Ed. 1862, 186, *Mass.*—Erichs. Archiv f. Nat. IX, ii, 231;—In. Bericht, 1842, 87, *Mass.*—Fitch, Amer. Journ. Agric. and Sc. VI, 146, *New*

York.—Scudd. Bost. Journ. Nat. Hist. VII, 474, *Mass. Maine, N. Hampshire, Vermont, Conn. Missouri, Southern Illinois.*

oxycephala Burm. Handb. d. Entom. II, 659, *Südcarolina.* See also *Acridium oxycephalum.*

parvipennis Harr. Hitche. Rep. 583; 2d Ed. 577;—In. Catal. 57;—In. Treat. Ed. 1841-2, 152; Ed. 1852, 162; Ed. 1862, 187, fig. 82, *Mass.*—Ericus. Archiv f. Nat. IX, ii, 231;—In. Bericht, 1842, 87, *Mass.*

polymorpha Burm. Handb. d. Entom.* II, 659, *Südcarolina.* See also *Acridium polymorphum.*

purpurascens Serv. Ann. Sc. Nat. XXII, 291, *Ile de la Trinité.*

quadrimaculata Harr. Treat. Ed. 1841-2, 151; Ed. 1852, 162; Ed. 1862, 186, *Mass.*—Ericus. Archiv f. Nat. IX, ii, 231;—In. Bericht, 1842, 87, *Mass.*

rugosa Scudd. Bost. Journ. Nat. Hist. VII. 476, *Northern Florida.*—Gerst. Archiv f. Nat. XXIX, ii, 358;—In. Bericht, 1862, 44, *Florida.*

sordida Harr. Hitche. Rep. 2d Ed. 577;—In. Catal. 57;—In. Treat. 1841-2, 151; Ed. 1852, 162; Ed. 1862, 187, *Mass.*—Ericus. Archiv f. Nat. IX, ii, 231;—In. Bericht, 1842, 87, *Mass.*

tolteca Sauss. Orthopt. nov. amer. II, 31;—In. Rev. et Mag. de Zool. 1861, 401, *Mexico calida.*—Gerst. Archiv f. Nat. XXVIII, ii, 317;—In. Bericht, 1861, 43, *Mexiko.*

triangularis Scudd. Bost. Journ. Nat. Hist. VII. 475, *Mass. Maine, N. Hampshire.*—Gerst. Archiv f. Nat. XXIX, ii, 358;—In. Bericht, 1862, 44, *Massachusetts.*

See also **Acridium.**

Thrincytes.

azteca Sauss. Orthopt. nov. amer. I, 2;—In. Rev. et Mag. de Zool. 1859, 61, *Mexico.*—Gerst. Archiv f. Nat. XXVI, ii, 402;—Bericht, 1859-60, 46, *Mexiko.*

chlorophaea ? Serv. Orthopt. 153, *New York.*

mexicana Sauss. Orthopt. nov. amer. II, 2;—In. Rev. et Mag. de Zool. 1861, 127, *Cordova, Mexico calida.*—Gerst. Archiv f. Nat. XXVIII, ii, 311;—In. Bericht, 1861, 39, *Mexiko.*

tolteca Sauss. Orthopt. nov. amer. I, 2;—In. Rev. et Mag. de Zool. 1859, 61, *Mexico.*—Gerst. Archiv f. Nat. XXVI, ii, 402;—In. Bericht, 1859-60, 46, *Mexiko.*

Thermaratris.

Sanssurei Dohrn, Entom. Zeit. Stett. XXIV, 62, *Cordova, Vera-cruz.*

Thorpia.

parva Serv. Ann. Sc. Nat. XXII, 53, *Amérique.* See also *Muntis parva.*
See also MANTIS.

Thyreonotus.

dorsalis Scudd. Bost. Journ. Nat. Hist. VII, 454, *Mass. Rhode Island, Maryland.*
pachymerus Scudd. Bost. Journ. Nat. Hist. VII, 453, *Connecticut, Mammoth Cave, Kentucky.*

Thyreocera.

cincta Burm. Handb. d. Entom. II, 499, *Mexico.*—Sauss. Orthopt. Amér. moy. 123, *Mexico.*—Brunn. Blatt. 122, *Mexique.*
discicollis ? Brunn. Blatt. 123, *Mexique.*
Gueriniana Sauss. Orthopt. nov. amer. III, 7; In. Rev. et Mag. de Zool. 1862, 168, *Mexico.*—In. Orthopt. Amér. moy. 121, *Mexique.*—Gerst. Archiv f. Nat. XXIX, 11, 354;—In. Bericht, 1862, 40, *Mexico.*—Brunn. Blatt. 126, *Mexique.*
mexicana Sauss. Orthopt. nov. amer. III, 6;—In. Rev. et Mag. de Zool. 1862, 168, *Mexico calida.*—In. Orthopt. Amér. moy. 122, *Les parties chaudes du Mexique, Cordova, Turtla, Alvarado.*—Gerst. Archiv f. Nat. XXIX, 11, 354;—In. Bericht, 1862, 40, *Mexico.*
oblongata Brunn. Blatt. 121, tab. iii, fig. 11, *Surinam, Bahia, Cayenn.*
Salleï Sauss. Orthopt. nov. amer. III, 7;—In. Rev. et Mag. de Zool. 1862, 164, *Mexico calida.*—In. Orthopt. Amér. moy. 123, *Les parties chaudes du Mexique; de la côte du golfe.*—Gerst. Archiv f. Nat. XXIX, 11, 354;—In. Bericht, 1862, 40, *Mexico.*
toltecа Sauss. Orthopt. nov. amer. III, 7;—In. Rev. et Mag. de Zool. 1862, 168, *Mexico calida.*—In. Orthopt. Amér. moy. 124, pl. i, fig. 21, *Les régions chaudes du Mexique: de Cordova et de la Cordillière orientale; dans les terres chaudes de la province de Mexico à Atlihuayan près Cuautla.*—Gerst. Archiv f. Nat. XXIX, 11, 354;—In. Bericht, 1862, 40, *Mexico.*—Brunn. Blatt. 125, *Mexique.*

Temnonotus.

mexicanus Sauss. Orthopt. nov. amer. II, 23;—In. Rev. et Mag. de Zool. 1861, 321, *Mexico temperata.*—Gerst. Archiv f. Nat. XXVIII, ii, 317;—In. Bericht, 1861, 43, *Mexico.*

Nietanus Saur. Orthopt. nov. amer. II, 24;—In. Rev. et Mag. de Zool. 1861, 321, *Mexico.*—Gerst. Archiv f. Nat. XXVIII, II, 317;—In. Bericht, 1861, 45, *Merika.*

otomitus Saur. Orthopt. nov. amer. II, 24;—In. Rev. et Mag. de Zool. 1861, 322, *Mexico orientalis.*—Gerst. Archiv f. Nat. XXVIII, II, 317;—In. Bericht, 1861, 45, *Merika.*

Zimmermanni Saur. Orthopt. nov. amer. I, 23;—In. Rev. et Mag. de Zool. 1861, 320, *Carolina.*—Gerst. Archiv f. Nat. XXVIII, II, 317;—In. Bericht, 1861, 45, *Carolina.*

Tragocephala.

infuscata Erichs. Archiv f. Nat. IX, II, 230;—In. Bericht, 1842, 86, *Mass.*—Scudd. Bost. Journ. Nat. Hist. VII, 461, *Mass. Maine, N. Hampshire, Connecticut.*—Gerst. Archiv f. Nat. XXIX, II, 358;—In. Bericht, 1862, 44, *Nord Amerika.* See also *Locusta infuscata.*

radiata Erichs. Archiv f. Nat. IX, II, 230;—In. Bericht, 1842, 86, *Mass.* See also *Locusta radiata.*

viridifasciata Erichs. Archiv f. Nat. IX, II, 230;—In. Bericht, 1842, 86, *Mass.*—Scudd. Bost. Journ. Nat. Hist. VII, 461, *Mass. Maine, Maryland, Conn.*—Gerst. Archiv f. Nat. XXIX, II, 358;—In. Bericht, 1862, 44, *Nord Amerika.* See also *Locusta viridifasciata.*

See also Locusta.

Tridactylum.

apicalis Say, Journ. Acad. Nat. Sc. Philad. IV, 310;—In. Entom. of N. Amer. Ed. LeConte, II, 239, *Southern and Western States.*—Burm. Handb. d. Entom. II, 742, *Südkarolina.*—Scudd. Bost. Journ. Nat. Hist. VII, 425, *Alabama, Kentucky.*—Thomas, Trans. Ill. St. Agric. Soc. V, 441, *Illinois.*

illinoisensis Thomas, Proc. Entom. Soc. Philad. I, 104;—In. Trans. Ill. St. Agric. Soc. V, 441, *Illinois.*

minutus Scudd. Bost. Journ. Nat. Hist. VII, 425, *Southern Illinois.*—Gerst. Archiv f. Nat. XXIX, II, 356;—In. Bericht, 1862, 42, *Illinois.*

terminalis Scudd. Bost. Journ. Nat. Hist. VII, 426, *Mass. Maryland, S. Illinois.*—Gerst. Archiv f. Nat. XXIX, II, 356;—In. Bericht, 1862, 42, *Massachusetts.*

tibialis Guér. Iconogr. Règne Anim. Ins. 336, *Nouvelle Orléans.*—Erichs. Archiv f. Nat. XIII, II, 139;—In. Bericht, 1846, 75, *New Orleans.*

TRIBONIUM, no PROSCRATEA.

Tropidischia.

xanthostoma SCUDD. Bost. Journ. Nat. Hist. VII, 441, *Crescent City, California.*

Tropinotus.

serratus FISCH. Index Orthopt. 16;—In. Bull. Soc. Imp. Nat. Mosc. XIX, 11, 481, *Am. mer.*

Truxalis.

brevicornis FABR. Syst. Entom. 279, *America.*—In. Spec. Ins. I, 352, *In America meridionali*—In. Entom. Syst. II, 28 ;—In. Nom. Entom. emend. Ed. 1797, 80; Ed. 1810, 80, *America.*—DILL. Enum. Ins. 64, *Amer.*—THUNB. Mém. Acad. St. Petersb. V, 264, *In India orientali et occidentali.*—In. Nov. Act. Upsal. IX, 84, *In India occidentali, America meridionali et Africa.*—BURM. Handb. d. Entom. II, 607, *Karolina, Brasilien.* See also *Gryllus brevicornis.*
cristatus MACQ. Catal. Mus. Lille, 329, *America meridionalis.*
dorsalis FAIRM. Ferr. Bull. So. Nat. XVII, 143, *Amérique méridionale, Brésil.*
giganteus HERBST, Fuessly, Archiv d. Ins. 1788, 191, tab. lii, fig. 6, *Amerika.* See also *Gryllus giganteus.*
nasutus THUNB. Mém. Acad. St. Petersb. V, 264, *In India orientali, Africa, Australi, China, Barthelemi.*—In. Nov. Act. Upsal. IX, 85, *In India orientali, Capite bonæ spei, insula Barthelemei et in China.*
notocolorus PAL. DE BEAUV. Insectes, 80, pl. lil, fig. 8, *Saint Domingue.*
obscurus FAIRO. Ferr. Bull. So. Nat. XVII, 143, *Amérique méridionale, Brésil.*
Sumichrasti [Acheta] SAUSS. Orthopt. nov. amer. II, 15;—In. Rev. et Mag. de Zool. 1861, 313, *Mexico temperata.*—[Acheta] GERST. Archiv f. Nat. XXVIII, 31, 317;—In. Bericht, 1861, 45, *Mexiko.*
viridulus PAL. DE BEAUV. Insectes, 81, pl. lil, fig. 4, *Saint Domingue.*
See also GRYLLUS.

Udeopsylla.

nigra SCUDD. Can. Nat. VII, 281;—In. Bost. Journ. Nat. Hist. VII, 413, *Minnesota, Red River of the North.*— GERST. Archiv f. Nat. XXIX, 11, 337;—In. Bericht, 1862, 43, *Red River.*
robusta SCUDD. Bost. Journ. Nat. Hist. VII, 442, *Nebraska.*

Xiphicera.

emarginata SERV. Orthopt. 612, *Brésil, Amérique septentrionale.*
pygmæa SAUSS. Orthopt. nov. amer. II, 6;—In. Rev. et Mag. de
    Zool. 1861, 156, *Mexico.*—GERST. Archiv f. Nat. XXVIII, II,
    316;—In. Bericht, 1861, 44, *Mexiko.*
serripes LAM. Hist. nat. Anim. sans Vert. IV, 244; 2ᵉ Éd. IV, 445;
    3ᵉ Éd. II, 153, *Les Indes.*

Xiphidium.

agile DURM. Handb. d. Entom. II, 707, *Süd-Karolina.* — THOMAS,
    Trans. Ill. St. Agric. Soc. V, 445, *Illinois.* See also *Locusta
    agilis.*
brevipenne SCUDD. Can. Nat. VII, 285, *Red River Settlements, British
    America.*—In. Bost. Journ. Nat. Hist. VII, 451, *Mass. Cape
    Cod, Maine*— GERST. Archiv f. Nat. XXIX, II, 357;— In.
    Bericht, 1862, 43, *Massachusetts.*
ensiferum SCUDD. Bost. Journ. Nat. Hist. VII, 451, *Illinois.*—GERST.
    Archiv f. Nat. XXIX, II, 357;—In. Bericht, 1862, 43, *Illinois.*
fasciatum SERV. Ann. Sc. Nat. XXII, 159, *Pennsylvanie.* — DURM.
    Handb. d. Entom. II, 708, *Mittel Amerika.*—? SCUDD. Can.
    Nat. VII, 285, *Red River Settlements, British America.* — In.
    Bost. Journ. Nat. Hist. VII, 451, *Mass. Cape Cod, Maine,
    Rhode Island, Conn. Vermont.*—THOMAS, Trans. Ill. St. Agric.
    Soc. V, 444, *Illinois.*
glaberrimum DURM. Handb. d. Entom. II, 707, *Süd-Karolina.* See
    also *Locusta glaberrima.*
mexicanum SAUSS. Orthopt. nov. amer. I, 11;—In. Rev. et Mag.
    de Zool. 1859, 208, *Mexico.* — GERST. Archiv f. Nat. XXVI,
    II, 405;—In. Bericht, 1859–60, 49, *Mexiko.*
    See also LOCUSTA.

Xya.

apicalis UHLER, Say, Entom. of N. Amer. Ed. LeConte, II, 239, *South-
    ern and Western States.*
mixta HALD. Proc. Acad. Nat. Sc. Philad. VI, 364, *Fort Gates, West-
    ern Texas.*—GERST. Archiv f. Nat. XX, II, 245;—In. Bericht,
    1853, 59, *Texas.*

Xiphodus.

adumbratus SAUSS. Orthopt. nov. amer. I, 4;—In. Rev. et Mag.
    de Zool. 1859, 62, *Portorico.*
    See also ACANTHODERUS.

Zetobora.

cicatricosa [Phortisca] SAUSS. Orthopt. Amér. moy. 213, *Cuba.*—
    BRUNN. Blatt. 291, *Para, Havane.* See also *Blatta cicatricosa.*
flavicollis BRUNN. Blatt. 292, *Cayenne, Ile de Cuba.*
verrucosa SAUSS. Blatt. nov. 26;—ID. Rev. et Mag. de Zool. 1864.
    344;—[Phortisca] ID. Orthopt. Amér. moy. 213, *Amérique mé-*
    ridionale.
    See also BLATTA.

www.ingramcontent.com/pod-product-compliance
Lightning Source LLC
Chambersburg PA
CBHW020806020726
47495CB00008B/2609